Mary Elizabeth Hewitt, Anna Jameson

Lives of Celebrated Female Sovereigns and Illustrious Women

including the Empress Josephine, Lady Jane Grey, Beatrice Cenci, Joan of Arc, Anne Boleyn, Charlotte Corday, Semiramis, Zenobia, Boadicea, Isabella of Castile, Berengeria, etc.

Mary Elizabeth Hewitt, Anna Jameson

Lives of Celebrated Female Sovereigns and Illustrious Women
*including the Empress Josephine, Lady Jane Grey, Beatrice Cenci, Joan of Arc, Anne Boleyn,
Charlotte Corday, Semiramis, Zenobia, Boadicea, Isabella of Castile, Berengeria, etc.*

ISBN/EAN: 9783337423155

Printed in Europe, USA, Canada, Australia, Japan

Cover: Foto ©Andreas Hilbeck / pixelio.de

More available books at **www.hansebooks.com**

LIVES

OF

Celebrated Female Sovereigns

AND

ILLUSTRIOUS WOMEN;

INCLUDING

THE EMPRESS JOSEPHINE, LADY JANE GREY, BEATRICE CENCI,
JOAN OF ARC, ANNE BOLEYN, CHARLOTTE CORDAY,
SEMIRAMIS, ZENOBIA, BOADICEA, ISABELLA
OF CASTILE, BERENGARIA, ETC.

BY MRS. ANNA JAMESON,

AUTHOR OF

"CHARACTERISTICS OF WOMEN," "LEGENDS OF THE MADONNA," ETC., ETC.

EDITED BY MARY E. HEWITT.

PHILADELPHIA:
PORTER & COATES,

PREFACE.

In the following pages, I have endeavored to present to the reader, as far as the limits of a single volume would permit, from a variety of sources, sketches of the lives of women, rendered illustrious by their heroism and their virtues.

To carry out this intention, then, to the letter, I ought, perhaps, to have omitted the sketch of Semiramis, who is described by one of her historians, as "a monster, possessed of every vice;" but she lived so far back in the ages of the world, that this account of her appears, to us, to be merely suppositious, and I have chosen to introduce her here, as an example of the indomitable courage and bravery, of purpose and action, sometimes displayed by woman, when placed in a situation to call them forth. That Semiramis lived in an idolatrous age, and was, like those of the time in which she flourished, a believer in the pagan doctrine of fatalism, will account for her seemingly puerile abandonment of her ambitious career, and cowardly submission to what she believed to be the incontrovertible decree of Destiny.

M. E. H.

CONTENTS.

Semiramis.

HEROINES OF HISTORY.

SEMIRAMIS.

SEMIRAMIS, Queen of Assyria, is the first female sovereign upon record who ever held undivided empire. All the accounts which have come down to us concerning this celebrated queen, are mixed up with so much exaggeration, absurdity, and mythological fiction, that she may be considered partly a fabulous and partly an historical personage. As beheld through the long lapse of ages, and in the dim distance of primeval time, with all her gorgeous and Babylonish associations around her, Semiramis appears to our fancy rather as a colossal emblem of female sovereignty, overshadowing the East, than as a real and distinct individual ; yet, that such a woman did once exist is more than probable, and her name has been repeated from age to age, till it has become so illustrious, and her exploits and character so frequently alluded to in history, in poetry, and in the arts, that it is obviously necessary to be acquainted with the traditions respecting her ; though quite unnecessary to give implicit credit to the relation of events resting on such vague, remote, and doubtful testimony, that, if it be difficult to believe, it is impossible to confute them. The time at which Semiramis lived is a matter of dispute ; and the authorities vary so extravagantly that we are tempted to exclaim, with Bryant, " What credit can possibly be given to the history of a person, the period of whose existence cannot be ascertained within 1500 years ?" Yet, so universal a celebrity must surely have had some foundation in truth.

According to Rollin, Semiramis flourished about 1950 years before the Christian era, that is, about 400 years after the Flood, and nearly about the time of Abraham. Other chronologists, with far more probability, place her reign about 600 years later; thus making her nearly contemporary with Gideon, Judge of Israel, and Theseus, King of Athens.

She was born at Ascalon, in Syria, and was the wife of Menones, one of the generals of Ninus, King of Assyria. At the siege of Bactria, whither she accompanied her husband, she distinguished herself by her prudence and courage, and through her sagacity the city was at length taken, after a protracted siege. She discovered a weak part in the fortifications, and led some soldiers up a by-path by night, by which means the walls were scaled, and the city entered. Ninus, struck with her wisdom and her charms, entreated her husband to resign Semiramis to him, offering his daughter, the Princess Sosana, in exchange, and threatening to put out the eyes of the husband if he refused. Menones, seeing the king resolved on his purpose, and the lady in all probability nothing loath, and unable to determine between the alternatives presented to him—the loss of his eyes, or the loss of his wife—hung himself in a fit of jealousy and despair and Ninus immediately afterward married his widow. Semiramis became the mother of a son named Ninias, and the king, dying soon afterward, bequeathed to her the government of his empire during the minority of his son. We have another version of this part of the story of Semiramis, which has afforded a fine subject for poets and satirists. It is recorded that Ninus, in the extravagance of his dotage, granted to his young and beautiful queen the absolute sovereignty of his empire for a single day. He seated her on his regal throne, placed his signet on her finger, commanded the officers of state and courtiers to do her homage, himself setting the first example, and her decrees during that brief space of time were to be considered absolute and irrevocable. Semiramis, with equal subtlety and audacity, instantly took advantage of her delegated power, and ordered her husband to be first imprisoned, and then strangled—a punishment which his folly would almost have deserved from any other hand. She declared herself his successor, and contrived to retain the supreme power during the remainder of her life. She was twenty years of age when she assumed the reins of empire, and resolved to immortalize her name by magnificent monuments and mighty enterprizes. She is said to have founded the city of Babylon, or at least to have adorned it with such prodigious and splendid works that they ranked among the wonders of the world. When we read the accounts of the " Great Babylon," of its walls and brazen gates, its temples, bridges, and hanging gardens, we should be inclined to treat the whole as a magnificent fiction of poetry, if the stupendous monuments of human art and labor still remaining in India and Upper Egypt, did not render credible the most extravagant of these descriptions, and prove on what a gigantic scale the ancients worked for immortality. We are also told that among the edifices erected by her was a mausoleum to the memory of the king, her husband, adjoining the great Tower of Babel, and adorned with statues of massive gold. When Semiramis had completed the adornment of her capital by the most wonderful works of art, she undertook a progress through her vast empire, and everywhere left behind her glorious me morials of her power and her benevolence. It seems to have been an article of faith among all the writers of antiquity, that Assyria had never been so great and so prosperous as under the dominion of this extraordinary woman. She built enormous aqueducts, connected the various cities by roads and causeways, in the construction of which she leveled hills and filled up valleys; and she was careful, like the imperial conqueror of modern times, to inscribe her name and the praises of her own munificence on all these monuments of her greatness. In one of these inscriptions she gives her own genealogy, in a long list of celestial progenitors; which shows that, like some other monarchs of the antique time, she had the weakness to disown her plebeian origin, and wished to lay claim to a divine and fictitious parentage :—

> " My father was Jupiter Belus ;
> My grandfather, Babylonian Saturn ;
> My great-grandfather, Ethiopian Saturn ;
> My great-grandfather's father, Egyptian Saturn ;
> And my great-grandfather's grandfather,
> Phœnix Cœlus Ogyges."

After reading this high-sounding catalogue of grandfathers and great-grandfathers, it is amusing to recollect that Semiramis has left posterity in some doubt whether she herself ever had a real existence, and may not be, after all, as imaginary a personage as any of her shadowy, heaven-sprung ancestors

There is another of the inscriptions of Semiramis, which is in a much finer spirit :—

" Nature bestowed on me the form of a woman ; my actions have surpassed those of the most valiant of men. · I ruled the empire of Ninus, which stretched eastward as far as the river Hyhanam, southward to the land of incense and of myrrh, and northward to the country of the Scythians and the Sogdians. Before me no Assyrian had seen the great sea. I beheld with my own eyes four seas, and their shores acknowledged my power. I constrained the mighty rivers to flow according to my will, and I led their waters to fertilize lands that had been before barren and without inhabitants. 1 raised impregnable towers; I constructed paved roads in ways hitherto untrodden but by the beasts of the forest; and in the midst of these mighty works I found time for pleasure and for friendship."

We are told that Semiramis was extremely active and vigilant in the administration of her affairs. One morning, as she was dressing, information was brought to her that a rebellion had broken out in the city; she immediately rushed forth, half-attired, her hair floating in disorder, appeased the tumultuous populace by her presence and her eloquence, and then returned to finish her toilette.

Not satisfied with being the foundress of mighty cities, and sovereign over the greatest empire of the earth, Semiramis was ambitious of military renown. She subdued the Medes, the Persians, the Libyans, and the Ethiopians, and afterward determined to invade India. She is the first monarch on record who penetrated beyond the Indus, for the expedition of Bacchus is evidently fabulous. The amount of her army appears to us absolutely incredible. She is said to have assembled three millions of foot-soldiers and five hundred thousand cavalry; and as the strength of the Indians consisted principally in the number of their elephants, she caused many thousand camels to be disguised and caparisoned like elephants of war, in hopes of deceiving and terrifying the enemy by this stratagem. Another historian informs us that she constructed machines in the shape of elephants, and that these machines were moved by some mechanical contrivance, which was worked by a single man in the interior of each. The Indian king or chief, whose name was Stabrobates, hearing of the stupendous armament which was moving against him, sent an ambassador to Semiramis, demanding who and what she was? and why, without any provocation, she was come to invade his dominions? To these very reasonable inquiries the Assyrian queen haughtily replied, "Go to your king, and tell him I will myself inform him who I am, and why I am come hither." Then, rushing onward at the head of her swarming battalions, she passed the river Indus in spite of all opposition, and advanced far into the country, the people flying before her unresisting, and apparently vanquished. But having thus insidiously led her on till she was surrounded by hostile lands, and beyond the reach of assistance from her own dominions, the Indian monarch suddenly attacked her, overwhelmed her mock elephants by the power and weight of his real ones, and completely routed her troops, who fled in all directions. The queen herself was wounded, and only saved by the swiftness of her Arabian steed, which bore her across the Indus; and she returned to her kingdom with scarce a third of her vast army. We are not informed whether the disasters of this war cured Semiramis of her passion for military glory; and all the researches of antiquarians have not enabled us to distinguish the vague and poetical from the true, or at least the probable events in the remainder of her story. We have no account of the state of manners and morals during her reign, and of the progress of civilization we can only judge by the great works imputed to her. Among the various accounts of her death the following is the most probable:—An oracle had foretold that Semiramis should reign until her son Ninias conspired against her; and after her return from her Indian expedition she discovered that Ninias had been plotting her destruction. She immediately called to mind the words of the oracle, and, without attempting to resist his designs, abdicated the throne at once, and retired from the world ; or, according to others, she was put to death by her son, after a reign of forty-two years. The Assyrians paid her divine honors under the form of a pigeon

Victoris.

NICTORIS,

NICTORIS succeeded Semiramis after an interval of five generations. Having observed the increasing power and restless spirit of the Medes, and that Ninevah, with other cities, had fallen a prey to their ambition, she proceeded to put her dominions in the strongest posture of defence. She sunk a number of canals above Babylon, which by their disposition rendered the Euphrates, which before flowed to the sea in an almost even line, so complicated by its windings, that in its passage to Babylon, it arrives three times at Ardericca, an Assyrian village; and to this hour, says Herodotus, they who wish to proceed from the sea up the Euphrates to Babylon, are compelled to touch at Ardericca three times on three different days. She raised banks also to restrain the river on each side, that were wonderful for their enormous height and substance. At a considerable distance above Babylon, turning aside a little from the stream, she ordered an immense lake to be dug, sinking it till they came to the water; its circumference was no less than four hundred and twenty furlongs. The earth of this was applied to the embankments of the river; and the sides of the lake were strengthened or lined with stones, brought thither for that purpose. Nictoris had in view by these works, first of all to break the violence of the current by the number of circumflexions, and also to render the navigation to Babylon as difficult as possible, with the farther view of keeping the Medes in ignorance of her affairs, by giving

them no comme\ .ial encouragement. Having rendered both of
these works stron; and secure, she next undertook to connect
both sides of the city, through which the river flowed, dividing
it into two parts, by the means of a bridge ; and the immense
lake which she had before sunk became the farther means of
extending her fame. It was a matter of general inconvenience
to the citizens, in the days of former kings, that whoever desired
to pass from one side of the city to the other, were obliged to
cross the water in a boat; but Nictoris changed the course of the
river by directing it into the canal prepared for its reception.
When this was full the natural bed of the river became dry, and
she then caused the embankments on each side, near those
smaller gates which led to the water, to be lined with bricks
hardened by fire. She afterwards erected a bridge, nearly in the
centre of the city, of large stones, strongly compacted with iron
and lead, and over this the inhabitants passed in the day time
by a square platform, which was removed in the evening to prevent acts of mutual depredation. When the canal was tho-
roughly filled with water, and the bridge completely finished and
adorned, the Euphrates was suffered to return to its original bed,
while the canal and the bridge were confessedly of the greatest
utility to the public.

Nictoris also caused her tomb to be erected over one of the
principal gates of the city,—in this instance deviating from the
customs of her country—the Assyrians, in their funeral rites,
imitating in all respects the Egyptians,—and placed upon it the
following inscription :—

" If any of the sovereigns, my successors, shall be in extreme
want of money, let him open my tomb and take as much as he
may think proper. If his necessity be not great, let him forbear ;
the experiment will perhaps be dangerous."

The tomb remained without injury till the time and reign of Darius. He was equally offended at the gate being rendered useless, from the general aversion to pass through the place over which a dead body was laid, and that the invitation thus held out to become affluent, should have been so long neglected. Darius opened the tomb ; but instead of riches he only found a corpse, with a label of this import—"If your avarice had not been equally base and insatiable, you would not have intruded on the repose of the dead."

Nictoris was succeeded by her son Labynatus, in whose reign Babylon was taken by Cyrus, during a day of festivity, while the citizens were engaged in dancing and merriment

Zenobia.

ZENOBIA,

QUEEN OF PALMYRA

OF the government and manners of the Arabians before the time of Mahomet, we have few and imperfect accounts; but from the remotest ages, they led the same unsettled and predatory life which they do at this day, dispersed in hordes, and dwelling under tents. It was not to those wild and wandering tribes that the superb Palmyra owed its rise and grandeur, though situated in the midst of their deserts, where it is now beheld in its melancholy beauty and ruined splendor, like an enchanted island in the midst of an ocean of sands. The merchants who trafficked between India and Europe, by the only route then known, first colonized this singular spot, which afforded them a convenient resting-place; and even in the days of Solomon it was the emporium for the gems and gold, the ivory, gums, spices, and silks of the far Eastern countries, which thus found their way to the remotest parts of Europe. The Palmyrenes were, therefore, a mixed race—their origin, and many of their customs, were Egyptian; their love of luxury and their manners were derived from Persia; their language, literature, and architecture, were Greek.

Thus, like Venice and Genoa, in more modern times, Palmyra owed its splendor to the opulence and public spirit of its merchants; but its chief fame and historical interest it owes to the genius and heroism of a woman!

Septimia Zenobia, for such is her classical appellation, was the daughter of an Arab chief, Amrou, the son of Dharb, the son of Hassan. Of her first husband we have no account; she was left a widow at a very early age, and married, secondly, Odenathus, chief of several tribes of the Desert, near Palmyra, and a prince of extraordinary valor, and boundless ambition. Odenathus was the ally of the Romans in their wars against Sapor, (or, more properly, Shah Poor), king of Persia. He gained several splendid victories over that powerful monarch, and twice pursued his armies even to the gates of Ctesiphon, (or Ispahan), his capital. Odenathus was as fond of the chase as of war; and in all his military hunting expeditions he was accompanied by his wife Zenobia, a circumstance which the Roman historians record with astonishment and admiration, as contrary to their manners, but which was the general custom of the Arab women of that time. Zenobia not only excelled her countrywomen in the qualities for which they were all remarkable—in courage, prudence, and fortitude, in patience of fatigue, and activity of mind and body—she also possessed a more enlarged understanding; her views were more enlightened, her habits more intellectual. The successes of Odenathus were partly attributed to her, and they were always considered as reigning jointly. She was also eminently beautiful—with the oriental eyes and complexion, teeth like pearls, and a voice of uncommon power and sweetness.

Odenathus obtained from the Romans the title of Augustus, and General of the East; he revenged the fate of Valerian, who had been taken captive and put to death by Shah Poor. The eastern king, with a luxurious barbarity truly oriental, is said to have used the unfortunate emperor as his footstool to mount his horse. But in the midst of his victories and conquests Odenathus became the victim of a domestic conspiracy, at the head of which was his nephew Mæonius. He was assassinated at Emessa during a hunting expedition, and with him his son by his first marriage. Zenobia avenged the death of her husband on his murderers; and as her sons were yet in their infancy, she first exercised the supreme power in their name; but afterward, apparently with the consent of the people, assumed the diadem with the titles of "Augusta" and "Queen of the East."

The Romans and their effeminate emperor Gallienus refused to acknowledge Zenobia's claim to the sovereignty of her husband's dominions, and Heraclianus was sent with a large army to reduce her to obedience; but Zenobia took the field against him, engaged and totally defeated him in a pitched battle. Not satisfied with this triumph over the haughty masters of the world, she sent her general Zabdas to attack them in Egypt, which she subdued and added to her territories, together with a part of Armenia and Asia Minor. Thus, her dominions extended from the Euphrates to the Mediterranean, and over all those vast and fertile countries formerly governed by Ptolemy and Seleucus. Jerusalem, Antioch, Damascus, and other cities famed in history, were included in her empire; but she fixed her residence at Palmyra, and in an interval of peace she turned her attention to the further adornment of her magnificent capital. It is related by historians, that many of those stupendous fabrics of which the mighty ruins are still existing, were either erected, or at least restored and embellished by this extraordinary woman. But that which we have most difficulty in reconciling with the manners of her age and country, was Zenobia's passion for study, and her taste for the Greek and Latin literature. She is said to have drawn up an epitome of history for her own use; the Greek historians, poets, and philosophers, were familiar to her; she invited Longinus, one of the most elegant writers of antiquity, to her splendid court, and appointed him her secretary and minister. For her he composed his famous " Treatise on the Sublime," a work which is not only admirable for its intrinsic excellence, but most valuable, as having preserved to our times many beautiful fragments of ancient poets whose works are now lost, particularly those of Sappho.

The classical studies of Zenobia seem to have inspired her with some contempt for her Arab ancestry. She was fond of deriving her origin from the Macedonian kings of Egypt, and of reckoning Cleopatra among her progenitors. In imitation of the famous Egyptian queen, she affected great splendor in her style of living, and in her attire ; and drank her wine out of cups of gold, richly carved and adorned with gems. It is, however, admitted that in female dignity and discretion, as well as in beauty, she far surpassed Cleopatra. She administered the government of her empire with such admirable prudence and policy, and in particular with such strict justice towards all classes of her subjects, that she was beloved by her own people, and respected and feared by the neighboring nations. She paid great attention to the education of her three sons, habited them in the Roman purple, and brought them up in the Roman fashion. But this predilection for the Greek and Roman manners appears to have displeased and alienated the Arab tribes ; for it is remarked that after this time their fleet cavalry, inured to the deserts and unequaled as horsemen, no longer formed the strength of her army.

While Gallienus and Claudius governed the Roman empire, Zenobia was allowed to pursue her conquests, rule her dominions, and enjoy her triumphs almost without opposition. But at length the fierce and active Aurelian was raised to the purple, and he was indignant that a woman should thus brave with impunity the offended majesty of Rome. Having subdued all his competitors in the West, he turned his arms against the Queen of the East. Zenobia, undismayed by the terrors of the Roman name, levied troops, placed herself at their head, and gave the second command to Zabdas, a brave and hitherto successful general. The first great battle took place near Antioch ; Zenobia was totally defeated after an obstinate conflict. But, not disheartened by this reverse, she retired upon Emessa, rallied her armies, and once more defied the Roman emperor. Being again defeated with great loss, and her army nearly dispersed, the high-spirited queen withdrew to Palmyra, collected her friends around her, strengthened her fortifications, and declared her resolution to defend her capital and her freedom to the last moment of her existence.

Zenobia was conscious of the great difficulties which would attend the seige of a great city, well stored with provisions, and naturally defended by surrounding deserts ; these deserts were infested by clouds of Arabs, who, appearing and disappearing with the swiftness and suddenness of a whirlwind, continually harrassed her enemies. Thus defended without, and supported by a strong garrison within, Zenobia braved her antagonist from the towers of Palmyra as boldly as she had defied him in the field of battle. The expectation of succors from the East added to her courage, and determined her to persevere to the last. "Those," said Aurelian in one of his letters, "who speak with contempt of the war I am waging against a woman are ignorant both of the character and power of Zenobia. It is impossible to enumerate her warlike preparations of stones, of arrows, and of every species of missile weapons and military engines."

Aurelian, in fact, became doubtful of the event of the seige,

and he offered the queen the most honorable terms of capitulation if she would surrender to his arms. But Zenobia, who was
aware that famine raged in the Roman camp, and daily looked
for the expected relief, rejected his proposals in a famous Greek
epistle, written with equal arrogance and eloquence ; she defiec'
the utmost of his power ; and, alluding to the fate of Cleopatra,
expressed her resolution to die like her rather than yield to the
Roman arms. Aurelian was incensed by this haughty letter,
even more than by dangers and delays attending the siege. He
redoubled his efforts—he cut off the succors she expected—he
found means to subsist his troops even in the midst of the desert—every day added to the number and strength of his army—
every day increased the difficulties of Zenobia, and the despair
of the Palmyrenes. The city would not hold out much longer,
and the queen resolved to fly, not to insure her own safety, but
to bring relief to the capital. Such at least is the excuse made
for part of her conduct, which certainly requires apology.
Mounted on a fleet dromedary she contrived to elude the
vigilance of the besiegers, and took the road to the Euphrates ;
but she was pursued by a party of the Roman light cavalry,
overtaken, and brought as a captive into the presence of Aurelian. He sternly demanded how she had dared to oppose the
power of Rome ! to which she replied, with a mixture of firmness and gentleness, " Because I disdained to acknowledge as
my masters such men as Aureolus and Gallienus. To Aurelian
I submit as my conqueror and my sovereign." Aurelian was
not displeased at the artful compliment implied in this answer ;
but he had not forgotten the insulting arrogance of her former
reply. While this conference was going forward in the tent of
the Roman emperor, the troops, who were enraged by her long
and obstinate resistance, and all-they had suffered during the

siege, assembled.in tumultuous bands calling out for vengeance, and with loud and fierce cries demanding her instant death. The unhappy queen, surrounded by the ferocious and insolent soldiery, forgot all her former vaunts and intrepidity. Her feminine terrors had perhaps been excusable if they had not rendered her base; but in her first panic she threw herself on the mercy of the emperor, accused her ministers as the cause of her determined resistance, and confessed that Longinus had written in her name that eloquent letter of defiance which had so incensed the emperor.

Longinus, with the rest of her immediate friends and counselors, were instantly sacrificed to the fury of the soldiers ; and the philosopher met death with all the fortitude which became a wise and great man, employing his last moments in endeavoring to console Zenobia and reconcile her to her fate.

Palmyra surrendered to the conqueror, who seized upon the treasures of the city, but spared the buildings and the lives of the inhabitants. Leaving in the place a garrison of Romans, he returned to Europe, carrying with him Zenobia and her family, who were destined to grace his triumphs.

But scarcely had Aurelian reached the Hellespont, when tidings were brought to him that the inhabitants of Palmyra had again revolted, and had put the Roman governor and garrison to the sword. Without a moment's deliberation the emperor turned back, reached Palmyra by rapid marches, and took a terrible vengeance on that miserable and devoted city. He commanded the indiscriminate massacre of all the inhabitants, men, women, and children ;—fired its magnificent edifices, and leveled its walls to the ground. He afterwards repented of his fury, and devoted a part of the captured treasures to reinstate some of the glories he had destroyed ; but it was too late—he conld not reanimate the dead, nor raise from its ruins the stupendous Temple of the Sun.   Palmyra became desolate; its very existence was forgotten, until about a century ago, when some English travelers discovered it by accident.   Thus the blind fury of one man extinguished life, happiness, industry, art and intelligence, through a vast extent of country, and severed a link which had long connected the eastern and western continents of the old world.

When Aurelian returned to Rome after the termination of this war, he celebrated his triumph with extraordinary pomp. A vast number of elephants, and tigers, and strange beasts from the conquered countries; sixteen hundred gladiators, an innumerable train of captives, and a gorgeous display of treasures—gold, silver, gems, plate, glittering raiment, and oriental luxuries and rarities, the rich plunder of Palmyra, were exhibited to the populace.   But every eye was fixed on the beautiful and majestic figure of the Syrian queen, who walked in the procession before her own sumptuous chariot, attired in her diadem and royal robes, blazing with jewels, her eyes fixed on the ground, and her delicate form drooping under the weight of her golden fetters, which were so heavy that two slaves were obliged to assist in supporting them on either side; while the Roman populace, at that time the most brutal and degraded in the whole world, gaped and stared upon her misery, and shouted in exultation over her fall.   Perhaps Zenobia may in that moment have thought upon Cleopatra, whose example she had once proposed to follow; and, according to the pagan ideas of greatness and fortitude, envied her destiny, and felt her own ignominy with all the bitterness of a vain repentance.

The captivity of Zenobia took place in the year 273, and in the fifth year of her reign.   There are two accounts of her subsequent fate, differing widely from each other. One author asserts that she starved herself to death, refusing to survive her own disgrace and the ruin of her country. But others inform us that the Emperor Aurelian bestowed on her a superb villa at Tivoli, where she resided in great honor, and that she was afterwards united to a Roman senator, with whom she lived many years. Her daughters married into Roman families, and it is said that some of her descendants remained so late as the fifth century.

The three sons of Zenobia are called in the Latin histories, Timolaus, Herennicanus, and Vaballathus. The youngest became king of part of Armenia; but of the two eldest we have no account.

3

Boadicea

BOADICEA,

THE history of ancient Rome is written in characters of blood, and over her whole wide-spread empire, from the Caledonian hills to the confines of India, from Torneo's rock to the cataracts of the Nile, the blood of slaughtered hecatombs of men, women, and children, has saddened the earth. Physical strength was her standard of right, and by that standard she measured her claims to every country of the globe, wherever her cohorts could gain and maintain a footing.

Intellectual Greece bowed to her yoke—the islands of the Mediterranean paid her homage—Carthage fell before her power—Iran acknowledged her authority—Egypt became her tributary, and even the remote Island of Britain did not escape the power of ambitious Ceasar, when Gaul lay prostrate at his feet. The estuaries of Britain were filled with his war-galleys, and the quiet of the happy island was broken by the clangor of Roman arms. A peaceful people, unaccustomed to the business of war, and illy armed, the Britons made but feeble resistance to their invaders, and soon another rich territory of earth was added to the collossal dominions of Rome. The whole island became subject to Roman authority; the country was divided into states, and a Roman governor was appointed over the whole. About the sixtieth year of our era, Seutonius Paulinus, one of the greatest generals of the age, was appointed governor of Britain, and allowed an army of about one hundred thousand men to keep the natives in subjection. The infamous Nero was at that time emperor of Rome, and Paulinus was a fit instrument to execute the orders of his master, who cared not how many people suffered, if his unbounded avarice and lust were satisfied. To fill the coffers of the emperor, the Britons were subjected to the most cruel taxation; and those who but recently were in the full enjoyment of peace and liberty, were reduced to the most abject slavery.

But the inherent principles of freedom, actively alive in the breast of the Briton, could not be destroyed, and when the oppressions of their conquerors became too severe to be borne, they raised the banner of revolt, around which every true Briton rallied. The spirit of revolution, prompted by a love of liberty, and keen resentment for wrongs inflicted, which had been increasing in intensity for a long time, broke out into open rebellion, at a time when Paulinus was absent upon the Island of Mona, or Anglesey. A peculiar act of cruelty on the part of the Romans, was the immediate cause of this general revolt; and to that act and its consequences we devote these pages.

Prasatugus, king of Iceni,* and a prince much beloved for his mildness and equity, when on his death-bed, made an equal division of his kingdom, one-half of which he bequeathed to the Roman emperor, and the other to his family. The reason for making this bequest to the emperor, was the vain hope, that it would so far satisfy his rapacity, as to secure his protection for his wife and children. But the moment that the death of Prasatugus came to the ears of Paulinus, he sent an army sufficient to take forcible possession of the *whole* of the wealth and the kingdom of the deceased prince. Against this unjust act,

---

* This State included that portion of England now known as the counties of Norfolk, Suffolk, Cambridge and Huntingdon.

his, queen Boadicea, a woman of extraordinary spirit, warmly remonstrated; but her remonstrance was met with the most brutal treatment from the minions of the governor. They even went so far as to scourge her publicly; and not content with this inhuman injury of her person, those brutal men ravished her daughters in the presence of the queen.

This outrage aroused the Iceni to revenge, and every man took a solemn oath to avenge this brutal wrong inflicted upon their queen and family. The Trinobantes next raised the war-cry, and in every part of the island where the injuries of the queen of the Iceni became known, the indignant Britons crowded around the standard of revolt, eager for the blood of the Roman barbarians.

Carnelodunum (London) was the only town that remained loyal; but even there the Romans were not safe. Throughout the whole island an indiscriminate massacre of men, women, and children, took place; and in one instance a legion of the Roman army, attempting to stay the dreadful retribution of the Iceni, were all slaughtered to a man. In London the revolters made terrible havoc. The Romans in great numbers fled to their principal temple for protection, but it was set on fire, and with its living contents entirely consumed. That outrage upon the queen of the Iceni, cost Rome eighty thousand of her citizens.

As soon as Paulinus heard of this revolt, he left Mona, and hastened to the assistance of his people. This the Britons expected; and the armies of the several states were combined, and, by unanimous consent, Boadicea was chosen commander-in-chief. The combined army of the Britons amounted to one hundred thousand men, while Paulinus could muster only about ten thousand. Alarmed at his comparatively weak condition, and the numerical strength of the revolters, the Roman general was perplexed to know what course to take. First he resolved to shut himself up in London, and bide the issue of a siege; but when he found the triumphant enemy marching toward the capital, he resolved to conquer them or die. The inhabitants of London begged him to remain in their defence, but he yielded to the solicitations of his soldiers, and the dictates of his own judgment, and resolved to do battle with the enemy.

The Roman army marched out into the open country and awaited the approach of the Britons. They chose for their camp a narrow strip of land, with a dense forest in the rear, while before them was spread out a spacious plain.

On this plain the host of Boadicea encamped, now numbering, (including the women and children who had been invited by the soldier-queen to witness the contest and share in the spoils of the undoubted victory,) two hundred and thirty thousand. Boadicea, still stung with the wrongs she had suffered, was eager to engage with Paulinus. With her daughters beside her, in a war-chariot, she traversed the ranks of the Britons, inflaming their zeal for her cause, and animating them with courage, by passionate addresses.

The description of her dress and appearance, on the morning of the battle that ended so disastrously for the royal amazon and her country, quoted from a Roman historian, is remarkably picturesque :—

" After she had dismounted from her chariot, in which she had been driving from rank to rank to encourage her troops, attended by her daughters and her numerous army, she proceeded to a throne of marshy turfs, appareled after the fashion of the Romans, in a loose gown of changeable colors, under which she wore a kirtle very thickly plaited, the tresses of her yellow hair hanging to the skirts of her dress. About her neck she wore a chain of gold, and bore a light spear in her hand, being tall, and of a comely, cheerful, and modest countenance; and so awhile she stood, pausing to survey her army, and being regarded with reverential silence, she addressed to them an impassioned and eloquent speech on the wrongs of her country."

" This is not the first time," cried she, " that Britons have been victorious under their queen. I come not here as one descended from royal progenitors, to fight for empire or riches, but as one of you—as a true Briton—to avenge the loss of liberty, the wrongs done to my own person, and the base violation of the chastity of my daughters. Roman lust has grown so strong, that nothing escapes its pollution; old and young are alike liable to its outrages. The gods have already begun to punish them according to their deserts. One legion that durst hazard a battle, was cut in pieces, and others have fled like cowards before us. Raise loud your war-shout, and their fears will make them flee. Consider your numbers and your motives for the war, and resolve to conquer or die. It is better to fall honorably in defence of liberty, than to submit to Roman outrage. Such, is *my* resolution; but, ye men, if ye choose, live and be slaves !"

When the brave queen had concluded her harangue, a loud shout ran along the lines of the British army, and exclamations of loyalty were heard on every side

But while these demonstrations denoted confidence of victory on the part of the Britons, Paulinus was unawed, and by forcible appeals to his soldiers, he raised their hopes and courage to the highest pitch. He pointed to the multitude of Britons, as a handful of men and immense numbers of women and children; he exorted them to believe the Britons to be cowards— charged them to keep close together so as to advance in an unbroken phalanx, and to fight sword in hand, after they had thrown their darts.

Then, ordering a charge to be sounded, the Romans advanced in a solid column, hurled their javelins with terrible effect, with desperate power broke into the ranks of the Britons, and with sword in hand spread death and desolation in their path. Such an unexpected and fierce onslaught, struck terror to the islanders, for they supposed the Romans would be awed by their numbers; and it was in vain that Boadicea encouraged them to repel the attack. They fled in dismay in every direction. The women and children were exposed to the fury of the Romans; neither age nor sex, nor even horses were spared; and when the sun set upon Britain that night, more than seventy thousand of her children lay dead upon that battle-field. Boadicea and her daughters narrowly escaped falling into the hands of the conquerors; but, stung with remorse and despair at her accumulated misfortunes, she took poison, and died.

Such, in brief, is a romantic chapter of the early history of Britain, and in it are shadowed forth many of the bolder features of the human character,—the tyranny of uncontrolled power, ambition, avarice, cruelty, lust; the generous heroism of woman, the strength of innate principles of freedom, the meanness of cowardice, and the suicidal tendency of misfortune and despair. And such are the leading features in almost every chapter of the world's history, where states and empires have changed masters. The record of the political progress of nations, is a wonderful romance, where truth and fable are combined in presenting to generation after generation, an entertaining volume for amusement and instruction; and, doubtless, Byron was not wide of the mark, when he denominated all history, " a splendid fiction."

Berengaria of Navarre.

BERENGARIA OF NAVARRE,

BERENGARIA, the beautiful daughter of Sancho the Wise, King of Navarre, was first seen by Richard Cœur de Lion, at a grand tournament given by her gallant brother, at Pampeluna, her native city. Richard was then captivated by the beauty of Berengaria, but his engagement to the fair and frail Alice of France prevented him from offering her his hand.

Berengaria may be considered a Provençal princess, by language and education, though she was Spanish by descent. Her mighty sire, Sancho the Wise, had for his immediate ancestor Sancho the Great, called the Emperor of all Spain. He inherited the little kingdom of Navarre, and married Beatrice, daughter to Alphonso, King of Castille, by whom he had three children, Berengaria, Blanche, and Sancho, surnamed the Strong, a hero celebrated by the Provençal poets for his gallant exploits against the Moors. He defeated the Miramolin, and broke the chains that guarded the camp of the infidel with his battle-axe, which chains were afterwards transferred to the armorial bearings of Navarre.

An ardent friendship had subsisted from boyhood between Richard and Sancho the Strong, the gallant brother of Berengaria. A similarity of pursuits strengthened the intimacy of Richard with the royal family of Navarre. The father and brother of Berengaria were celebrated for their skill and judgment in Provençal poetry. Berengaria was herself a learned princess ; and Richard, who was not only a troubadour poet but, as acting sovereign of Aquitaine, was the prince and judge of all troubadours, became naturally drawn into close bonds of amity with a family, whose tastes and pursuits were similar to his own.

No one can marvel that the love of the ardent Richard should be strengthened when he met the beautiful, the cultivated, and virtuous Berengaria, in the familiar intercourse which sprang from his friendship with her gallant brother ; but a long and secret engagement, replete with " hope deferred," was the fate of Richard the Lion-hearted and the fair flower of Navarre.

Our early historians first mention the attachment of Richard and Berengaria about the year 1177. If we take that event for a datum, even allowing the princess to have been very young when she attracted the love of Richard, she must have been twenty-six at least before the death of his father placed him at liberty to demand her hand. Richard had another motive for his extreme desire for this alliance ; he considered that this beloved mother, Queen Eleanora, was deeply indebted to King Sancho, the father of Berengaria, because he had pleaded her cause with Henry II., and obtained some amelioration of her imprisonment.

Soon after Richard ascended the English throne he sent his mother, Queen Eleanora, to the court of her friend, Sancho the Wise, to demand the Princess Berengaria in marriage, "for," says Vinisauf, " he had long loved the elegant girl." Sancho the Wise not only received the proposition with joy, but intrusted Berengaria to the care of Queen Eleanora. The royal ladies traveled from the court of Navarre together, across Italy to Naples, where they found the ships belonging to Eleanora had arrived in the bay. But etiquette forbade Berengaria to approach her lover till he was free from the claims of Alice ; therefore she sojourned with Queen Eleanora at Brindisi, in the spring of 1191, waiting the message from King Richard, announcing that he was free to receive the hand of the Princess of Navarre.

It was at Messina that the question of the engagement between the Princess Alice and King of England was debate with Philip Augustus, her brother ; and more than once, the potentates assembled, for the crusade expected that the forces of France and England would be called into action, to decide the right of King Richard to give his hand to another lady than the sister of the King of France.

The rhymes of Piers of Langtoft, recapitulate these events with brevity and quaintness :—

> " Then spake King Philip,
> And in grief said,
>   ' My sister Alice
> Is now forsaken,
>   Since one of more riches
> Of Navarre hast thou taken.'
>   When King Richard understood
> What King Philip had sworn,
>   Before clergy he stood,
> And proved on that morn,
>   That Alice to his father
> A child had borne,
>   Which his sire King Henry
> Held for his own.
>   A maiden child it was,
> And now dead it is.
>   ' This was a great trespass,
> And against my own witte,
>   If I Alice take.' "

King Philip then contends that Richard held in hand his sister's dower, the good city of Gisors. Upon this, the King of England brings the matter to a conclusion in these words :—

> " Now, said King Richard,
>   That menace may not be,
> For thou shall have ward
>   Of Gisors thy citée,
> And treasure ilk a deal.
>   Richard yielded him his right,
> His treasure and his town,
>   Before witness at sight,
> (Of clerk and eke baron,)
>   His sister he might marry,
> Wherever God might like,
>   And, to make certainty,
> Richard a quittance took."

The French contemporary chroniclers, who are exceedingly indignant at the repudiation of their princess, attribute it solely to Eleanora's influence. Bernard, the treasurer, says, " The old queen could not endure that Richard should espouse Alice, but demanded the sister of the King of Navarre for a wife for her son. At this the King of Navarre was right joyful, and she traveled with Queen Eleanora to Messina. When she arrived Richard was absent, but Queen Joanna was there, preparing herself to embark next day. The Queen of England could not tarry, but said to Joanna—' Fair daughter, take this damsel for me to the king your brother, and tell him I command him to espouse her speedily.' Joanna received her willingly, and Eleanora returned to France."

Piers of Langtoft resumes :—

> " She be left Berengere,
>   At Richard's cottage,
>   Queen Joanne held her dear ;
>   They lived as doves in cage."

King Richard and King Tancred were absent on a pilgrimage to the shrine of St. Agatha at Catania, where Tancred must have devoutly prayed for the riddance of his guest. Richard here presented the Sicilian king with a famous sword, pretending it was Caliburn, the brand of King Arthur, lately found at Glastonbury, during his father's antiquarian researches for the tomb of that king.

Richard then embarked in his favorite galley, named by him Trenc the-mere.* He had previously, in honor of his betrothment, instituted an order of twenty-four knights, who pledged themselves in a fraternity with the king to scale the walls of Acre ; and that they might be known in the storming of that city, the king appointed them to wear a blue band of leather on the left leg, from which they were called Knights of the Blue Thong.

The season of Lent prevented the immediate marriage of Richard and his betrothed ; and, as etiquette did not permit the unwedded maiden, Berengaria, to embark in the Trenc-the-mere under the immediate protection of her lover, she sailed in company with Queen Joanna, in one of the strongest ships, under the care of a brave knight, called Stephen de Turnham.

After these arrangements Richard led the van of the fleet in Trenc-the-mere, bearing a huge lantern at her poop, to rally

* Literally meaning, *cut-the-sea.*

4

the fleet in the darkness of night.   Thus, with a hundred and
fifty ships and fifty galleys, did Lion-hearted Richard and his
bride and sister, hoist sail for Palestine, where Philip Augustus
had already indolently commenced the siege of Acre.

> "Syrian virgins wail and weep,
>   English Richard ploughs the deep."

But we must turn a deaf ear to the bewitching metre of polished verse, and quote details taken by Piers of Langtoft from
the Provençal comrade of Richard and Berengaria's crusade
voyage :—

> " Till King Richard be forward,
>   He may have no rest,
>   Acres then is his tryste,
>   Upon Saracen fiends,
>   To venge Jesu Christ,
>   Hitherward he wends.
>   The king's sister Joanne,
>   And Lady Berengare,
>   Foremost sailed of ilk one ;
>   Next them his chancellor
>   Roger Mancel.
>   The chancellor so hight,
>   His tide fell not well ;
>   A tempest on him light,
>   His ship was down borne,
>   Himself there to die ;
>   The king's seal was lost,
>   With other gallies tway.
>   Lady Joanna she
>   The Lord Jesu besought,
>   In Cyprus she might be
>   To haven quickly brought,

The maiden Berengare,
She was sore afright,
That neither far nor near,
Her king rode in sight."

Queen Joanna was alarmed for herself; but the maiden Berengaria only thought of Richard's safety.

Bernard, the treasurer, does not allow that Joanna was quite so much frightened. We translate his words:—"Queen Joanna's galley sheltered in the harbor of Limoussa, when Isaac, the Lord of Cyprus, sent two boats, and demanded if the queen would land. She declined the offer, saying, 'All she wanted was to know whether the King of England had passed.' They replied, 'They did not know.' At that juncture Isaac approached with a great power, upon which the cavaliers, who guarded the royal ladies, got the galley in order to be rowed out of the harbor at the first indication of hostility. Meantime Isaac, who saw Berengaria on board, demanded, 'What damsel that was with them?' They declared, 'She was the sister of the King of Navarre, whom the King of England's mother had brought for him to espouse.' Isaac seemed so angry at this intelligence, that Stephen de Turnham gave signal to heave up the anchor, and the queen's galley rowed with all speed into the offing."

When the gale had somewhat abated, King Richard, after mustering his navy, found not only that the ship was missing, wherein were drowned both the chancellor of England and the great seal, but the galley that bore the precious freight of his sister and his bride. He immediately sailed from a friendly Cretan harbor in search of his lost ships. When arrived off Cyprus, he entered the bay of Famagusta, and beheld the galley 'hat contained his princesses, laboring heavily and tossing in the offing. He became infuriated with the thought that some wrong had been offered to them, and leaped, armed as he was, into the first boat that could be prepared. His anger increased on learning that the queen's galley had put into the bay in the storm, but had been driven inhospitably from shelter by the threats of the Greek despot.*

At the time of Richard's landing, Isaac and all his islanders were busily employed in plundering the wreck of the chancellor's ship and two English transports, then stranded on the Cypriot shore. As this self-styled emperor, though in behavior worse than a pagan, professed to be a Christian, Richard, at his first landing, sent him a civil message, suggesting the propriety of leaving off plundering his wrecks. To this Isaac returned an impertinent answer, saying, " that whatever goods the sea threw on his island he should take, without asking any one."

" They shall be bought full dear, by Jesu, heaven's king !"

With this saying, Richard, battle-axe in hand, led his crusaders so boldly to the rescue, that the mock emperor and his Cypriots scampered into Limoussa, the capital of the island, much faster than they had left it.

Freed from the presence of the inhospitable despot, King Richard made signals for Joanna's galley to enter the harbor. Berengaria, half dead with fatigue and terror, was welcomed on shore by the conquering king, "when," says the chronicler, " there was joy and love enow."

As soon as Isaac Comnenus was safe behind the walls of his citadel, he sent a message to request a conference with King Richard, who expected he had a little lowered the despot's

* *Despot* was a title g'ven to the petty Greek potentates.

pride; but when they met, Isaac was so full of vaporing and boasting, that he elicited from King Richard an aside in English; and as Cœur de Lion then uttered the only words in our language he ever was known to speak, it is well they have been recorded by chronicle :—

"Ha! de debil!" exclaimed King Richard, "he speak like a fole Breton."*

As Isaac and Richard could not come to any terms of pacification, the despot retreated to a strong-hold in a neighboring mountain; while Richard, after making a speech to the Londoners, (we hope in more choice English than the above), instigating them to the storm of the Cypriot capital with promise of plunder, led them on to the attack, axe in hand. The Londoners easily captured Limoussa.

Directly the coast was clear of Isaac and his myrmidons; magnificent preparations were made at Limoussa for the nuptials and coronation of King Richard and Berengaria. We are able to describe the appearance made by these royal personages at this high solemnity. King Richard's costume, we may suppose, varied little from that in which he gave audience to the despot Isaac, a day after the marriage took place.

" A satin tunic of rose-color was belted round his waist—his mantle was of striped silver tissue, brocaded with silver half-moons—his sword of fine Damascus steel, had a hilt of gold, and a silver-scaled sheath—on his head he wore a scarlet bonnet, brocaded in gold, with figures of animals. He bore a truncheon in his hand. His Spanish steed was led before him, saddled,

* This speech implied no offence to the English, but was meant as a reproach ' the Bretons, who are to this day proverbial in France for their willfulness. Besides, Richard was bitter against the Bretons, who deprived him of the society of his then acknowledged heir, Arthur, their duke.—(*Vinisauf.*)

and bitted with gold, and the saddle was inlaid with precious stones. Two little golden lions were fixed on it, in the place of a crupper. They were figured with their paws raised in act to strike each other." In this attire, Vinisauf adds, Richard, who had yellow curls, a bright complexion, and a figure like Mars himself, appeared a perfect model of military and manly grace.

The effigy of Queen Berengaria at Espan certainly presents her as a bride—a circumstance which is ascertained by the flowing tresses—royal matrons always wearing their hair covered, or else closely braided.

Her hair is parted, *à la vierge*, on the brow; a transparent veil, open on each side, like the Spanish mantillas, hangs behind, and covers the rich tresses at their length. The veil is confined by a regal diadem of peculiar splendor, studded with several bands of gems, and surmounted by *fleurs-de-lis*, to which so much foliage is added as to give it the appearance of a double crown, perhaps because she was crowned queen of Cyprus as well as England. Our antiquarians affirm, that the peculiar character of Berengaria's elegant but singular style of beauty brings conviction to every one who looks on her effigy that it is a carefully finished portrait.

At his marriage King Richard proclaimed a grand feast.

> " To Limoussa the lady was led,
> His feast the king did cry,
> Berengere will be wed,
> And sojourn thereby
> The third day of the feast;
> Bishop Bernard of Bayone
> Newed oft the geste
> To the queen he gave the crown."

"And there, in the joyous month of May, 1191," says an ancient writer, "in the flourishing and spacious isle of Cyprus, celebrated as the very abode of the goddess of love, did King Richard solemnly take to wife his beloved lady Berengaria. By the consent of the Cypriots, wearied of Isaac's tyranny, and by the advice of the allied crusaders, who came to assist at his nuptials, Richard was crowned King of Cyprus, and his bride Queen of England and Cyprus.

Soon after, the fair heiress of Cyprus, daughter to the despot Isaac, came and threw herself at the feet of Richard. "Lord King," she said, "have mercy on me;" when the king courteously put forth his hand to lift her from the ground, and sent her to his wife and his sister Joanna. As many historical scandals are afloat respecting the Cypriot princess, implying that Richard, captivated by the distressed beauty, from that moment forsook his queen, it is well to observe the words of an eye-witness, who declares that Richard sent the lady directly to his queen, from whom she never parted till after their return to Europe.

The surrender of the Cypriot princess was followed by the capture of her father, whom the King of England bound in silver chains richly guilt, and presented to Queen Berengaria as her captive.*

After the conclusion of the nuptials and coronation of Berengaria, her royal bridegroom once more hoisted his flag on his good galley Trenc-the-mere, and set sail in beautiful summer weather for Palestine. Berengaria and her sister-in-law again

---

* Isaac afterwards entered among the Templars, and in their order died. Richard presented his island to Guy de Lusignan, his friend, as a compensation for the loss of Jerusalem. This dethronement of Isaac, and the captivity of his daughter, were the origin of Richard's imprisonment in Germany, as we shall presently see.

sailed under the protection of Sir Stephen de Turnham, it being
safer than companionship with the warlike Richard. Their
alley made the port of Acre before the Trenc-the-mere.

"On their arrival at Acre, though," says Bernard le Treso-
rier, " it was very grievous to the king of France to know that
Richard was married to any other than his sister ; yet he received Berengaria with great courtesy, taking her in his arms,
and lifting her on shore himself from the boat to the beach."

Richard appeared before Acre on the long bright day of St.
Barnabas, when the whole allied army, elated by the naval victory he had won by the way, marched to the beach to welcome
their champion. " The earth shook with footsteps of the Christians, and the sound of their shouts."

When Acre was taken, Richard established his queen and
sister safely there. They remained at Acre with the Cypriot
princess, during the whole of the Syrian campaign, under the
care of Richard's Castellans, Bertrand de Verbun and Stephen
de Munchenis.

To the left of the mosque at Acre are the ruins of a palace,
called, to this day, King Richard's Palace.* This was doubtless
the abode of Berengaria

There is not a more pleasant spot in history than the tender
friendship of Berengaria and Joanna, who formed an attachment
amidst the perils and terrors of storm and siege, ending only
with their lives. How quaintly, yet expressively, is their gentle
and feminine love for each other marked by the sweet simplicity
of the words,

> " They held each other dear,
> And lived like doves in cage !"

---

* Dr. Clarke's Travels. The tradition is that Richard built the Palace ; but he
had no time for any such work. This architecture is Saracenic, and was doubtless a palace of the resident emir of Acre.

nuting, at tne same time, tne harem-like seclusion in which the royal ladies dwelt, while sharing the crusade campaign.

It was from the citadel of Acre that Richard tore down the banner of Leopold, archduke of Austria, who was the uncle of the Cypriot lady. Her captivity was the real matter of dispute

We have little space to dwell on Richard's deeds of romantic valor in Palestine, on the capture of Ascalon, or the battle of Jaffa, before which city was killed Richard's good steed, named Fanuelle, whose feats in battle are nearly as much celebrated by the troubadours as those of his master.*

After the death of Fanuelle, Richard was obliged to fight on foot. The courteous Saladin, who saw him thus battling, was shocked that so accomplished a cavalier should be dismounted, and sent him as a present a magnificent Arab charger. Richard had the precaution to order one of his knights to mount the charger first. The headstrong beast no sooner found a stranger on his back, than he took the bit between his teeth, and, refusing all control, galloped back to his own quarters, carrying the Christian knight into the midst of Saladin's camp. If King Richard had ridden the wilful animal, he would in like manner have been at the mercy of the Saracens ; and Saladin was so much ashamed of the misbehavior of his present, that he could scarcely look up while he apologized to the Christian knight ; for it appeared as if he had laid a trap for the liberty of King Richard. He sent back the knight, mounted on a more manageable steed, n which Richard rode to the end of the campaign.

King Richard, during his Syrian campaign, was once within

* By some called Favelle, probably Flavel, meaning yellow-colored. Vinisauf declares this peerless charger was taken among the spoils of Cyprus, with another named Lyard. The cavaliers in ancient times named their steeds from their color, as *Bayard*, bay-color. *Lyard*, gray ; *Ferraunt*, black as iron ; *Flaret*, yellow, or very light sorrel.

sight of Jerusalem, but never took it. While he was with his queen, Berengaria, at Acre, an incident befell him, of which de Joinville, the companion in arms of St. Louis, has thus preserved the memory :—

" In those times, when Hugh, Duke of Burgundy, and King Richard of England, were abiding at Acre, they received intelligence that they might take Jerusalem if they chose, for its garrison had gone to the assistance of Damascus. The Duke of Burgundy and King Richard accordingly marched towards the holy city, King Richard's battalions leading the way, while Burgundy's force brought up the rear. But when King Richard drew near to Jerusalem, intelligence was brought him that the Duke of Burgundy had turned back with his division, out of pure envy, that it might not be said that the King of England had taken Jerusalem. As these tidings were discussing, one of the King of England's knights cried out,

" ' Sire, sire, only come hither, and I will show you Jerusalem.'

" But the king, throwing down his weapons, said, with tears in his eyes, and hands uplifted to heaven—

" ' Ah ! Lord God, I pray thee that I may never see thy holy city Jerusalem, since things thus happen, and since I cannot deliver it from the hands of thine enemies !' Richard could do nothing more than return to his queen and sister at Acre.

" You must know that this King Richard performed such deeds of prowess when he was in the Holy Land, that the Saracens, on seeing their horses frightened at a shadow or a bush, cried out to them, ' What ! dost think Melech-Ric is there ?' This they were accustomed to say from the many times he had vanquished them. In like manner, when the children of

Turks or Saracens cried, their mothers said to them, ' Hush, hush ! or I will give you to King Richard ;' and from the terror of these words the babes were instantly quiet."

The Provençal historian affirms, that the final truce between Richard and Saladin was concluded in a fair flowery meadow near Mount Tabor, where Richard was so much charmed with the gallant bearing of the Prince of Miscreants, as Saladin is civilly termed in the crusading treaties, that he declared he would rather be the friend of that brave and honest pagan, than the ally of the crafty Philip or the brutal Leopold.

The autumn of 1192 had commenced, when King Richard concluded his peace with Saladin, and prepared to return, covered with fruitless glory, to his native dominions   A mysterious estrangement had at this time taken place between him and Berengaria ; yet the chroniclers do not mention that any rival had supplanted the queen, but merely that accidents of war had divided him from her company. As for the Cypriot princess, if he were estranged from his queen, he must likewise have been separated from the fair captive, since she always remained with Berengaria.

The king bade farewell to his queen and sister, and saw them embark the very evening of his own departure. The queens were accompanied by the Cypriot princess, and sailed from Acre, under the care of Stephen de Turnham, September the 29th. Richard meant to return by a different route across Europe. He traveled in the disguise of a Templar, and embarked in a ship belonging to the master of the Temple. This vessel was wrecked off the coast of Istria, which forced Richard to proceed homewards through the domains of his enemy, Leopold of Austria. But to his ignorance of geography is attributed his near approach to Leopold's capital. After several narrow escapes, a page sent by Richard to purchase provisions at a village near Vienna, was recognized by an officer who had made the late crusade with Leopold. The boy was seized, and, after enduring cruel torments, he confessed where he had left his master.

When Leopold received certain intelligence where Richard harbored, the inn was searched, but not a soul found there who bore any appearance of a king. "No," said the people, "there is no one here, without he be the Templar in the kitchen, now turning the fowls which are roasting for dinner." The officers of Leopold took the hint and went into the kitchen, where in fact was seated a Templar very busy turning the spit. The Austrian chevalier, who had served in the crusade, knew him, and said quickly, "There he is—seize him!"

Cœur de Lion started from the spit, and did battle for his liberty right valiantly, but was overborne by numbers.

The revengeful Leopold immediately imprisoned his gallant enemy, and immured him so closely in a Styrian castle, called Tenebreuse, that for months no one knew whether the lion-hearted king was alive or dead. Richard, whose heroic name was the theme of admiration in Europe, and the burden of every song, seemed vanished from the face of the earth.

Better fortune attended the vessel that bore the fair freight of the three royal ladies. Stephen de Turnham's galley arrived without accident at Naples, where Berengaria, Joanna, and the Cypriot princess, landed safely, and, under the care of Sir Stephen, journeyed to Rome.

The Provençal traditions declare, that, here Berengaria first took the alarm that some disaster had happened to her lord, from seeing a belt of jewels offered for sale, which she knew had been in his possession when she parted from him. At Rome she likewise heard some vague reports of his shipwreck, and of the enmity of the emperor Henry VI.

Berengaria was detained at Rome with her royal companions, by her fear of the emperor, for upwards of half a year. At length the pope, moved by her distress and earnest entreaties, sent them under the care of Messire Mellar, one of the cardinals, to Pisa, whence they proceeded to Genoa, where they took shipping to Marseilles. At Marseilles, Berengaria was met by her friend and kinsman, the King of Arragon, who showed the royal ladies every mark of reverence, gave them safe conduct through his Provençal domains, and sent them on under the escort of the Count de Sancto Egidio.

This Egidio is doubtless the gallant Raymond Count St. Gilles, who, traveling from Rome with a strong escort, offered his protection to the distressed queens ; and though his father, the Count of Toulouse, had during Richard's crusade invaded Guienne, and drawn on himself a severe chastisement from Berengaria's faithful brother, Sancho the Strong ; yet the young count so well acquitted himself of his charge, that he won the affections of the fair widow, Queen Joanna, on the journey. The attachment of these lovers healed the enmity that had long subsisted between the house of Aquitaine and that of the Counts of Toulouse, on account of the superior claims of Queen Eleanora on that great fief. When Eleanora found the love that subsisted between her youngest child and the heir of Toulouse, she conciliated his father by giving up her rights to her daughter, and Berengaria had the satisfaction of seeing her two friends united after she arrived at Poitou.

Now Queen Berengaria is left safely in her own dominions, it is time to return to her unfortunate lord, who seems to have been destined by the malice of Leopold to a life-long incarceration. The royal prisoner almost despaired of liberty when he wrote that pathetic passage in his well-known Provençal tenson, saying, " Now know I for a certainty that there exists for me neither friend nor parent, or for the lack of gold and silver I should not so long remain a prisoner."

He scarcely did justice to his affectionate mother, who, directly she learned his captivity, never ceased exerting herself for his release.

Without giving any credence to the ballad story of King Richard and the Lion's heart, which solely seems to have arisen from a metaphorical epithet of the troubadour Peyrols,* and is not even alluded to by the most imaginative of contemporary chroniclers, it really appears that Richard was ill-treated during his German captivity. Matthew Paris declares, he was thrown into a dungeon, from whence no other man ever escaped with life, and was loaded with irons; yet his countenance was ever serene, and his conversation pleasant and facetious, with the crowds of armed guards by whom he was surrounded day and night.

It was a long time before Richard's friends could with any certainty make out his locality. He was utterly lost for some months. Blondel, a troubadour knight and poet, who had been shipwrecked with him on the coast of Istria, and who had

In the beautiful crusade *sirrente* extant by Peyrols, he calls the king *lion-hearted Richard*. Peyrols was his fellow-soldier.—(*Sismondi*.)

The earliest chronicler who mentions the lion legend is Rastall, the brother-in-law of Sir Thomas More, who had no better means of knowing the truth than we have. Here are his quaint sayings on the subject :—

" It is said that a lyon was put to King Richard, being in prison, to have devoured him, and when the lyon was gaping he put his arm in his mouth and *pulled the lion by the heart so hard* that he slew the lyon, and therefore is called Cœur de Lyon ; while others say he is called Cœur de Lyon, because of his boldness and hardy stomach."

sought him through the cities of southern Germany, sang, beneath the tower Tenebreuse in which he was confined, a *tenson* which Richard and he had composed together. Scarcely had he finished the first stanza, when Richard replied with the second. Blondel directly went to Queen Eleanora, and gave her tidings of the existence of her son, and she took measures for his release. Her letters to the pope are written with a passionate eloquence, highly illustrative of that tradition of the south which names her among the poets of her country :—

" Mother of pity," she says, " look upon a mother of so many afflictions! or, if thy holy Son, the fountain of mercy, afflicts my son for my transgression, oh, let me, who am the cause, endure alone the punishment.

" Two sons alone remain for my succor, who but indeed survive for my misery ; for King Richard exists in fetters, while Prince John, brother to the captive, depopulates with the sword, and wastes with fire. The Lord is against me, his wrath fights against me ; therefore do my children fight against each other !"

The queen-mother here alludes to the strife raised by Prince John. He had obtained his brother's leave to abide in England on condition that he submitted to the government established there. Queen Eleanora had intended to fix her residence at Rouen, as a central situation between her own dominions and those of King Richard. But the confused state of affairs in England summoned her thither, February 11, 1192. She found John in open rebellion, for, stimulated by messages from Philip Augustus, offering him all Richard's continental provinces and the hand of Alice rejected by Richard, he aimed at nothing less than the English crown. The arrival of his mother curbed his turbulence ; she told him to touch his brother's rights under peru of her curse ; sne forbade his disgraceful intention of allying himself with Alice ; and, to render such mischievous project impossible, she left that princess in close confinement at Rouen, instead of delivering her ·to Philip Augustus, as King Richard had agreed ; so little truth is there in the common assertion, that the worthless character of John might be attributed to the encouragement his vices received from his mother ; but it was the doting affection of Henry II. for his youngest son that had this effect, as he was the child of his old age and constantly near him, while the queen was kept in confinement at a distance from her family.

When Queen Eleanora and the chief justiciary heard of the detention of King Richard, they sent two abbots to confer with him in Germany. They met him with his guards on the road to Worms, where a diet of the empire was soon to be held, and were received by him with his usual spirit and animation. He inquired into the state of his friends, his subjects, and his dominions, and particularly after the health of the King of Scotland, on whose honor, he said, he entirely relied ; and certainly he was not deceived in his judgment of the character of that hero. On hearing of the base conduct of his brother John, he was shocked and looked grave ; but presently recovering his cheerfulness, he said, with a smile, " My brother John was never made for conquering kingdoms !"

Richard defended himself before the diet with eloquence and pathos that drew tears from most of his hearers ; and the mediation of the princes of the empire induced the emperor to accept as ransom one hundred thousand marks of silver.

Meantime the ransom was collected in England, Normandy, and Aquitaine, to which Queen Eleanora largely contributed. When the first installment was ready, this affectionate mother and the chief justiciary set out for Germany, a little before Christmas. Queen Eleanora was accompanied by her granddaughter, Eleanora, surnamed the Pearl of Brittany. This young princess was promised, by the ransom-treaty, in marriage to the heir of Leopold of Austria. The Cypriot princess was likewise taken from the keeping of Queen Berengaria, on the demand of the emperor, and surrendered to her German relatives.

It was owing to the exertions of the gallant Guelphic princes, his relations, that the actual liberation of Cœur de Lion was at last effected. Henry the Lion, Duke of Saxony, and his sons appeared before the diet, and pleaded the cause of the English hero with the most passionate eloquence; they pledged their credit for the payment of the remainder of his ransom, and actually left William of Winchester, the youngest Guelphic prince, in pawn with the emperor for the rest of the ransom.

After an absence of four years, three months, and nine days, King Richard landed at Sandwich, in April, the Sunday after St. George's day, in company with his royal mother, who had the pleasure of surrendering to him his dominions, both insular and continental, without diminution.

Eleanora's detention of the Princess Alice in Normandy had drawn on that country a fierce invasion from Philip Augustus, the result of which would have been doubtful, if the tears of Berengaria, then newly arrived in Aquitaine, had not prevailed on her noble brother, Sancho the Strong, to traverse France with two hundred choice knights. By the valor of this hero, and his chivalric reinforcement, Normandy was delivered from the King of France.

Berengaria, during the imprisonment of her royal husband, lost her father, Sancho the Wise, King of Navarre, who died in 1194, after a glorious reign of forty-four years.

5

After a second coronation, Richard went in progress throughout England, with his royal mother, to sit in judgment on those Castellans who had betrayed their fortresses to his brother John. At all these councils Queen Eleanora assisted him, being treated by her son with the utmost reverence, and sitting in state at his right hand.

The magnanimous Cœur de Lion treated these rebels with great lenity ; and when Prince John, on the arrival of the king at Rouen, being introduced by Queen Eleanora, knelt at his brother's feet for pardon, he raised him with this remarkable expression—" I forgive you, John, and I wish I could as easily forget your offence as you will my pardon."

King Richard finished his progress by residing some months in his Angevin territories.   Although he was in the vicinity of the loving and faithful Berengaria, he did not return to her society.   The reason of this estrangement was, that the king had renewed his connection with a number of profligate and worthless associates, the companions of his long bachelor-hood in his father's lifetime.   His conduct at this time infinitely scandalized all his subjects, as he abandoned himself to drinking and great infamy ; for which various virtuous churchmen reproved him boldly, to their credit be it spoken.

" The spring of 1195, Richard was hunting in one of his Norman forests, when he was met by a hermit, who recognized him, and preached him a very eloquent sermon on his irregular life, finishing by prophesying, that unless he repented, his end and punishment were close at hand.   The king answered slightingly, and went his way ; but the Easter following he was seized with a most severe illness, which threatened to be fatal, when he remembered the saying of the hermit-prophet, and, greatly alarmed, he began to repent of his sins."

Richard sent for all the monks within ten miles round, and made public confession of his iniquities, vowing, that if Queen Berengaria would forgive him, he would send for her, and never forsake her again.

The final restoration of Berengaria to the affections of her royal husband took place a few months after, when Richard proceeded to Poictiers, where he was reconciled to his queen, and kept Christmas and the new year of 1196 in that city, with princely state and hospitality. It was a year of great scarcity and famine, and the beneficent queen exerted her restored influence over the heart of the king, by persuading him to give all his superfluous money in bountiful alms to the poor; and through her goodness many were kept from perishing. From that time Queen Berengaria and King Richard were never parted. She found it best to accompany him in all his campaigns; and we find her with him at the hour of his death.

Higden, in the Polychronichon, gives this testimony to the love that Berengaria bore to Richard :—" The king took home to him his queen Berengaria, whose society he had for a long time neglected, though she were a royal, eloquent, and beauteous lady, and for his love had ventured with him through the world."

The same year the king, despairing of heirs by his consort, sent for young Arthur, Duke of Bretagne, that the boy might be educated at his court as future king of England. His mother, Constance, out of enmity to Queen Eleanora, unwisely refused this request, and she finished her folly by declaring for the king of France, then waging a fierce war against Richard. This step cost her hapless child his inheritance, and finally his life. From this time Richard acknowledged his brother John as his heir.

The remaining three years of Richard's life was spent in petty provincial wars with the king of France. In one of his treaties, the Princess Alice was at last surrendered to her brother, who gave her, with (a tarnished reputation, and) the dowry of the county of Ponthieu, in marriage to the Count of Aumerle, when she had arrived at her thirty-fifth year.

After the reconciliation between Richard and Berengaria, the royal revenues arising from the tin-mines in Cornwall and Devon, valued at two thousand marks per annum, were confirmed to the queen for her dower. Her continental dower was the city of Bigorre in Aquitaine, and the whole county of Mans.

It was the lively imagination of Richard, heated by the splendid fictions of Arabian romance, that hurried him to his end. A report was brought to him that a peasant plowing in the fields of Vidomar, Lord of Chaluz, in Aquitaine, had struck upon a trap-door which concealed an enchanted treasure, and going down into a cave discovered several golden statues with vases full of diamonds, all of which had been secured in the castle of Chaluz, for the private use of the Sieur de Vidomar. Richard, when he heard this fine tale, sent to Vidomar, demanding, as sovereign of the country, his share of the golden statues. The poor Castellan declared that no such treasure had been found; nothing but a pot of Roman coins had been discovered, and those he was welcome to have.

As Richard had set his mind on golden statues and vases of diamonds, and had thriven so well when he demanded the golden furniture from King Tancred, it was not probable he could lower his ideas to the reality stated by the unfortunate Lord of Vidomar. Accordingly he marched to besiege the Castle of Chaluz, sending word to Vidomar either to deliver the statues, or abide the storming of the castle. To this siege Queen Berengaria accompanied the king. Here Richard met his death, being pierced from the walls by an arrow from an arbalista, or crossbow, aimed by the hand of Bertrand de Gordon. It was the unskillfulness of the surgeon, who mangled the king's shoulder in cutting out the arrow, joined to Richard's own willfulness in neglecting the regimen of his physicians, that caused the mortification of a trifling wound, and occasioned the death of a hero, who to many faults joined a redeeming generosity that showed itself in his last moments. After enduring great agony from his wound, as he drew near to death, the Castle of Chaluz was taken. He caused Bertrand de Gordon to be brought before him, and telling him he was dying, asked him whether he had discharged the fatal arrow with the intention of slaying him ?

" Yes, tyrant," replied Gordon ; " for to you I owe the deaths of my father and my brother, and my first wish was to be revenged on you."

Notwithstanding the boldness of this avowal, the dying king commanded Gordon to be set at liberty, and it was not his fault that his detestable mercenary general, the Fleming, Marcade, caused him to be put to a cruel death.

Richard's death took place April 6th, 1199 ; his queen unquestionably was with him when he died. She corroborated the testimony that he left his dominions and two-thirds of his treasures to his brother John.

Richard appears to have borne some personal resemblance to his great uncle, William Rufus. Like him, his hair and complexion were warm in color, and his eyes blue and fiercely sparkling. Like Rufus, his strength was prodigious, but he had the advantage of a tall majestic figure. There are some points of resemblance in character between Richard and his collateral ancestor, though Richard must be considered a more learned and elegant prince, and susceptible, withal, of more frequent impulses of generosity and penitence. They both seem to have excelled in the same species of wit and lively repartee.

At the time of King Richard's death, Matthew Paris declares Queen Eleanora, his mother, was governing England, " where," adds that historian, " she was exceedingly respected and beloved."

Before the body of Cœur de Lion was committed to the grave, an additional load of anguish assailed the heart of his royal widow, through the calamities that befell Joanna, her friend, and Richard's favorite sister. The persecution on account of religion that afterwards visited Joanna's gallant son, in the well-known war against the Albigenses, had already attacked his father incipiently. Owing to the secret agitations of the Catholic clergy, the Barons of Toulouse were in arms against the gallant Raymond. Queen Joanna, though in a state little consistent with such exertions, flew to arms for the relief of her adored lord. We translate the following mournful passage from Guillaúme de Puy-Laurens :—" Queen Joanna was a woman of great courage, and was highly sensitive to the injuries of her husband. She laid siege to the Castle of Ceasar ; but, owing to the treachery of her attendants, her camp was fired—she escaped with difficulty from the burning tents, much scorched and hurt. Unsubdued by this accident, she hastened to lay her wrongs before her beloved brother, King Richard. She found he had just expired as she arrived. The pains of premature child-birth seized her as she heard the dire intelligence, and she sank under the double affliction of mental and corporeal agony. With her last breath she begged to be laid near her brother Richard." To Berengaria the request was made, and the cold remains of the royal brother and sister, the dearest objects of the sorrowing queen's affections, were laid, by her pious care, side by side in the stately abbey of Fontevraud.

The death of Joanna was immediately succeeded by that of Berengaria's only sister Blanche. This princess had been given in marriage by Cœur de Lion to his nephew and friend, the troubadour-prince, Thibaut of Champagne. The Princess Blanche died the day after the birth of a son, who afterwards was the heir both of Sancho and Berengaria, and finally King of Navarre. Thus, in the course of a few short weeks, was the Queen of England bereft of all that were near and dear to her; the world had become a desert to Berengaria before she left it for a life of conventual seclusion.

Queen Berengaria fixed her residence at Mans in the Orleannois, where she held a great part of her foreign dower. Here she founded the noble Abbey of L'Espan.

Once Queen Berengaria left her widowed retirement, when she met her brother-in-law, King John, and his fair young bride, at Chinon, her husband's treasure city. Here she compounded with the English monarch, for the dower she held in England, for two thousand marks per annum, to be paid half-yearly. After being entertained with royal magnificence, and receiving every mark of respect from the English court, the royal widow bade farewell to public splendor, and retired to conventual seclusion, and the practice of constant charity. But no sooner was John fixed firmly on the English throne, than he began to neglect the payment of the dower for which his sister-in-law had compounded; and in 1206, there appears in the Fœdera a passport for the queen-dowager to come to England for the purpose of conferring with King John; but there exists no authority whereby we can prove that she arrived in England.

The records of 1209 present a most elaborate epistle from Pope Innocent, setting forth the wrongs and wants of his dear daughter in Christ, Berengaria, who, he says, had appealed to him " with floods of tears streaming down her cheeks, and with audible cries"—which, we trust, were flowers of rhetoric of the pope's secretary. As Pope Innocent threatens John with an interdict, it is pretty certain that the wrongs of Berengaria formed a clause in the subsequent excommunication of the felon king.

In 1214, when the excommunication was taken off, there exists a letter from John to his dear sister, the illustrious Berengaria, praying that the pope's nuncio might arbitrate what was due to her. The next year brings a piteous letter from King John, praying that his dearly-beloved sister will excuse his delay of payment, seeing the " greatness of his adversity by reason of the wickedness of his magnates and barons," who had invited Prince Louis of France to spoil her estates ; " but when," says King John, " these clouds that have overcast our serenity shall disperse, and our kingdom be full of joyful tranquillity, then the pecuniary debt owed to our dear sister shall be paid joyfully and thankfully."

This precious epistle was penned July 8th, 1216, by John but he died the succeeding October, and Berengaria's debt was added to the vast sum of his other trespasses ; for " joyful tranquillity" never came for him, nor of course her time of payment.

In the reign of Henry III., Berengaria had again to require the pope's assistance for the payment of her annuity. Her arrears at that time amounted to £4040 sterling ; but the Templars became guarantees and agents for her payments ; and from that time the pecuniary troubles of Berengaria cease to form a feature in our national records.

The date of Berengaria's death has generally been fixed about the year 1230, but that was only the year of the completion of her Abbey of Espan, and of her final retirement from the world, as from that time she took up her abode within its walls, and finished there her blameless life, at an advanced age, some years afterwards.

Berengaria was interred in her own stately abbey. The following most interesting particulars of her monument we transcribe from the noble work of the late Mr. Stothard, edited by his accomplished widow, Mrs. Bray :—

" When Mr. Stothard visited the Abbey of L'Espan, near Mans, in search of the effigy of Berengaria, he found the church converted into a barn, and the object of his inquiry in a mutilated state, concealed under a quantity of wheat. It was in excellent preservation, with the exception of the left arm. By the effigy were lying the bones of the queen, the silent witnesses of the sacrilegious demolition of the tomb. After some search, a portion of the arm belonging to the statue was recovered." Three men who had assisted in the work of destruction, stated, " that the monument with the figure upon it stood in the centre of the aisle, at the east end of the church ; that there was no coffin within it, but a small square box, containing bones, pieces of linen, some stuff embroidered with gold, and a slate, on which was found an inscription." The slate was found in possession of a canon of the church of St. Julien, at Mans ; upon it was engraven an inscription, of which the following is a translation :—

" The tomb of the most serene Berengaria, Queen of England, the noble founder of this monastery, was restored and removed to this more sacred place. In it were deposited the bones which were found in the ancient sepulchre, on the 27th May, in the year of our Lord 1672."

The sides of the tomb are ornamented with deep quatrefoils. The effigy which was upon it is in high relief. It represents the queen with her hair unconfined, but partly concealed by the coverchief, over which is placed an elegant crown. Her mantle is fastened by a narrow band crossing her breast; a large fermail, or brooch, richly set with stones, confines her tunic a the neck. To an ornamental girdle, which encircles her waist, is attached a small aumoniere or purse. This greatly resembles a modern reticule, with a chain and clasped top. The queen holds in her hands a box, singular from the circumstance of its having embossed on the cover a second representation of herself, as lying on a bier, with waxen torches burning in candlesticks on either side of her.

From early youth to her grave, Berengaria manifested devoted love for Richard—uncomplaining when deserted by him, forgiving when he returned, and faithful to his memory unto death. The royal Berengaria, Queen of England, though never *in* England, little deserves to be forgotten by any admirer of feminine and conjugal virtue.

Laura.

LAURA.

Laura, rendered immortal by the love and lyre of Petrarch
was the daughter of Audibert de Noves, who was of the *haute
noblesse* of Avignon. He died in the infancy of Laura, leaving
her a dowry of one thousand gold crowns, (about fifty thousand
dollars,) a magnificent portion for those times. She was married
at the age of eighteen to Hugh de Sade, a young noble only a
few years older than his bride, but not distinguished by any advantages either of person or mind. The marriage contract is
dated in January, 1325, two years before her first meeting with
Petrarch ; and in it her mother, the Lady Ermessende, and her
brother, John de Noves, stipulate to pay the dower left by her
father ; and also to bestow on the bride two magnificent dresses
for state occasions—one of green, embroidered with violets, the
other of crimson, trimmed with feathers. In all the portraits
of Laura now extant, she is represented in one of these two
dresses, and they are frequently alluded to by Petrarch. He
tells us expressly that, when he first met her at matins in the
church of Saint Claire, she was habited in a robe of green spotted
with violets. Mention is also made of a coronal of silver with
which she wreathed her hair—of her necklaces and ornaments
of pearls. Diamonds are not once alluded to, because the art
of cutting them had not then been invented. From all which it
appears that Laura was opulent, and moved in the first class of
society. It was customary for women of rank in those times to

dress with extreme simplicity on ordinary occasions, but with the most gorgeous splendor when they appeared in public.

There are some beautiful descriptions of Laura surrounded by her young female companions, divested of all her splendid apparel, in a simple white robe and a few flowers in her hair, but still preëminent over all by her superior loveliness.

She was in person a fair, Madonna-like beauty, with soft dark eyes, and a profusion of pale golden hair parted on her brow, and falling in rich curls over her neck. The general character of her beauty must have been pensive, soft, unobtrusive, and even somewhat languid. This softness and repose must have been far removed from insipidity, for Petrarch dwells on the rare and varying expression of her loveliness, the lightening of her smile, and the tender magic of her voice, which was felt in the inmost heart. He dwells on the celestial grace of her figure and movements, and describes the beauty of her hand and the loveliness of her mouth. She had a habit of veiling her eyes with her hand, and her looks were generally bent on the earth.

In a portrait of Laura, in the Laurentinian library at Florence, the eyes have this characteristic downcast look.

Laura was distinguished, then, by her rank and fortune, but more by her loveliness, her sweetness, and the untainted purity of her life and manners in the midst of a society noted for its licentiousness. Now she is known as the subject of Petrarch's verses, as the woman who inspired an immortal passion, and, kindling into living fire the dormant sensibility of the poet, gave origin to the most beautiful and refined, the most passionate and yet the most delicate amatory poetry that exists in the world.

Petrarch was twenty-three years of age when he first felt the power of a violent and inextinguishable passion. At six in the morning on the sixth of April, A. D. 1327, (he often fondly records the exact year, day and hour,) on the occasion of the festival of Easter, he visited the church of Saint Claire at Avignon, and beheld, for the first time, Laura de Sade. She was just twenty years of age, and in the bloom of beauty—a beauty so touching and heavenly, so irradiated by purity and smiling innocence, and so adorned by gentleness and modesty, that the first sight stamped the image in the poet's heart, never thereafter to be erased.

Petrarch beheld the loveliness and sweetness of the young beauty, and was transfixed. He sought acquaintance with her; and while the manners of the times prevented his entering her house, he enjoyed many opportunities of meeting her in society, and of conversing with her. He would have declared his love, but her reserve enforced silence. " She opened my breast and took my heart into her hand, saying ' speak no word of this,' " he writes. Yet the reverence inspired by her modesty and dignity was not always sufficient to restrain her lover. Being alone with her on one occasion, and she appearing more gracious than usual, Petrarch tremblingly and fearfully confessed his passion ; but she, with altered looks, replied, " I am not the person you take me for !" Her displeasure froze the very heart of the poet, so that he fled from her presence in grief and dismay.

No attentions on his part could make any impression on her steady and virtuous mind. While love and youth drove him on, she remained impregnable and firm ; and when she found that he still rushed wildly forward, she preferred forsaking to following him to the precipice down which he would have hurried her. Meanwhile, as he gazed on her angelic countenance, and saw purity painted on it, his love grew spotless as herself. Love transforms the true lover into a resemblance of the object of his passion In a town, which was the asylum of vice, calumny never breathed a taint upon Laura's name; her actions, her words, the very expression of her countenance, and her slightest gestures were replete with modest reserve combined with sweetness, and won the applause of all.

Francesco Petrarch was of Florentine extraction, and the son of a notary, who, being held in great esteem by his fellow-citizens, had filled several public offices.

When the Ghibelines were banished Florence, in 1302, Petraccolo was included in the number of exiles; his property was confiscated, and he retired with his wife, Eletta Canigiani, whom he had lately married, to the town of Arrezzo, in Tuscany. And here on the night of the 20th of July, 1304, Petrarch first saw the light. When the child was seven months old his mother was permitted to return from banishment, and she established herself at a country house belonging to her husband, near Ancisa, a small town fifteen miles from Florence. The infant who, at his birth, it was supposed would not survive, was exposed to imminent peril during this journey. In fording a rapid stream, the man who had charge of him carried him, wrapped in swaddling clothes, at the end of a stick; he fell from his horse, and the babe slipped from the fastenings into the water, from which, however, he was rescued, uninjured.

The youth of Petrarch was obscure in point of fortune, but it was attended by all the happiness that springs from family concord, and the excellent character of his parents. At the age of fifteen he was sent to study in the University of Montpellier, then frequented by a vast concourse of students. His father intended his son to pursue the study of the law, as the profession best suited to insure his reputation and fortune; but to this pursuit Francesco was invincibly repugnant. He was soon after sent to Bologna, where, as at Montpellier, he continued to dis-

play great taste for literature, much to his father's dissatisfaction.

At Bologna, Petrarch made considerable progress in the
study of the law, moved thereto, doubtless, by the entreaties of
his excellent parent.

After three years spent at Bologna, Petrarch was recalled to
France by the death of his father. Soon after his mother died
also, and he and his brother were left entirely to their own
guidance, with very slender means, and those diminished by the
dishonesty of those whom his father named as trustees to their
fortune. Under these circumstances Petrarch entirely abandoned the profession of the law, as it occurred to both him and
his brother that the clerical profession was their best resource in
a city where the priesthood reigned supreme. They resided at
Avignon, and became the favorites and companions of the ecclesiastical and lay nobles who formed the papal court. His talents
and accomplishments were of course the cause of this distinction,
besides that his personal advantages were such as to prepossess
every one in his favor. He was so handsome as frequently to
attract observation when he passed along the streets. When,
to the utmost simplicity and singleness of mind, were added
splendid talents, the charm of poetry, so highly valued in the
country of the Troubadours, an affectionate and generous disposition, vivacious and pleasing manners, an engaging and attrac-
tive exterior, we cannot wonder that Petrarch was the darling
of his age, the associate of its greatest men, and the man whom
princes delighted to honor.

The passion of Petrarch for Laura was purified and exalted
at the same time. She filled him with noble aspirations, and
divided him from the common herd. He felt that her influence
made him superior to vulgar ambition, and rendered him wise,

6

truc, and great She saved him in the dangerous period of youth, and gave a worthy aim to all his endeavors. The manners of his age permitted one solace—a Platonic attachment was the fashion of the day. The Troubadours had each a lady to adore, to wait upon, and to celebrate in song, without its being supposed that she made him any return beyond a gracious acceptance of his devoirs, and allowing him to make her the heroine of his verses. Petrarch endeavored to merge the living passion of his soul into this airy and unsubstantial devotion. Laura permitted the homage; she perceived his merit and was proud of his admiration; she felt the truth of his affection, and indulged the wish of preserving it and her own honor at the same time. Without her inflexibility, this had been a dangerous experiment; but she always kept her lover distant from her— rewarding his reserve with smiles, and repressing by frowns all the overflowings of his heart.

By her resolute severity, she incurred the danger of ceasing to be the object of his attachment, and of losing the gift of an immortal name, which he has conferred upon her. But Petrarch's constancy was proof against hopelessness and time. He had too fervent an admiration of her qualifications ever to change ; he controlled the vivacity of his feelings, and they became deeper rooted. "Untouched by my prayers," he says, "unvanquished by my arguments, unmoved by my flattery, she remained faithful to her sex's honor; she resisted her own young heart, and mine, and a thousand, thousand things, which must have conquered any other. She remained unshaken. A woman taught me the duty of a man ! to persuade me to keep the path of virtue, her conduct was at once an example and a reproach."

But whether, in this long conflict, Laura preserved her heart untouched, as well as her virtue immaculate; whether she shared the love she inspired, or whether she escaped from the captivating assiduities and intoxicating homage of her lover, "fancy free;" whether coldness, or prudence, or pride, or virtue, or the mere heartless love of admiration, or a mixture of all together, dictated her conduct, is at least as well worth inquiry as the color of her eyes, or the form of her nose, upon which we have pages of grave discussion. She might have been *coquette par instinct*, if not *par calent;* she might have felt, with feminine *tacte*, that, to preserve her influence over Petrarch, it was necessary to preserve his respect. She was evidently proud of her conquest—she had else been more or less than woman; and at every hazard, but that of self-respect, she was resolved to retain him. If Petrarch absented himself for a few days, he was generally better treated on his return. If he avoided her, then her eye followed him with a softer expression. When he looked pale from sickness of heart and agitation of spirits, Laura would address him with a few words of pitying tenderness. When he presumed on this benignity, he was again repulsed with frowns. He flew to solitude —solitude! Never let the proud and torn heart, wrung with the sense of injury, and sick with unrequited passion, seek that worst resource against pain, for there grief grows by contemplating itself, and every feeling is sharpened by collision. Petrarch sought to "mitigate the fever of his heart" amid the shades of Vaucluse, a spot so gloomy, and so solitary, that his very servants forsook him; and Vaucluse, its fountains, its forests, and its hanging cliffs, reflected only the image of Laura.

He passed several years thus, cut off from society. His books were his great resource; he was never without one in his hand. Often he remained in silence from morning till night, wandering

among the hills when the sun was yet low, and taking refuge,
during the heat of the day, in his shady garden. At night, after
performing his clerical duties, (for he was canon of Lombes),
he rambled among the hills—often entering, at midnight, the
cavern, whose gloom, even during the day, struck his soul with
awe. "Fool that I was!" he exclaims in after-life, "not to
have remembered the first school-boy lesson—that solitude is
the nurse of love!"

While living at Vaucluse, Petrarch, invited to Rome by the
Roman Senate, repaired thither to receive the laurel crown of
poesy. The ceremony was performed in the Capitol with great
solemnity, in the presence of all the nobles and high-born ladies
of the city. Leaving Rome soon after his coronation, he repaired to Parma, where Clement VI. rewarded him for subsequent political services by naming him prior of Migliarino in
the diocese of Pisa.

Petrarch returned to Avignon. The sight of Laura gave
fresh energy to a passion which had survived the lapse of fifteen
years. She was no longer the blooming girl who had first
charmed him. The cares of life had dimmed her beauty. She
was the mother of many children, and had been afflicted at
various times by illness. Her home was not happy. Her husband, without loving or appreciating her, was ill-tempered and
jealous. Petrarch acknowledged that if her personal charms
had been her sole attraction he had already ceased to love her.
But his passion was nourished by sympathy and esteem ; and,
above all, by that mysterious tyranny of love, which, while it
exists, the mind of man seems to have no power of resisting,
though in feebler minds it sometimes vanishes like a dream.
Petrarch was also changed in personal appearance. His hair
was sprinkled with gray, and lines of care and sorrow trenched

his face. On both sides the tenderness of affection began to replace, in him the violence of passion, in her the coyness and severity she had found necessary to check his pursuit. The jealousy of her husband opposed obstacles to their seeing each other. They met as they could in public walks and assemblies. Laura sang to him, and a soothing familiarity grew up between them as her fears became allayed, and he looked forward to the time when they might sit together and converse without dread.

At length he resolved to leave Laura and Avignon forever, and instead of plunging into solitude, to seek the wiser resource of travel and society. Laura saw him depart with regret. When he went to take leave of her, he found her surrounded by a circle of her ladies. Her mien was dejected; a cloud overcast her face, whose expression seemed to say, " Who takes my faithful friend from me ?" Petrarch was struck to the heart by a sad presentiment—the emotion was mutual—they both seemed to feel that they should never meet again.

Petrarch departed. The plague, which had been extending its ravages over Asia, entered Europe. It spread far and wide ; nearly one half the population of the world became its prey. Petrarch saw thousands die around him, and he trembled for his friends. He heard that it was at Avignon. A thousand sad presentiments haunted his mind. At last the fatal truth reached him, Laura was dead ! By a singular coincidence, she died on the anniversary of the day when he first saw her. She was taken ill on the third of April, and languished but three days. As soon as the symptoms of the plague declared themselves, she prepared to die. She made her will, which is dated on the third of April, and received the sacraments of the church. On the sixth she died, surrounded by her friends and the noble ladies of Avignon, who braved the dangers of infection to attend on one so lovely and so beloved.   On tne evening of the same day on which she died, she was interred in the chapel of the Cross which her husband had lately built in the church of the Minor Friars at Avignon.

Her tomb was discovered and opened in 1533, in the presence of Francis the First, whose celebrated stanzas on the occasion are well known.

Of the fame which, even in her lifetime, the love, and the poetical adoration of Petrarch had thrown around his Laura, curious instance is given which will characterize the manners of the age.   When Charles of Luxembourg (afterwards Emperor) was at Avignon, a grand fête was given, in his honor, at which all the noblesse were present.   He desired that Petrarch's Laura should be pointed out to him ; and when she was introduced, he made a sign with his hand that the other ladies present should fall back ; then going up to Laura, and for a moment contemplating her with interest, he kissed her respectively on the forehead and on the eyelids.

Petrarch survived her twenty-six years, dying in 1374.   He was found lifeless one morning in his study, his hand resting on a book.

Joan of Arc.

JOAN OF ARC,

THE MAID OF ORLEANS.

ALTHOUGH woman is so physically constituted as to render the more tender and delicate offices of human duty her appropriate sphere of action, yet this by no means justifies the illiberal but common error that her mental abilities are only equal to her corporeal energies. We might adduce numberless instances to disprove this inference, for the history of the past is rife with the records of the mental strength and moral courage of woman. When the holy impulse of maternal or conjugal affection, the noble sentiments of true patriotism, the angelic spirit of genuine benevolence, or the awful presence of great danger or death have awakened in its fullest strength the more masculine energies of the female character, where can we look for more cool deliberation, sagacious forethought, or firmness of purpose, than such occasions have exhibited? The pages of holy writ, the annals of Greece and Rome, the book of Christian martyrs, the records of our revolutionary struggles, all exhibit, in their brightest hues, the moral excellences, and unsubdued strength of wo man. But for undaunted courage, a connection with a series of brilliant achievements, and an exhibition of almost superhuman strength of character, under every circumstance, history furnishes but rare parallels to her whose name stands at the head of this article. Nor can history present a more damning stain upon the human character than is pictured in the details of her death.

Jeanne, or *Joan d' Arc*, commonly called the Maid of Orleans, was the daughter of a poor peasant of Domremy, a town
situated in the north-east part of France, upon the borders of
Loraine.   The poverty of her parents rendered her earlier years
a scene of toil in menial services, and even the rudiments of education were denied her by the arbitrary power of circumstances.
Filled with that true piety which burns with so pure a flame in
the hearts of many of the rural peasantry of the French provinces, her mother was a fit tutor in schooling her child in that
knowledge which is so essential to the correct formation of
human character, and she taught her the mysteries of revealed
religion.

Joan was always of a very imaginative temperament; and,
when yet a mere child, she would often stray away from her
companions into the forest shades, and there hold imaginary
intercourse with celestial visitants.   The ruling passion of her
life was religion, and upon that topic all her thoughts, and conversation, and actions hinged.

Although circumscribed by poverty to a narrow and humble
sphere, yet, as she approached toward womanhood, her rare
personal charms and strongly-developed intellect won for her
the admiration and esteem of all.   She left her father's house,
and engaged as a seamstress in the neighboring town of Neuf-
chateau, where she pursued her new avocation with industry for
five years.   Her beauty attracted universal attention, and many
advantageous proposals of marriage were made, but by her
promptly refused.   Her affections were too firmly set upon religion to be disturbed by or divided with the things of earth,
and she sought no other intercourse than the presence of angels
and saints.   Her monomania in that respect increased with her
years; and with asseverations of truth, she frequently declared

that she had held audible conversation with the angels Michael and Gabriel, and saints Catherine, Margaret, &c.

She declared the delight she experienced while sitting in the solitary forest and listening with rapt attention to the melodies of heaven, and seemed truly astonished at the fact that none but herself were permitted to enjoy those celestial concerts.

At the age of sixteen another passion, equally strong with religion, claimed a share of her affections.

This sentiment was *patriotism*—pure, unadulterated love of country, and a sincere desire for the promotion of her country's welfare. Peculiar circumstances conspired to render this passion strong to its fullest extent, and opened a wide field for its perfect development. At this time, (1428,) England claimed the sovereignty of France, and by the power of the sword, and the right of might, held possession of a greater part of the kingdom. The Duke of Bedford, uncle to Henry VI., the reigning monarch of England, resided in Paris, and acted as regent for his nephew ; while Charles VII., the lawful emperor of France, by birth—possession of the throne—and the almost undivided love of the people, was a refugee in one of the frontier towns. English troops were garrisoned in all the cities and considerable towns, and a powerful army was daily extending its unlawful encroachments. Cruel retribution followed every resistance of the inhabitants, and fields and vineyards, towns and hamlets, were destroyed by the invading foe.

These events made a strong impression upon the ardent imagination of Joan, and she conceived the bold idea that she was commissioned by heaven to be an instrument in effecting the deliverance of her country. Conscious of what was the proper sphere of woman, she felt that her sex was degrading to her spirit, for it denied her the privilege of engaging in the martial pursuits necessary to the fulfilling of her mission. But her enthusiasm broke down every barrier, and she engaged in every manly exercise calculated to invigorate her frame and give her that knowledge she so much needed in the enterprise in which she was about to embark. She soon became an unrivaled equestrian, and managed her horse with all the skill of the bravest knight. These exercises gave an increased glow to her beauty, and she became an object almost of adoration. The superstition of the times invested her with divine attributes, and the idea took possession of the minds of many of the lower class that she was the Virgin Mary, sent at this inauspicious moment to deliver France from a foreign yoke.

On the 24th of February, 1429, Joan first entered the royal presence, and offered her services in restoring to the emperor his crown, and to her country its liberty. Charles was at this time at Chinon, a little distance from Orleans. The latter city had warmly espoused his cause, and at the time in question was strongly besieged by the English, led on by the traitor Duke of Burgundy, who had been one of the most powerful vassals of the French crown.

The emperor had heard of the extraordinary young maiden now before him, but he had conceived her to be a tattered menial, urged on by fanaticism that had displaced weak judgment from a weak head, and at first refused her an audience. But, when assured that the applicant was no crazed mendicant, he gave her permission to enter. The emperor was filled with astonishment ; nay, some secret impulse awakened feelings of awful reverence in his bosom, when the maiden, armed *cap-a-pié*, stood upright before him, without paying even that obeisance expected from every subject. She uncovered her head, and her dark hair fell in profusion upon her mailed shoulders. The excitement of the moment gave increased animation to her countenance, and she seemed to the astonished monarch as a lovely angel, truly commissioned by Heaven for some mighty deed. Joan first broke silence.

"I come," said she, " not in the strength of steel, but mailed in the panoply of righteousness, to offer my services to my king and country. I ask not the royal signet as a proof of my commission; my credentials are from Heaven—my chief sovereign, the Lord God Omnipotent. I have heard a voice of wail go up from hill and valley. I have seen the rich vineyard trampled down by mercenary warriors. I have beheld the frequent glare at midnight of consuming villages and hamlets, and yet, amid all this desolation, I have been obliged to sit and sigh over the weakness of my countrymen, and the uncurbed strength of the foe. The darkness has deepened over my beloved land, but light now streams upon it. The arm of a woman, in the hands of God to effect a mighty deliverance; will an earthly sovereign refuse her permission to lead his armies? At this moment the walls of Orleans are giving way to the battle-axes of the enemy, and Chinon will be next invested by English soldiers, and thus the last hope of France will depart. Heaven has issued its mandate; be thine concurrent, and Joan d' Arc will on to the rescue!"

Charles hesitated not a moment in granting the young enthusiast the boon she asked, and preparations were immediately made to execute the enterprise. The monarch was a man of much sagacity, and he employed every means to invest the maiden, and everything appertaining to her, with a supernal character, for he knew that the prevailing superstitions of the time would, in such a connection, give increased vigor to the soldiery. Everything being in readiness, the maid mounted a white steed, and with a banner of the same hue, dashed forward at the head of brave and enthusiastic troops for Orleans. She charged upon the enemy with terrible force, and despite the most desperate efforts of the foe, she succeeded in entering the beleagured city. Fresh courage animated soldiers and citizens, and on the eighth of May, the English, who had encompassed the city for more than six months, raised the siege, and retired in terror and confusion. This was but a beginning of her achievement. A few days after, she was victorious at the battle of Patay, where two thousand five hundred Englishmen were slain, and more than twelve hundred taken prisoners, among whom was the generalissimo, the brave Talbot. This, with the capture of Orleans, was a death-blow to English power in France; and town after town now opened its gates to the French troops, led on by Joan d' Arc. Rheims at length surrendered, and on the 17th of July, scarcely five months after this extraordinary young woman first grasped the sword, in her country's cause, the dethroned monarch was solemnly consecrated and crowned in the cathedral of this last conquered city.

Having executed the mission which she deemed Heaven to have given her, Joan laid aside the panoply of war, again assumed the costume of her sex, and, in the character of a meek and humble woman, presented herself before the emperor, and petitioned his leave for her to retire to the quiet and obscurity of her native village. But the monarch, truly grateful, entreated and even commanded her to remain in public life. Honors were lavished upon her; letters of nobility were granted to herself and family; a medal was struck, in commemoration of her achievements, and the name of Joan d' Arc became familiar in every place and cottage in Europe. At the earnest solicitation of Charles, she again took command of his troops, and for more than a year her career was one of brilliant exploits, in contending against the English, who yet lingered on the borders of France with the vain hope of regaining the territory they had lost.

But how pure soever the spirit, however noble the soul, however valorous and great, wise and good, an individual may be, the invidious monster, jealousy, will ever be creating a progeny of calumniators, or worse foes, to frustrate his designs and eclipse his well-earned glory. Such was the case of the Maid of Orleans. When all was commotion—when victory after victory, in rapid succession, was working out the political redemption of France, all were ready, from monarch to vassal, to bow the knee of reverence to the instrument of good. But the tempest at length subsided, and French generals felt themselves disgraced in being led on to battle by a woman; and even the French monarch forgot the services of a brave conqueror in restoring to him his crown, in the reflection that she was but a *poor country girl!*

On the 24th of May, 1430, while valorously defending Compeigne from the attacks of the army of the Duke of Burgundy, the treacherous governor shut her out from the very city she was gallantly defending ; and after performing prodigies of valor, comparatively alone, she was overpowered by superior numbers, and compelled to surrender to the enemy. She fell into the hands of John of Luxemburg, and a short time afterward, she was actually sold by him to the Duke of Bedford, for ten thousand livres ! She was then taken to Rouen, and there arraigned before the ecclesiastical tribunal, charged with being a *sorceress.* From the time of her capture till the moment in question, the ungrateful monarch to whom she had given a crown and a kingdom, made not a single effort for her liberation, and the poor girl was left entirely to the mercy of a personal foe, and a foe to her common country.

At that age, when even suspicion was sufficient to convict of heresy in religion, and with such powerful accusers as charged her with sorcery, Joan had but little mercy to expect from a tribunal of corrupt bigots. Every device was used to afford sufficient testimony to give the coloring of an excuse to their unholy proceedings, and she was vexed with a thousand questions irrelevant to the subject, with the hope of eliciting some answer that might be construed into heresy. For nearly four months she was daily brought out of prison, where she was kept on bread and water, and obliged to pass the ordeal of severe questioning—questioning, often the most absurd. On one occasion she was asked, whether at the coronation of Charles, she had not displayed a standard, consecrated by magical incantation? She replied, " My trust was in the Almighty, whose image was impressed upon the banner, and having encountered the dangers of the field, I was entitled to share the glory of Rheims. I serve," continued she, with uplifted hands, " I serve but one master—acknowledge but one sovereign, and he is our common Father. Ye have threatened me with excommunication—ye have threatened me with stripes, and chained me in a dungeon, and now ye threaten me with the fire and fagot. Ye may burn this tabernacle, but the soul that dwelleth in it, ye cannot harm ; and that God whose arm bears me up in this affliction, is also your Judge. My faith is in Christ the Lord, and your threatenings fall upon my ear and heart like idle words. Do with me as ye see fit—your reward will soon follow."

During all of her examinations, she betrayed no weakness ; and when at length she was excommunicated and sentenced to be burned at the stake, her strength failed her not. On the

12th of May, 1431, she was taken from the prison under an escort of one hundred and twenty armed men. She was clad in female apparel, and upon her head was placed a paper crown, inscribed, " Apostate, heretic, idolatress." She was supported by two Dominican friars, and as she passed through the thronged streets, she exclaimed, " Oh, Rouen ! Rouen ! must thou be my last abode !" She uttered blessings on the people as she passed, and supplicated Heaven to have mercy upon her accusers, judges, and executioners. Seated upon the scaffold was the English cardinal of Winchester, the Bishop of Terouanne, Chancellor of France, Bishop of Beauvois, and the other judges. To these the heavily-fettered maiden was delivered, and she ascended the scaffold with her face bathed in tears. Her funeral sermon was then preached !—yes, in view of heaven, a professed ambassador of the meek and merciful Jesus—preached the funeral sermon of a living, weak, defenceless, *innocent* girl ! and she was then handed over to the secular officers to be put to death. Before she descended to mount the fatal pile, she knelt down and prayed Heaven to forgive all. Nor was the ungrateful Charles forgotten in her last moments, and she invoked the blessing of Heaven upon him and her country.

As she arose from her knees, one of the judges said, " take her away !" and the executioner, trembling like an aspen, advanced, received her from the guards, and led her to the funeral pile. She asked for a crucifix, which being given her, she kissed it, and pressed it to her bosom. The fagots were lighted, and in a few moments she was surrounded with flames. An awful silence pervaded the multitude, and no voice was heard but that of the dying martyr, whose lips, until scared by flames, uttered the name of Jesus, mingled with the groans

7

whicl. the violence ot her anguish extorted from her.—By order of the Bishop of Winchester, her ashes were collected and thrown into the river.

Thus died this extraordinary maiden at the age of nineteen years, to whom, Hume justly observed, " the more liberal and generous superstitions of the ancients would have erected altars." This last tragedy in the drama of her wonderful career, is an eternal stigma, not only on the two nations immediately concerned, but upon the age in which she lived ; and the actors in the scene, however much they may be robed in sacerdotal dignity and reverence, should receive the execrations of the good in all ages, as fit brethren for the Neros and Caligulas of ancient Rome. Twenty years afterward her mother demanded and obtained a reversal of her sentence, and by the Bishop of Paris her character was fully cleared from every imputation of guilt of the crimes of which she was accused. At Orleans, Rouen, and various parts of France, monuments were erected to her honor ; and by a bull of Pope Calixtus III., she was declared a martyr to her religion, her country, and her king

Isabella of Castile.

ISABELLA OF CASTILE.

SHOULD we seek through the pages of history for a sovereign, such as the Supreme Spirit of Good might indeed own for his vice-regent here on earth, where should we find one more blameless and beautiful than that of Isabella? Or, should we point out a reign, distinguished by great events—events of such magnitude as to involve in their consequences, not particular kings and nations, but the whole universe, and future ages to the end of time—where could we find a reign such as that of Isabella, who added a new world to her hereditary kingdom? Or, did we wish to prove that no virtues, talents, graces, though dignifying and adorning a double crown and treble sceptre; nor the possession of a throne fixed in the hearts of her people; nor a long course of the most splendid prosperity, could exempt a great queen from the burthen of sorrow, which is the lot of her sex and of humanity; where could we find an instance so forcible as in the history of Isabella?

This illustrious woman was the daughter of John the Second, King of Castile and Leon, and born in 1450, four years before the death of her father. King John, after a long, turbulent, and unhappy reign, died at Medina-del-Campo, leaving by his first wife, Maria of Arragon, a son, Don Henry, who succeeded him; and by his second wife, Isabella of Portugal, two children in their infancy, Alphonso and Isabella.

Among the many princes who sought the hand of Isabella,

Don Ferdinand, son of the King of Arragon, was preferred by
the young princess, and their marriage was accordingly performed at Valladolia, privately—the king, her brother, Henry
the Fourth of Castile, who was a vicious prince, and whose acts
of misgovernment had already led to a general revolt, at the
head of which was the Archbishop of Toledo, and the chief
nobility—being opposed to this alliance from motives of interest.

At the period of her marriage, (in 1469), Isabella had just
entered her twentieth year. In person she was well formed,
of middle size, with great dignity and gracefulness of deportment, and a mingled gravity and sweetness of demeanor. Her
complexion was fair; her hair auburn, inclining to red; her eyes
were of a clear blue, with a benign expression, and there was
a singular modesty in her countenance, gracing, as it did, a
wonderful firmness of purpose and earnestness of spirit. She
exceeded her husband in beauty, in personal dignity, in acute-
ness of genius, and grandeur of soul. She combined a masculine energy of purpose with the utmost tenderness of heart, and
a softness of temper and manner truly feminine. Her self-
command was not allied to coldness, nor her prudence to dissimulation, and her generous and magnanimous spirit disdained
all indirect measures, and all the little crooked arts of policy.
While all her public thoughts and acts were princely and august,
her private habits were simple, frugal, and unostentatious.
Without being learned, she was fond of literature; and being
possessed of a fine understanding, had cultivated many branches
of knowledge with success. She encouraged and patronized the
arts, and was the soul of every undertaking which tended to
promote the improvement and happiness of her subjects. Her
only fault—most pardonable in her sex, her situation, and the
age in which she lived—was, that her piety tended to bigotry,

and placed her too much at the disposal of her priestly advisers.
This led her into some errors, sad to think of, and fraught with
evil consequences to her people—they are a subject of regret—
they cannot be a subject of reproach to this glorious creature,
who, in an age of superstition and ignorance, was sometimes
mistaken and misled, but never perverted.

Ferdinand, when he received the hand of Isabella, was a few
months younger than his bride.   He was of the middle stature,
well proportioned, and hardy, from athletic exercise; his carriage was free, erect, and majestic; he had an ample forehead,
and hair of a bright chestnut color; his eyes were clear; his
complexion rather florid, but scorched to a manly brown by the
toils of war; his mouth was handsome and gracious in its ex
pression; his voice sharp; his speech quick and fluent.   His
courage was cool and undaunted, not impetuous; his temper
close and unyielding, and his demeanor grave.   His ambition
was boundless, but it was also selfish, grasping, and unchecked
by any scruple of principle, any impulse of generosity.   He had
great vigor of mind and great promptitude of action, but he
never knew what it was to be impelled by a disinterested motive; and even his excessive bigotry, which afterwards obtained
for him and his successors the title of " Most Catholic," was still
made subservient to his selfish views and his insatiate thirst for
dominion.   Yet, however repulsive his character may appear to
us who can contemplate at one glance the events of his long
reign, and see his subtle, perfidious policy dissected and laid
bare by the severe pen of history, he did not appear thus in the
eyes of Isabella when they met at Valladolid.   He was in the
bloom of youth, handsome, brave, and accomplished; the vices
of his character were yet undeveloped, his best qualities alone
apparent.   Animated by the wish to please, and no doubt

pleased himself to find in the woman whom ambition had made his bride, all the charms and excellencies that could engage his attachment, we cannot wonder that Ferdinand at this time obtained and long fixed the tenderness and respect of his wife whose disposition was in the highest degree confiding and affectionate.

The furious civil war that had raged for two or three years between King Henry and his young brother Alphonso, and his partisans, previous to the marriage of Isabella, had been terminated by the death of the prince at the age of fifteen, and the nobles opposed to Henry then resolved to place Isabella at their head. Isabella rejected the offered crown, and Henry, willing to purchase at any price, however humiliating, for a few years longer, the empty title of King, concluded a treaty with the chiefs, whereby he acknowledged his reputed daughter, Joanna, illegitimate, setting aside her claims entirely, and declared Isabella his heiress and successor.

When Henry found that this marriage had been solemnized without his knowledge or consent, he was struck with rage and terror; he revoked the treaty he had made in Isabella's favor, declared his daughter Joanna his only legal heir, and civil war again distracted and desolated the kingdom for more than three years. The death of Henry in 1474, finally opened a sure road to peace; and Ferdinand and Isabella were immediately, and almost without opposition, proclaimed King and Queen of Castile.

The Archbishop of Toledo, who had been so instrumental in placing Isabella on the throne, and the chief negotiator of her marriage, believed himself now at the summit of power, and expected everything, from the gratitude and weakness of the young queen, but was surprised to find that Isabella was not of a character to leave the government in the hands of another. Disappointed in his ambitious views, the Archbishop quitted the court in a fit of jealousy and disgust, and threw himself into the party of Joanna, whose pretensions were supported by the young Marquis of Gillena, and other nobles. Alphonso, King of Portugal, also espoused the cause of Joanna, and invaded Castile with a powerful army, and Joanna was proclaimed Queen at Placentia. The Portuguese were, however, defeated at Toro, by Ferdinand, and Alphonso was obliged to retire to his own kingdom. The disaffected nobles submitted one after another to the power of Isabella, and Castile breathed at last from the horrors of civil war.

The poor Princess Joanna at last sought refuge in a convent, where she took the veil at the age of twenty, and died a nun.

Thus Isabella remained without a competitor, and was acknowledged as Queen of Castile and Leon; and three years after the battle of Toro, the death of his father raised Ferdinand to the throne of Arragon. The kingdoms of Castile and Arragon were thenceforward united indissolubly, though still independent of each other. There arose at first some contest relative to the order of precedence. Castile and Leon had hitherto been allowed the precedence over Arragon in all political transactions; but Ferdinand now insisted that, as king and husband, his titles should precede those of his wife.

It was a very delicate point of conjugal and state etiquette, and Isabella was placed in a difficult situation; she conducted herself, however, with that mixture of gentleness, prudence, and magnanimity, which distinguished her character. She acknowledged, as a wife, the supremacy of Ferdinand, as her husband: in public and private she yielded to him all the obedience, honor, and duty he could require, naming him on every occasion her lord, her master, her sovereign; but she would not concede one lota of the dignity of her kingdom. She maintained that the Queen of Castile should never yield the precedence to the King of Arragon, and in the end she overruled all opposition. It was decided that in all public acts promulgated in their joint names, the titles of Castile and Leon should precede those of Arragon and Sicily. Isabella managed this delicate affair with a firmness which endeared her to her Castilian nobles, who were haughtily jealous of the honor of their country ; yet she upheld her rights with so much sweetness and feminine address as to gain rather than lose in the affections of her husband ; while her influence in his councils, and the respect of his ministers, were evidently increased by the resolution she had shown in maintaining what was considered a point of national honor.

In the same year that the kingdoms of Castile and Arragon were united, Queen Isabella was at Toledo, and gave birth to her second daughter, the Infanta Joanna, afterwards the mother of Charles the Fifth.

The first great event of the reign of the two sovereigns was the war of Granada. Hostility against the Moors seems to have been the hereditary appanage of the Crown of Castile ; and it was one of the principal articles in Isabella's marriage-treaty, that Ferdinand should lead the armies of the queen against the infidels as soon as the affairs of the kingdom allowed him to do so. Isabella has always been represented as a principal adviser and instigator of this sanguinary war, and, during its continuance, the animating soul of all the daring enterprises and deeds of arms achieved by others ; and though the Spanish historians have added this to the rest of her merits, yet, disguise it as we will, there is something revolting to female nature in the idea of a woman thus interested and engaged in carrying on a war, not defensive, but offensive, and almost exterminating. We ought, therefore, in justice to Isabella, to look into the motives by which she was impelled—to consider the situation of the two countries at the time, the opinions and spirit of the age, and the deep-seated religious prejudices on both sides, which gave a tincture of fierce zeal to this great and terrible contest. It was bigotry on one side opposed to fanaticism on the other. The Spaniards fought for honor, dominion, and the interests of the church. The Moors fought for their homes and hearths, their faith, their country, their very existence as a nation.

Isabella, in undertaking this war, which had been in a measure transmitted to her with her crown, was certainly swayed by motives of which we can hardly estimate the full force, unless we transport ourselves in fancy back to the very times in which she lived. For seven hundred years the existence of a Moorish kingdom in the south of Spain had been like a thorn in the side of Christendom. Isabella deemed it a reproach that her frontiers should be endangered—her power defied, by a people occupying a slip of land between her kingdom and the sea; and a sense of religion, sincere though pitiably mistaken, made her regard the conversion of the Moors as a necessary consequence of their subjection, and a war against them, even to extremity, as good and acceptable service to Heaven. On the other hand, the policy of Ferdinand in conducting this war, though cloaked under an appearance of religious zeal, was far more deep and selfish. With him it was not only the desire of extending his dominions and increasing his revenues, but, in accordance with a deep-laid plan, to aggrandize the crown at the expense of the power of the nobility and the liberties of the people—a plan which he pursued through his whole reign with the most profound sagacity and the most unwearied perseverance. And he well knew that a popular war, which should place an immense

army at his disposal, and ·exhaus⁺ the resources and the ardent
spirit of the nobles in the general service, would be an effectual
step to the object he had in view.

The kingdom of Granada extended along the south of Spain
for about one hundred and eighty miles, and between the mountains and the sea its breadth was about seventy miles ; yet this
narrow space was filled with populous cities, enriched by agriculture and commerce, defended by strong fortresses, and inhabited by a wealthy, warlike, industrious, and polished race
of people. Nearly in the centre of the kingdom stood the
royal city of Granada, on two lofty hills, the one crowned by the
glorious palace of the. Alhambra, within whose splendid courts
forty thousand persons might have been lodged and entertained ;
the other by the citadel of Alcazaba. The sides of these hills
and the valley between them were occupied by houses and
palaces to the number of seventy thousand, and Granada alone
could send forth from her gates twenty thousand fighting men.
Around this noble city stretched the Vega or Plain of Granada,
which resembled one vast and beautiful garden in the highest
state of cultivation ; there flourished the citron and the orange,
the pomegranate and the fig-tree—there the olive poured forth
its oil, and the vine its purple juice. On one side, a range of
snowy mountains seemed to fence it from its hostile neighbors ,
on the other, the blue Mediterranean washed its shores, and
poured into its harbors the treasures of Africa and the Levant.
Nor were the inhabitants of this terrestrial Eden unmindful or
unworthy of its glorious loveliness. They believed themselves
peculiarly favored by Heaven in being placed in a spot of earth
so enchanting, that they fancied the celestial Paradise must be
suspended immediately over it, and could alone exceed it in de-
lights. Their patriotism had in it something romantic and

tender, like the passion of a lover for his mistress.—They clung
to their beautiful country with a yearning affection ; they poured
their blood like water in its defence ; they celebrated its charms,
and lamented its desolation in those sweet and mournful ballads
which are still extant, and which can yet draw tears from their
Christian conquerors.

Long before the last invasion of Ferdinand and Isabella the
Moorish power had been on the decline.   They had once possessed nearly the whole of the peninsula, from the Strait of
Gibraltar to the Pyrenees, but had, by degrees, been driven
southward by the Christian powers, until they were circumscribed within the boundaries of Granada.   Even this they had
held for some time as tributary to their enemies, paying annu-
ally two thousand pistoles of gold and sixteen hundred Christian
captives or Moorish slaves to the sovereigns of Castile.

During the weak government of Henry the Fourth, and the
civil wars which had distracted the kingdoms of Castile and
Arragon, this tribute had fallen into disuse ; it had not been
paid for several years.   And while the Christian monarchs were
weakened by internal and mutual warfare, the Moors had been
increasing in wealth and power, and had even extended their
dominions by the addition of several tracts and towns lying on
their frontiers.   Their king, Muley Aben Hassan, was a tyrant
in his family, and, at this time, distracted by domestic feuds ;
but he was a man of strong mind, with talents both for war and
government.   He had been distinguished in his youth for personal valor, and still retained in old age the fiery spirit and
haughty bearing of his earlier years.   Such, in a few words, was
the state of the two nations when the war began.

The first step taken by Ferdinand and Isabella was, to send a
solemn embassy to the Moorish king, requiring the payment of

the long arrears of tribute due to the monarchs of Castile. Aben Hassan received the ambassador in the state-chamber of the Alhambra, and to the haughty requisition he replied as haughtily, "Tell your sovereigns that the kings of Granada who were used to pay tribute in money to the Castilian crown are dead. Our mint at present coins nothing but blades of cimeters and heads of lances." The ambassador, Don Juan de Vera, probably longed to hurl back this proud defiance in the teeth of the infidels; but it was then no time to answer it in the same spirit. The contest with Portugal was still pending; the claims of Isabella to her throne still undecided. It was not till 1481 that Ferdinand and Isabella, having signed a treaty with the King of Portugal, were enabled to turn their whole attention to the long-meditated, long-deferred war with Granada.

The Moorish king, aware of their intentions, and of the vast preparations making against him, was resolved to strike the first blow. He attacked Zahara, a celebrated fortress, perched on the summit of a mountain, and deemed so impregnable from its situation, as well as the strength of its defences, that a woman of severe and inaccessible chastity was proverbially called a Zahareña. In the dead of the night, Zahara was surprised by the Moors, the garrison massacred, and the rest of the inhabitants driven into captivity and sold as slaves. Although this inroad had only anticipated the intentions of Ferdinand and Isabella, and had given them a fair pretext for carrying the war into Granada, they affected the strongest indignation, and at their command all the chivalry of Castile flew to arms.

Among the nobles who first lifted their banners in this war, and afterward became celebrated for their exploits, four were especially distinguished:—Don Rodrigo Ponce de Leon, Marquis of Cadiz; Don Alonzo de Aguilar, (the elder brother of Gon-

salvo de Cordova); the Count de Cabra; and the Duke of
Medina Sidonia. All these were in fact feudal sovereigns.
They were often engaged in petty wars with each other; and
there was not one of them who could not bring a small army of
his own retainers into the field. The Marquis of Cadiz had immense possessions in Andalusia, including even populous cities
ánd strong fortresses. His near neighborhood to the Moors, and
frequent and mutual inroads, had kept up a constant feeling of
hostility and hatred between them. This nobleman was the first
to avenge the capture of Zahara; and his measures were taken
with equal celerity and secrecy. He assembled his friends and
followers, made a descent on the territories of the enemy, and
took by storm the strong town of Alhama, situated within a few
leagues of the Moorish capital.

When the news of the capture of Alhama was brought to
Granada, it filled the whole city with consternation. The old
men tore their garments, and scattered ashes on their heads;
the women rent their hair and ran about weeping and wailing—
with their children in their arms, they forced their way into the
presence of the king, denouncing woe on his head, for having
this brought down the horrors of war on their happy and
beautiful country. "Accursed be the day," they exclaimed,
"when the flame of war was kindled by thee in our land! May
the holy Prophet bear witness before Allah, that we and our
children are innocent of this act! Upon thy head, and upon
the heads of thy posterity to the end of the world, rest the sin
of the destruction of Zahara!"*

* The lament of the Moors on the loss of Alhama is perpetuated in the little
Spanish ballad so happily and so faithfully translated by Lord Byron—

"The Moorish king rides up and down
Through Granada's royal town," &c.

Aben Hassan, unmoved by these feminine lamentations, assembled his army in all haste, and flew to the relief of Alhama; he invested it with three thousand horse and fifty thousand foot, and Alhama would assuredly have been retaken by this overwhelming force, but for the courage and magnanimity of a woman.

When news was brought to the Marchioness of Cadiz that her valiant husband was thus hard beset within the fortress of Alhama—so that he must needs yield or perish, unless succor should be afforded him, and that speedily—she sent immediately to the Duke of Medina Sidonia, the most powerful of the neighboring chiefs, requiring of him, as a Christian knight and a gentleman, to fly to the assistance of the marquis. Now, between the family of the Duke and that of the Marquis of Cadiz, there was an hereditary feud, which had lasted more than a century, and they were moreover personal enemies; yet, in that fine spirit of courtesy and generosity which mingled with the ferocity and ignorance of those times, the aid demanded with such magnanimous confidence by the high-hearted wife of De Leon, was as nobly and as frankly granted by the Duke of Medina Sidonia. Without a moment's hesitation he called together his followers and his friends, and such was his power and resources, that five thousand horse and fifty thousand foot assembled round his banner at Seville. With this numerous and splendid army he hastened to the relief of Alhama ere it should be overwhelmed by the enemy. In fact, the small but gallant band which still held its walls against the fierce attacks of the Moor, were now reduced to the last extremity, and must in a few days have capitulated.

Ferdinand and Isabella were at Medina del Campo when tidings successively arrived of the capture of Alhama, of the

terrible situation of the Marquis of Cadiz, and the generous
expedition of Medina Sidonia. The king, when he heard of
this vast armament, and the glory to be acquired by the relief
of Alhama, sent forward couriers to the duke with orders to
await his coming, that he might himself take the command of
the forces ; and then, with a few attendants, he spurred towards
the scene of action, leaving the queen to follow.

But the Duke of Medina Sidonia was not inclined to share
with another—not even with his sovereign—the glory of an expedition undertaken from such motives, and at his own care and
cost : moreover, every hour of delay was of the utmost consequence, and threatened the safety of the besieged ; instead,
therefore, of attending to the commands of the king, or awaiting his arrival, the army of Medina Sidonia pressed forward to
Alhama. On the approach of the Duke, Aben Hassan, who
had already lost a vast number of his troops through the gallant
defence of the besieged, saw that all farther efforts were in vain.
Gnashing his teeth, and tearing up his beard by the roots, with
choler and disappointment, he retired to his city of Granada.
Meantime the Marquis of Cadiz and his brave and generous
deliverer met and embraced before the walls of Alhama ; the
Duke of Medina Sidonia refused for himself and his followers
any share in the rich spoils of the city ; and from that time
forth, these noble cavaliers, laying aside their hereditary animosity, became firm and faithful friends.

These were the feats which distinguished the opening of the
war ; they have been extracted at some length, as illustrating
the spirit and manners of the age, and the character of this
memorable contest. The other events of the war, except as far
as Isabella was personally concerned, must be passed over more
rapidly. She had followed the king from Medina del Campo,

8

and arrived at Cordova just as the council was deliberating what was to be done with the fortress of Alhama. Many were of opinion that it was better to demolish it at once than to maintain it with so much danger and cost in the midst of the enemy's territory. " What !" exclaimed Isabella, indignant that so much blood and valor should have been expended in vain; " what, then, shall we destroy the first fruits of our victories? shall we abandon the first place we have wrested from the Moors ? Never let us suffer such an idea to occupy our minds It would give new courage to the enemy, arguing fear or feebleness in our councils. You talk of the toil and expense of maintaining Alhama ; did we doubt, on undertaking this war, that it was to be a war of infinite cost, labor, and bloodshed ? and shall we shrink from the cost, the moment a victory is obtained, and the question is merely to guard or abandon its glorious trophy ? Let us hear no more of the destruction of Alhama ; let us maintain its walls sacred, as a strong-hold granted us by Heaven in the centre of this hostile land, and let our only consideration be, how to extend our conquest, and capture the surrounding cities."[*] This spirited advice was applauded by all. The city of Alhama was strongly garrisoned, and maintained thenceforward, in despite of the Moors.

From this time we find Isabella present at every succeeding campaign, animating her husband and his generals by her courage and undaunted perseverance ; providing for the support of the armies by her forethought and economy ; comforting them under their reverses by her sweet and gracious speeches, and pious confidence in Heaven ; and by her active humanity and her benevolent sympathy, extended to friend and foe, softening, as far as possible, the horrors and miseries of war. Isabella was

* Chronicle of the Conquest of Granada, vol. 1, p. 81.

the first who instituted regular military surgeons to attend the movements of the army, and be at hand on the field of battle. These surgeons were paid out of her own revenues; and she also provided six spacious tents, furnished with beds and all things requisite, for the sick and wounded, which were called the " Queen's Hospital."

Thus, to the compassionate heart of a woman, directed by energy and judgment, the civilized world was first indebted for an expedient which has since saved so many lives, and done so much towards alleviating the most frightful evils of war.

It were long to tell of all the battles and encounters, the skirmishes and the forays, the fierce mutual inroads for massacre or plunder, which took place before the crescent was finally plucked down, and the cross reared in its stead ; or, to describe the valorous sieges and obstinate defences of the fortresses of Ronda, Zalca, Moclin, and Baza ; nor how often the banks of the Xenil were stained with blood, while down its silver current

> " Chiefs confused in mutual slaughter,
> Moor and Christian, roll'd along !"

The Castilian sovereigns, great as were their power and resources, had to endure some signal reverses ; the most memorable of which was the disgraceful repulse of Ferdinand before the walls of Loxa, in 1482, and the terrible defeat of the Christians in the passes of the mountains of Malaga, which occurred in 1483. On that disastrous day, which is still remembered in the songs of Andalusia, three of the most celebrated commanders of Castile, with the pride of her chivalry, were encountered by a determined band of Moorish peasantry. All the brothers of the Marquis of Cadiz perished at his side ; the Master of Santiago fled ; the royal standard-bearer was taken prisoner ; and the

Marquis of Cadiz, and his friend Don Alonzo de Aguilar, escaped with difficulty, and wounded almost to death. In truth, the Moors made a glorious stand for their national honor and independence ; and, had it not been for their own internal divisions and distracted councils, which gave them over a prey to their conquerors, their subjection which cost such a lavish expenditure of blood, and toil, and reasure, had been more dearly purchased—perhaps the issue had been altogether different.

The feuds between the Zegris and the Abencerrages, and the domestic cruelties of Aben Hassan, had rendered Granada a scene of tumult and horror, and stained the halls of the Alhambra with blood. Boabdil, the eldest son of Aben Hassan, (called by the Spanish historians, " el Rey Chiquito," or " el Chico," the little King), had rebelled against his father, or rather had been forced into rebellion by the tyranny of the latter. The old monarch was driven from the city of Granada, and took up his residence at Malaga, while Boabdil reigned in the Alhambra. The character of Boabdil was the reverse of that of his ferocious sire ; he was personally brave, generous, magnificent, and humane ; but indolent, vacillating in temper, and strongly and fatally influenced by an old tradition or prophecy, which foretold that he would be the last king of his race, and that he was destined to witness the destruction of the Moorish power in Spain. Roused, however, by the remonstrances of his heroic mother, the Sultana Ayxa, Boabdil resolved to signalize his reign by some daring exploit against the Christians. He assembled a gallant army, and led them to invade the Castilian territory   In the plains of Lucena he was met by the Count de Cabra, who, after a long-contested and sanguinary battle, defeated and dispersed his troops. Boabdil himself, distinguished above the rest, not less by his daring valor than by his golden armor and his turban that blazed with jewels, was taken prisoner, and carried by the Count de Cabra to his castle of Vaena.

The mother of Boabdil, the Sultana Ayxa, and his young and beautiful wife Morayma, had daily watched from the loftiest tower of the Alhambra to see his banners returning in triumph through the gate of Elvira; a few cavaliers, fugitives from the battle of Lucena, and covered with dust and blood, came spurring across the Vega, with the news of his defeat and capture— and who can speak the sorrow of the wife and the mother? Isabella herself, when the tidings of this great victory were brought to her, wept in the midst of her exultation for the fate of the Moorish prince. She sent him a message full of courtesy and kindness; and when the council met to consider whether it would be advisable to deliver Boabdil into the hands of his cruel father, who had offered large terms to get him into his power, Isabella rejected such barbarous policy with horror. By her advice and influence, Boabdil was liberated and restored to his kingdom, on conditions which, considering all the circumstances, might be accounted favorable: it was stipulated that he should acknowledge himself the vassal of the Castilian crown; pay an annual tribute, and release from slavery four hundred Christian captives, who had long languished in chains; and that he should leave his only son and the sons of several nobles of his family as hostages for his faith. Having subscribed to these conditions, Boabdil was received by Ferdinand and Isabella at Cordova, embraced as a friend, and restored to his kingdom, with gifts and princely honors.

In liberating Boabdil, the politic Ferdinand was impelled by motives far different from those which actuated his generous queen. He wisely calculated that the release of the Moorish prince would prove far more advantageous than his detention, by prolonging the civil discords of the kingdom of Granada, and dividing its forces. The event showed he had not been mistaken. No sooner was Boabdil restored to freedom than the wrath of the fiery old king, Aben Hassan, again turned upon his son, and the most furious contests raged between the two parties.

This was the miserable and distracted state of Granada, while King Ferdinand continued to push his conquests, taking first one city or castle, then another—ravaging the luxuriant Vega, and carrying away the inhabitants into captivity; while Boabdil, bound by the treaty into which he had entered, wept to behold his beautiful country desolated with fire and sword, and dared not raise his arm to defend it. In the midst of these troubles, old Aben Hassan, becoming blind and infirm, was deposed by his brother Abdalla el Zagal, who proclaimed himself king; and, denouncing his nephew Boabdil as an ally of the Christians and a traitor to his faith and country, he prepared to carry on the war with vigor. The military skill of El Zagal was equal to his ferocity; and the Christians found in him a determined and formidable opponent.

The fortress of Ronda, in the Serrania, which had long been considered impregnable from its strength and situation, was taken from the Moors in 1485, after a long and fierce resistance. The isolated rock on which this strong-hold was perched, like the aëry of the vulture, was hollowed into dungeons deep and dark, in which were a vast number of Christian captives, who had been taken in the Moorish forays. It is recorded that among them were several young men of high rank, who had surrendered themselves slaves in lieu of their parents, not being able to pay the ransom demanded; and many had pined for years in these eceptacles of misery. Being released from their fetters, they were all collected together, and sent to the queen at Cordova. When Isabella beheld them she melted into tears. She ordered hem to be provided with clothes and money, and all other necessaries, and conveyed to their respective homes; while the chains they had worn were solemnly suspended in the church of St. John, at Toledo, in sign of thanksgiving to Heaven. This was the spirit in which Isabella triumphed in success—an instance of the gentle and magnanimous temper with which she could sustain a reverse which occurred soon afterward.

A short time after the siege of Ronda, Isabella took up her residence at Vaena, a strong castle on the frontiers of Andalusia, belonging to the renowned and valiant Count de Cabra, the same who had won the battle of Lucena and taken Boabdil prisoner. The influence which Isabella exercised over her warlike nobles was not merely that of a queen, but that of a beautiful and virtuous woman, whose praise was honor, and whose smiles were cheaply purchased by their blood. The Count de Cabra, while he entertained his royal and adored mistress within his castle walls, burned to distinguish himself by some doughty deed of arms, which should win him grace and favor in her eyes. The Moor El Zagal was encamped near Moclin; to capture another king, to bring him in chains to the feet of his mistress—what a glorious exploit for a Christian knight and a devoted cavalier! The ardent count beheld only the hoped success—he overlooked the dangers of the undertaking. With a handful of followers, he attacked the fierce El Zagal—was defeated—and himself and his retainers driven back upon Vaena, with " rout and confusion following at their heels."

Isabella waited the issue of this expedition within the walls of the castle. She was seated in the balcony of a lofty tower, overlooking the vale beneath, and at her side were her daughter Isabella and her infant son Don Juan.   Her chief minister and counsellor, the venerable Cardinal Mendoza, stood near her. They looked along the mountain-road which led towards Moclin, and beheld couriers spurring their steeds through the defiles with furious haste, and galloping into the town ; and in the same moment the shrieks and wailings which rose from below informed Isabella of the nature of their tidings ere they were summoned to her presence.   For a moment her tenderness of heart prevailed over her courage and fortitude ; the loss of so many devoted friends, the defeat of one of her bravest knights, the advantage and triumph gained by the enemy almost in her presence, and the heart-rending lamentations of those who had lost sons, brothers, lovers, husbands, in this disastrous battle, almost overwhelmed her.   But when some of the couriers present endeavored to comfort her by laying the blame on the rashness of De Cabra, and would have lessened him in her opinion, she was roused to generous indignation :—" The enterprise," she said, " was rash, but not more rash than that of Lucena, which had been crowned with success, and which all had applauded as the height of heroism.   Had the Count de Cabra succeeded in capturing the uncle, as he did the nephew, who would not have praised him to the skies ?"

The successful enterprise of the Christians against Zalea concluded the eventful campaign of 1485.   Isabella retired from the seat of war to Alcada de Henares, where, in the month of December, she gave birth to her third daughter, the Infanta Catherine of Arragon, afterward the wife of Henry the Eighth of England.

The next year, 1486, was one of the most memorable during the war.   Early in the spring, Isabella and her husband repaired to Cordova, and a gallant and splendid array of the feudal chieftains of Castile assembled round them. That ancient city, with all the fair valley along the banks of the Guadalquiver, resounded with warlike preparation ; the waving of banners, the glancing of spears, the flashing of armor, the braying of trumpets, the neighing of steeds, the gorgeous accoutrements of the knights and their retainers, must have formed a moving scene of surpassing interest and magnificence. There was the brave Marquis of Cadiz, justly styled the mirror of Andalusian chivalry. When the women who were obliged to attend Queen Isabella to the wars, and who possessed not her noble contempt of danger, beheld the Marquis of Cadiz, they rejoiced, and felt secure under the protection of one so renowned for his courtesy to their sex, and of whom it was said, that no injured woman had ever applied to him in vain for redress. There was the valiant Count de Cabra, who had captured Boabdil, and the famous Don Alonzo de Aguilar, renowned for his deeds of arms in history and in song ; and there was his brother Gonsalvo de Cordova, then captain of Isabella's guards. There was the young Duke of Infantado, with his five hundred followers, all glittering in silken vests and scarfs, and armor inlaid with silver and gold ; and the Duke of Medina Sidonia, and the Duke of Medina Celi, names at once so harmonious in their sound, and so chivalrous in their associations, that they dwell upon the ear like the prolonged note of a silver clarion. Besides these, were many worthy cavaliers of England, France, and Germany, who were induced partly by the fame of this holy expedition, (such it was then deemed), partly by the wish to distinguish themselves in the sight of a beautiful and gracious queen, to join the banners of Isabella and Ferdinand, at Cordova. The most conspicuous of these foreign auxiliaries was Lord Rivers of England, a

near relation of Elizabeth of York, and the son of that accomplished Lord Rivers who was beheaded at Pomfret   After the
battle of Bosworth-field, he joined the camp of the Catholic
sovereigns with three hundred retainers, and astonished the
Spaniards by the magnificence of his appointments, his courtesy,
his valor, and the ponderous strength and determined courage
of his men.   There was also the accomplished French knight
Gaston de Léon of Toulóuse, with a band of followers, all gallant
and gay, " all plumed like ostriches that wing the wind," and
ready alike for the dance or the mélee—for lady's bower or battle field—and many more.

The presence of Isabella and her court lent to this martial
pomp an added grace, dignity, and interest.   She was surrounded by many ladies of noble birth and distinguished beauty,
the wives, or mothers, or sisters of the brave men who were
engaged in the war.   The most remarkable were, the Infanta
Isabella, at this time about fourteen, and who, as she grew in
years, became the inseparable companion and bosom friend of
her mother; the high-minded Marchioness of Cadiz, and the
Marchioness of Moya, both honored by the queen's intimacy, and
the latter eminent for her talents as well as her virtues.   A
number of ecclesiastics of high rank and influence also attended
on Isabella.   The grand cardinal, Gonzalez de Mendoza, was
always at her side, and was at this time and during his life her
chief minister and adviser.   He is described as "a man of a
clear understanding, eloquent, judicious, and of great quickness
and capacity in business, simple yet nice in his apparel, lofty
and venerable in his deportment."   He was an elegant scholar,
but of course imbued with all the prejudices of his age and
calling; and notwithstanding his clerical profession, he had a
noble band of warriors in his pay.   There were also the pope's

nuncio, the Prior of Prado, the warlike Bishop of Jaen, and many others.

Amid this assemblage of haughty nobles and fierce soldiers, men who knew no arts but those of war, and courted no glory which was not sown and reaped in blood—amid all these high-born dames and proud and stately prelates—moved one in lowly garb and peaceful guise, overlooked, unheeded, when not repulsed with scorn by the great, or abandoned to the derision of the vulgar, yet bearing on his serene brow the stamp of greatness—one before whose enduring and universal fame the transient glory of these fighting warriors faded away, like tapers in the blaze of a noontide sun, and compared with whose sublime achievements their loftiest deeds were mere infant play. This was the man—

> "By Heaven design'd
> To lift the veil that cover'd half mankind"—

Columbus!—he first appeared as a suiter in the court of Castile in the spring of the year 1486. In the midst of the hurry and tumult of martial preparation, and all the vicissitudes and pressing exigencies of a tremendous and expensive war, we can hardly wonder if his magnificent but (as they then appeared) extravagant speculations should at first meet with little attention or encouragement. During the spring and autumn of this year he remained at Cordova, but though warmly patronized by the Cardinal Mendozo, he could not obtain an audience of the sovereigns.

Nor was Isabella to blame in this. It appears that while Ferdinand proceeded to lay siege to Loxa, the queen was wholly engrossed by the care of supplying the armies, the administration of the revenues, and all the multiplied anxieties of foreign and domestic government, wnich, in the absence of Ferdinand, devolved solely upon her. She gave her attention unremittingly to these complicated affairs, sparing neither time nor fatigue, and conducted all things with consummate judgment, as well as the most astonishing order and activity. It is not surprising that, under such circumstances, Columbus, then an obscure individual, should have found it difficult to obtain an audience, or that his splendid views, as yet unrealized, should have appeared, amid the immediate cares and interests and dangers pressing around her, somewhat remote and visionary, and fail to seize on her instant attention.

In the meantime the war proceeded. Loxa was taken after an obstinate defence, and a terrible slaughter of the miserable inhabitants. Boabdil, " the Unlucky," was retaken at Loxa, but released again, on renewing his oath of vassalage, to foment the troubles of his wretched country.*

After the capture of Loxa, Ferdinand wrote to Isabella, requesting her presence in his camp, that he might consult with her on the treatment of Boabdil, and the administration of their new dominions.

In ready obedience to her husband's wish, Isabella took her departure from the city of Cordova on the 12th of June. She was accompanied by her favorite daughter, the Princess Isabella, and a numerous train of noble ladies and valiant cavaliers, with

---

* In one of the suburbs of Loxa, a poor weaver was at his work during the hottest of the assault. His wife urged him to fly. "Why should I fly?" said the Moor; "to be rescued for hunger and slavery? I tell you, wife, I will abide here; for better is it to die quickly by the steel than to perish piecemeal in chains and dungeons." Having said this he coolly resumed his work, and was slain at his loom by the furious assailants.—Vide Conquest of Granada. This reminds us of Archimedes only that the Moorish weaver was the greater philosopher of the two, and did not stick to his loom through mere absence of mind.

courtiers, statesmen, and prelates of rank. On the frontiers oi Granada she was met by the Marquis of Cadiz, who, with a gallant company of knights and retainers, had come to escort nei through the lately-conqui red territories to the camp, which was now removed to Moclin, another formidable place of strength, whizh Ferdinand had invested with his whole army. On her journey thither Isabella made a short stay at Loxa, where she and the young Infanta visitea · the sick and wounded soldiers, distributing among them money and raiment, and medical aid, according to their need. Thence Isabella proceeded through the mountain-roads toward Moclin, still respectfully escorted by the brave Marquis of Cadiz, who attended at her bridle-rein, and was treated by her with all the distinction due to so valiant and courteous a knight. When she approached the camp, the young Duke del Infantado, with all his retainers, in their usual gorgeous array, met her at the distance of several miles ; and when they came in view of the tents, the king rode forth to receive her, at the head of the grandees, and attended by all the chivalry of his army, glittering in their coats of mail and embroidered vests, with waving plumes, and standards and pennons floating in the summer air. " The queen," says the Chronicle, " was mounted on a chestnut mule, in a saddle-chair of state ; the housings were of fine crimson cloth embroidered with gold ; the reins and head-piece were of satin, curiously wrought with needlework. The queen wore a skirt of velvet over petticoats of brocade ; a scarlet mantle hung from her shoulders, and her hat was of black velvet embroidered with gold." The dress of the young Infanta was all of black, and a black mantilla, ornamented in the Moorish fashion, hung on her shoulders. The ladies of the court, all richly dressed, followed on forty mules. The meeting between Ferdinand and Isabella on this occasion was arranged with true Spanish gravity and etiquette. Laying their conjugal character aside for the present, they approached each other as sovereigns—each alighting at some paces' distance, made three profound reverences before they embraced. The queen, it is remarked, took off her embroidered hat, and remained with her head uncovered, except by a silken net which confined her hair. Ferdinand then kissed her respectfully on the cheek, and, turning to his daughter, he took her in his arms, gave her a father's blessing, and kissed her on the lips. They then re-mounted, and the splendid procession moved onward to the camp, the Earl of Rivers riding next to the king and queen.

Isabella and her daughter were present during the whole of the siege of Moclin, which was reduced with great difficulty, and principally through the skill of the Lombard engineers. It appears that in the use of all fire-arms the Spaniards greatly excelled the Moors ; and in the sciences of fortification and gunnery, which were still in their infancy, the Italians at this time exceeded all Europe. Moclin fell before the Spanish batteries, and the inhabitants capitulated ; and Isabella and her husband entered the city in solemn state with their band of warriors. They were preceded by the standard of the cross, and a company of priests, with the choir of the royal chapel, chanting the *Te Deum*. As they moved thus in solemn procession through the smoking and deserted streets of the fallen city, they suddenly heard a number of voices, as if from under the earth, responding to the chorus of priests, and singing aloud, " Blessed is he that cometh in the name of the Lord." There was a pause of astonishment ; and it was discovered that these were the voices of certain Christian captives who had been confined in the subterraneous dungeons of the fortress. Isabella, overcome with a variety of emotions, wept, and commanded that these captives should be instantly brought before her ; she then ordered them to be clothed and comforted, and conveyed in safety to their several homes.

The queen remained for some weeks at Moclin, healing, as far as she was able, the calamities of war—introducing regular government and good order into her new dominions—converting mosques into churches and convents, and founding colleges for the instruction and conversion of the Moors. It should not be omitted, that with all her zeal for religion, Isabella uniformly opposed herself to all measures of persecution or severity. The oppression and cruelty afterward exercised towards the conquered Moors did not originate with her ; but, on the contrary, were most abhorrent to her benign temper and her natural sense of justice. She was ever their advocate and protectress, even while she lent all the energies of her mind to the prosecution of the national and religious war she waged against them. Hence, she was hardly more beloved and revered by her Catholic than by her Moslem subjects.

Ferdinand, meantime, marched forward, and ravaged the Vega, even to the very gates of Granada. He then returned to join the queen at Moclin ; and, at the conclusion of this triumphant campaign, the two sovereigns retired to the city of Cordova, leaving young Frederick de Toledo, (already distinguished for his military talents, and afterward the Duke of Alva of terrible memory,) to command upon the frontiers of their new conquests.

From Cordova, Isabella removed to Salamanca, where the plans and proposals of Columbus were for the first time laid before a council appointed to consider them. When we read in history of the absurd reasoning, the narrow-minded objections, the superstitious scruples, which grave statesmen and learned doctors opposed to the philosophical arguments. and enthusiastic eloquence of Columbus, we cannot wonder that Isabella herself should doubt and hesitate. Her venerable minister, the Cardinal Mendoza, favored Columbus, but her confessor, Ferdinand de Talavera, was decidedly inimical to all plans of discovery, and by his private influence over the queen, he was enabled to throw a thousand impediments in the way of the great navigator, and defer his access to Isabella.

The winter passed away before the council at Salamanca came to any decision. Early in the spring of 1487, King Ferdinand took the field with twenty thousand cavalry and fifty thousand foot; while Isabella remained at Cordova, to preside as usual over the affairs of government, and make arrangements for conveying to this vast army the necessary and regular supplies. It was the design of Ferdinand to attack Malaga, the principal seaport of Granada, and the second city of the kingdom, and thus cut off any succors that might be expected from the Mahometan states of Africa. It was necessary to reduce several strong places before the army could invest the city of Malaga, and among others, Velez Malaga. Before this last-mentioned town, the king exhibited a trait of personal valor which had nearly proved fatal to him. The camp being endangered by a sudden attack of the Moors, he rushed into the battle, armed only with his lance; his equery was slain at his side, and Ferdinand instantly transfixed with his spear the Moor who had killed his attendant. He was thus left without a weapon, surrounded by the enemy, and, had not the Marquis of Cadiz and others of his nobles galloped to his rescue, he must have perished. On his return to the camp in safety, he made a vow to the Virgin, never again to enter the battle without his sword girded to his side.

When Isabella was informed of this incident, she was greatly
agitated. The gallantry and danger of her husband appear to
have left a strong impression on her imagination, for long afterward she granted to the inhabitants of Velez Malaga, as the
arms of their city, an escutcheon, representing the figure of the
king on horseback, with the equery dead at his feet, and the
Moors flying before him.

In the beginning of May, Ferdinand undertook the memorable
siege of Malaga, which lasted more than three months. The
city was strongly fortified, and, contrary to the wishes of the
opulent and peaceful merchants, was most obstinately defended
by Hamet el Zegri, a valiant old Moor, who had the command
of the garrison. To him the horrible sufferings inflicted on the
inhabitants by a protracted siege appeared quite unworthy the
consideration of a soldier, whose duty it was to defend the fortress intrusted to him. The difficulties, dangers, and delays
which attended this siege, so dispirited the Spaniards, that many
thought of abandoning it altogether. A report that such was
the intention of the sovereigns was circulated among the Christians and the Moors, and gave fresh courage to the latter. To
disprove it in the sight of both nations, Queen Isabella, attended
by her daughter and the whole retinue of her court, arrived to
take up her residence in the camp.

Isabella was received by her army with shouts of exultation.
Immediately on her arrival, she gave a proof of the benignity
of her disposition, by entreating that the attacks on the city
might be discontinued, and offers of peace sent in her name to
the besieged. The firing accordingly ceased for that day, and
gladly would the inhabitants of Malaga have accepted her overtures ; but the fierce Hamet el Zegri disdainfully rejected them,

9

and even threatened with death the first person who should propose to capitulate.

The Marquis of Cadiz invited the queen and the infanta to a banquet in his tent, which crowned with its floating banners and silken draperies the summit of a lofty hill, opposite to the citadel of Malaga. While he was pointing out to Isabella the various arrangements of the royal camp, which. filled with warlike tumult the valley at their feet—while he was explaining the operations of the siege, the strong defences of the city, and the effects of the tremendous ordnance—he suddenly beheld from one of the enemy's towers his own family-banner hung out in scorn and defiance ; it was the same which had been captured by the Moors, in the terrible defeat among the mountains, in 1483. Whatever the marquis might have felt at this insult offered to him in the presence of his queen and the noblest ladies of her court, he suppressed his indignation. While his kinsmen and followers breathed deep vows of revenge, he alone maintained a grave silence, and seemed unmindful of the insolent taunt ; but within a few days afterward, the tower from which his banner had been displayed in mockery, lay a heap of ruins.

While Isabella remained in the camp before Malaga, her life, which her virtues had rendered dear and valuable to her people, had nearly been brought to a tragical close. A Moorish fanatic named Agerbi, who had among his own people the reputation of a santon, or holy prophet, undertook to deliver his country from its enemies. He found means to introduce himself into the Christian camp, where his wild and mysterious appearance excited equal astonishment and curiosity ; he pretended to the gift of prophecy, and required to be conducted to the king and queen, to whom he promised to reveal the event of the siege and other secrets of importance. By command of the Marquis of Cadiz, he was conducted to the royal tents. It happened, fortunately, that the king was then asleep. The queen, though impatient and curious to behold this extraordinary prophet, of whom her attendants had made such a wonderful report, yet, with her usual delicacy toward her husband, refused to receive the Moor, or listen to his communications, until the king should wake ; he was, therefore, conducted into a tent in which the Marchioness of Moya and Don Alvaro were playing at chess—a few attendants were standing round. From the dress and high bearing of these personages, and the magnificent decorations of the pavilion, the Moorish santon believed himself in presence of the king and queen ; and while they were gazing on him with wonder and curiosity, he drew a cimeter from beneath his robe, struck Don Alvaro to the earth, and turning on the marchioness, aimed a blow at her head, which had been fatal, if the point of his weapon had not caught in the hangings of the tent, and thus arrested its force, so that it lighted harmless on the golden ornaments in her hair. This passed like lightning. In the next moment the assassin was flung to the earth by a friar and the queen's treasurer, and instantly massacred by the guards, who rushed in upon hearing the deadly struggle. The soldiers, in a paroxysm of indignation, seized on his body, and threw it into the city from one of their military engines. Don Alvaro recovered from his wound, and an additional guard, composed of twelve hundred cavaliers of rank, was stationed round the royal tents. Isabella, though struck at first with consternation and horror at this treacherous attempt on her life, was still anxious to spare the miserable inhabitants of Malaga. By her advice, terms of capitulation were again offered to the city, but in vain ; Hamet el Zegri, encouraged by a certain Moorish necromancer whom he entertained in his household, and who fed him with false hopes and predictions, again rejected her overtures with contempt.

It appears, that among those who joined the court of Isabella before Malaga, was Columbus, whose expenses on this occasion were defrayed from the royal treasury.* But amid the clash and din of arms, and the dangers and anxieties of the siege—the murderous sallies and fierce assaults, only relieved now and then by solemn religious festivals, or by the princely banquets given by the various commanders at their respective quarters—there was no time to bestow on the considerations of plans for the discovery of distant worlds; the issue of a long and terrible war hung upon the event of an hour, and the present crisis engrossed the thoughts of all.

In the meantime the siege continued—famine raged within the city, and the people, seized with despair, were no longer restrained by the threats or the power of Hamet el Zegri. They pursued him with curses and lamentations as he rode through the streets—mothers threw down their starving infants before his horses. "Better," they exclaimed, "that thou shouldst trample them to death at once, than that we should behold them perish by inches, and listen to their famished cries." Hamet, unable to stem the tide of popular fury, withdrew into the fortress of the citadel, called the Gibralfaro, and abandoned the town and its inhabitants to their fate; they immediately surrendered at discretion, and were forced to ransom themselves from slavery on hard and cruel terms, which very few were able to fulfill. The fortress yielded soon afterward. Hamet el Zegri was thrown into a dungeon, and the garrison sold into slavery. Sixteen hundred Christian captives were found in the city of Malaga; they were sent to Queen Isabella, as the most accept-

* Vide Life and Voyages of Columbus.

able trophy of her success; and yet the same Isabella, who received these poor people with compassionate tenderness—who took off their fetters with her own hands, relieved their wants, and restored them to their families and houses—the same Isabella sent fifty beautiful Moorish girls as a present to the Queen of Naples—thirty to the Queen of Portugal, and others she reserved for herself and for the favorite ladies of her household.

In the following year (1488) Ferdinand led his army to attack the Moors on the eastern side of Granada. This campaign was short, and by no means successful, owing to the military prowess of El Zagal, who ruled in these provinces. Isabella spent the ensuing winter at Saragossa and Valladolid, occupied in the domestic affairs of her kingdom, and in the education of . her children. Voltaire asserts, that Isabella and her husband "neither loved nor hated each other, and that they lived together less as husband and wife than as allied and independent sovereigns;" but on closer examination of their history, this does not appear to be true. Isabella's marriage had been a union of inclination as well as of policy. In her youth she had both loved and admired her husband. As his cold and selfish character disclosed itself, she may possibly have felt her esteem and affection decline; and it is remarked by Voltaire himself, that she deeply suffered as a woman and a wife, not only from her husband's coldness, but from his frequent infidelities. Yet, if they had private disagreements, they were never betrayed to the prying eyes of the courtiers. In this respect she maintained her own dignity and his with admirable self-command. She found consolation for her domestic sorrows in the society of her eldest daughter, the Infanta Isabella, and in the excellent qualities of her son Don Juan Her second daughter, Joanna, had been from her infancy subject to fits, which in the course of years disordered her intellect. Her youngest daughter, Catherine who has obtained a mournful celebrity in history as Catherine of Arragon, was about this time demanded in marriage by Henry VII. of England for his son Prince Arthur. This infant marriage sealed a commercial and political treaty between the two countries, which remained unbroken till the time of Philip II. and Queen Elizabeth.

The year 1489 was rendered memorable by the siege of Baza, a fortress situated on the eastern confines of Granada. On the reduction of this place depended the event of the war, and the king invested it with an army of twenty-five thousand men While he was before the place, displaying his military skill and leading on his gallant chivalry, a far more difficult task devolved on Queen Isabella; she had to attend to the affairs of government, and at the same time to provide all things for supplying a large army, inclosed in the enemy's country, and to which there was no access but over difficult mountain-roads and dangerous passes. The incredible expenses and difficulties she met and overcame, and the expedients to which she had recourse, give us the most extraordinary idea of her talents, her activity, and her masculine energy of mind. The undertaking was in fact so hazardous, that those who usually contracted for the supply of the army now refused to do it on any terms. Isabella was therefore left to her own resources. She constructed roads through the rugged mountainous frontier for the conveyance of the convoys—she hired fourteen thousand mules, which were incessantly employed in the transport of grain and other necessaries. To supply the almost incredible expense, she had not recourse to any oppressive measures of taxation; many prelates and convents opened to her their treasures she pledged her own plate; and it is related that many wealthy individuals readily lent her large sums of money on no other security than her word—such was the character she bore among her subjects, such their confidence in her faith and truth. "And thus," says the Chronicle, "through the wonderful activity, judgment and enterprise of this heroic and magnanimous woman, a great host, encamped in the heart of a warlike country, accessible only over mountain-roads, was maintained in continual abundance;" and to her the ultimate success of the undertaking may be attributed. After the siege had lasted nearly seven months at an immense cost of treasure and waste of life, Isabella came with her daughter and all her retinue, and took up her residence in the camp. When from the towers of Baza the Moors beheld the queen and all her splendid train emerging from the defiles, and descending the mountain-roads in a long and gorgeous array, they beat their breasts, and exclaimed, "Now is the fate of Baza decided!" yet such was the admiration and reverence which this extraordinary woman commanded even among her enemies, that not a gun was fired, not a shaft discharged, nor the slightest interruption offered to her progress. On her arrival there was at once a cessation of all hostilities, as if by mutual though tacit consent, and shortly after Baza surrendered on honorable terms. The chief of the Moorish garrison, Prince Cidi Yahye, was so captivated by the winning grace and courtesy with which Isabella received him, that he vowed never more to draw his sword against her; the queen accepted him as her knight, and replied to his animated expressions of devotion with much sweetness, saying, "that now he was no longer opposed to her, she considered the war of Granada as already terminated."

Baza surrendered in December, 1489, and was soon followed

by the submission of the haughty Moor El Zagal, who, driven from place to place, and unable any longer to contend against the Christian forces, yielded up that part of the kingdom of Granada which yet acknowledged him as sovereign, and did homage to Ferdinand and Isabella as their vassal.

King Boabdil yet ruled in Granada, and the treaty of his friendship between him and the Catholic king had been duly observed as long as it suited the policy of Ferdinand; but no sooner had El Zagal surrendered than Boabdil was called upon to yield up his capital, and receive in lieu of it the revenues of certain Moorish towns. Boabdil might possibly have accepted these terms, but the citizens of Granada and the warriors who had assembled within it, rose up against him, and under the command of Muza, a noble and valiant Moor, they returned a haughty defiance to Ferdinand, declaring that they would perish beneath the walls of their glorious city, ere they would surrender the seat of Moorish power into the hands of unbelievers. Ferdinand and Isabella deferred for a time the completion of their conquest, and retired after this campaign to the city of Seville. In the spring of 1490, the Infanta Isabella was united to Don Alphonso, the Prince of Portugal; and for some weeks after the celebration of these nuptials, the court at Seville presented a continual scene of splendor and revelry, banquets, feasts, and tournaments. In the midst of these external rejoicings the heart of Isabella bled over her approaching separation from her beloved daughter, and the young princess herself wore a look of settled melancholy, which seemed prophetic of the woes of her short-lived marriage.

It was just at this crisis that Columbus renewed his solicitations, and pressed for a decided answer to his propositions. He was referred as before to a council or board of inquiry, and the

final report of this committee of " scientific men" is too edify-
ing to be omitted here. It was their opinion, " that the
scheme proposed was vain and impossible, and that it did not
become such great princes to engage in an enterprise of the
kind, on such weak grounds as had been advanced."*

Notwithstanding this unfavorable report, and the ill offices of
Fernando de Talavera, the sovereigns did not wholly dismiss
Columbus, but still held out a hope that at a future period, and
after the conclusion of the war, they would probably renew the
treaty with him. But Columbus had been wearied and disgusted by his long attendance on the court, and he would no
longer listen to these evasive and indefinite promises. He quitted
Seville in deep disappointment and indignation, at the very time
that Ferdinand and Isabella were assembling the army destined
for the siege of Granada, little suspecting, that while they were
devoting all their energies and expending all their resources in
the conquest of a petty kingdom, they were blindly rejecting
the acquisition of a world.

On the 11th of April, 1491, King Ferdinand took the field
for this last campaign. His army consisted of forty thousand in-
fantry and ten thousand cavalry. He was accompanied by his
son, Don Juan, then a fine youth of sixteen, and by all the
chivalry of Castile and Arragon, including the Marquis of
Cadiz, and the Marquis of Villena—the Counts de Cabre, de
Tendilla, Cifuentes, and Ureña, Don Alonzo de Aguilar, and
Gonsalvo de Cordova, all names renowned in the annals of
Spain. Isabella with her family and retinue remained for a
time at Alcala la Real, a strong place on the frontiers; but
they soon afterward quitted this fortress, and took up their

* Vide Life and Voyages of Columbus

residence in the camp before Granada.   The Moors, excited by the enthusiasm and example of Muza, their heroic commander, defended their city with courageous obstinacy, and the environs of Granada were the scene of many romantic exploits and renowned deeds of arms.   One or two of these adventures, in which Isabella was personally interested, ought to find a place here.

It happened on a certain day, when the siege had already lasted about two months, that a fierce Moorish chief, named El Tarfe, made a sally from the walls, with a band of followers. He galloped almost alone up to the Christian camp, leaped the intrenchments, flung his lance into the midst of the royal tents, and then turning his horse, sprung again over the barriers, and galloped back to the city with a speed which left his pursuers far behind.   When the tumult of surprise had ceased, the lance of El Tarfe was found quivering in the earth, and affixed to it a label, purporting that it was intended for the Queen Isabella.

Such an audacious insult offered to their adored and sovereign lady, filled the whole Christian host with astonishment and indignation.   A Castilian knight, named Perez de Pulgar, deeply swore to retort this insolent bravado on the enemy.   Accompanied by a few valiant friends, he forced his way through one of the gates of Granada, galloped up to the principal mosque, and there, throwing himself from his horse, he knelt down, and solemnly took possession of it, in the name of the Blessed Virgin.   Then taking a tablet, on which were inscribed the words AVE MARIA, he nailed it to the portal of the mosque with his dagger, re-mounted his horse, and safely regained the camp, slaying or overturning all his opponents.

On the day which succeeded this daring exploit, Queen Isabella and her daughters expressed a wish to have a nearer view of the city, and of the glorious palace of the Alhambra, than they could obtain from the camp. The noble Marquis of Cadiz immediately prepared to gratify this natural but perilous curiosity ; assembling a brilliant and numerous escort, composed of chosen warriors, he conducted Isabella and her retinue to a rising ground nearer the city, whence they might view to advantage the towers and heights of the Alhambra.

When the Moors beheld this splendid and warlike array approaching their city, they sent forth a body of their bravest youth, who challenged the Christians to the fight. But Isabella, unwilling that her curiosity should cost the life of one human being, absolutely forbade the combat ; and her knights obeyed, but sorely against their will. All at once, the fierce and insolent El Tarfe, armed at all points, was seen to advance ; he slowly paraded close to the Christian ranks, dragging at his horse's tail the inscription " Ave Maria," which Pulgar had affixed to the mosque a few hours before. On beholding this abominable sacrilege, all the zeal, the pride, the long-restrained fury of the Castilians burst forth at once. Pulgar was not present, but one of his intimate friends, Garcilaso de la Vega,* threw himself at the feet of the queen, and so earnestly entreated her permission to avenge this insult, that his request was granted ; he encountered and slew the Moor in single combat, and the engagement immediately became general. Isabella, at once shocked by the consequences of her curiosity, and terrified by the sudden onset and din of arms, threw herself on her knees with all her ladies, and prayed earnestly, while " lance to lance, and horse to horse," the battle fiercely raged around her. At length, victory decided for the Christians, and the Moors were driven back with loss upon the city. The

* This Garcilaso de la Vega is said to have been the father of the great poet.

Marquis of Cadiz then rode up to the queen, and while she yet trembled with agitation, he, with grave courtesy, apologized for the combat which had taken place, as if it had been a mere breach of etiquette, and gallantly attributed the victory to her presence. On the spot where this battle was fought Isabella founded a convent, which still exists, and in its garden is a laurel which, according to the tradition of the place, was planted by her own hand.

Not long afterward Isabella was exposed to still greater danger. One sultry night in the month of July, she had been lying on her couch, reading by the light of a taper. About midnight she arose and went into her oratory to perform her devotions; and one of her attendants, in removing the taper, placed it too near the silken curtains which divided her magnificent pavilion into various compartments; the hangings, moved by the evening breeze, caught fire, and were instantly in a blaze—the conflagration spread from tent to tent, and in a few moments the whole of this division of the camp was in flames.

The queen had scarcely time to extricate herself from the burning draperies, and her first thought was for the safety of her husband. She flew to his tent. The king, upon the first alarm, and uncertain of the nature of the danger, had leaped from his bed, and was rushing forth half-dressed, with his sword in his hand. The king being in safety, Isabella's next thought was for her son; but he had already been extricated by his attendant, and carried to the tent of the Marquis of Cubra. No lives were lost, but the whole of the queen's wardrobe and an immense quantity of arms and treasure were destroyed.

The Moors, who from their walls beheld this conflagration, entertained some hopes that such a terrible disaster and the approach of winter would induce the sovereigns to abandon the siege. Their astonishment was great when they saw a noble and regular city rise from the ruins of the camp. It owed its existence to the piety and magnanimity of Isabella, who founded it as a memorial of her gratitude to Heaven, and at the same time to manifest the determination of herself and her husband never to relinquish the siege while Granada remained standing. The army wished to call this new city by the name of their beloved queen; but the piety of Isabella disclaimed this compliment, and she named it La Santa Fé.

It was during the erection of this city that Queen Isabella once more dispatched a missive to Columbus, desiring his return to the court, that she might have farther conference with him; and she sent him at the same time, with that benevolence which characterized her, a sum of money to bear his expenses, and to provide him with a mule for his journey, and habiliments fitted to appear in the royal presence. He arrived at the city of Santa Fé just as Granada, reduced to the last extremity by famine and the loss of its bravest inhabitants, had surrendered on terms of capitulation, and the standard of the Cross and the great banner of Castile were seen floating together on the lofty watch-tower of the Alhambra. It was on the 6th of January, 1492, that Isabella and Ferdinand made their triumphal entry into the fallen city. The unfortunate Boabdil met them, and surrendered the keys to King Ferdinand. He would have dismounted and tendered the usual token of vassalage, by kissing the hands of the king and queen, but they generously declined it; and Isabella, with many kind and courteous words, delivered to Boabdil his only son, who had hitherto been detained as a hostage. The Moorish monarch, accompanied by all his family and suite, then took his melancholy way towards the province which had been assigned to him as his future residence. On reaching a hill above Granada, (which has since been called by the Spaniards *El Ultimo Suspiro del Moro*, " the last sigh of the Moor "), Boabdil turned, and, casting a last look back on the beautiful Vega, and the glorious city of his forefathers, he burst into tears. " You do well," said his high-spirited mother, Ayxa, " to weep like a woman for what you knew not how to defend like a man !" The reproof might have been just, but in such a moment the cruel taunt ill became a mother's heart or lips.   Boabdil afterward retired to Africa, and resided in the territories of the King of Fez.   He survived the conquest of Granada thirty-four years, and died at last on the field, valiantly fighting in defence of the kingdom of Fez.

The war of Granada lasted ten years, and with the surrender of the capital terminated the dominion of the Moors in Spain, which, dating from the defeat of Roderick, the last of the Goths, had endured seven hundred and seventy-eight years.   When the tumult of this great triumph had in some degree subsided, Isabella had leisure to attend to Columbus, and the negotiation with him was renewed.   The terms, however, on which he insisted with a lofty enthusiasm, appeared so exorbitant when compared with his lowly condition and the vague nature of his views, that his old adversary, Fernando de Talavera, now Archbishop of Granada, again interposed between him and the kind intentions of the queen, and said so much that Isabella, after some hesitation, declared his pretensions to be inadmissible. Columbus, on the other hand, would not abate one iota of his demands.   In bitterness of spirit he saddled his mule, and turned his back on Santa Fé.   Scarcely had he departed when two of his most enthusiastic friends, who were besides high in the royal favor,* waited on the queen.   They vindicated Colum-

* Luis de St. Angel and Alonzo de Quintanilla.

bus from the aspersions of Talavera ; they entreated, they remonstrated with all the zeal which their friendship for him and their loyalty to the queen could inspire. The Marchioness of Moya added to their arguments the most eloquent persuasions. Isabella listened. She had ever been friendly to this great and glorious enterprise, and her enthusiasm was now kindled by that of her friend. She still hesitated for one moment, recollecting how completely the royal treasury was drained by the late war, and that the king, her husband, was coldly averse to the measure. At length she exclaimed, "It shall be so—I will undertake the enterprise for my own kingdom of Castile, and will pledge my jewels for the necessary sum !" "This," says the historian of Columbus, " was the proudest moment in the life of Isabella. It stamped her renown forever as the patroness of the discovery of the New World."

A courier was immediately dispatched to recall Columbus, who had already reached the bridge of Piños, two or three leagues from Granada. He hesitated at first, but when he was informed that the messenger came from the queen herself, and bore her pledge and promise, confiding in her royal word, he turned his mule at once, and retraced his steps to Santa Fé. The compact between the two sovereigns and Columbus was signed in April, 1492, Isabella undertaking all the expenses except one-eighth, which was borne by the admiral ; and in the following August Columbus set sail from Palos.

The history of his voyages and discoveries does not properly enter into the personal history of Queen Isabella. It may be remarked generally, that in all her conduct toward Columbus, and all her views and decrees in the government of the newly-discovered world, we find the same beautiful consistency, the same generous feeling, and the same rectitude of intention.

Next to that moment in which Isabella declared herself the sole patroness of Columbus, and undertook the voyage of discovery for her " own kingdom of Castile," the most memorable epoch of her life was his return from the New World, when she received him in state at Barcelona; and, when laying at her feet the productions of those unknown lands, he gave her a detailed narrative of his wonderful voyage.

Isabella was particularly struck by his account of the inhabitants of these new-found regions; she took a tender interest in their welfare, and often reiterated her special commands to Columbus that they should be treated with kindness, and converted or civilized only by the gentlest means. Of the variety of circumstances which interposed between these poor people and her benevolent intentions we can only judge by a detailed account of the events which followed, and the characters of those intrusted with the management of the new discoveries. When the most pious churchmen and enlightened statesmen of her time could not determine whether it was or was not lawful, and, according to the Christian religion, to enslave the Indians— when Columbus himself pressed the measure as a political necessity, and at once condemned to slavery those who offered the slightest opposition to the Spanish invaders—Isabella settled the matter according to the dictates of her own merciful heart and upright mind. She ordered that all the Indians should be conveyed back to their respective homes, and forbade absolutely all harsh measures toward them on any pretence. Unable at such a distance to measure all the difficulties with which Columbus had to contend, her indignation fell on him; and the cruelties which his followers exercised, at least under the sanction of his name, drew on him her deep displeasure.

While under the immediate auspices of Isabella these grand

discoveries were proceeding in the New World, Ferdinand was engrossed by ambitious projects nearer home. Naples had been invaded by Charles VIII. in 1494, and Gonsalvo de Cordova had been sent to oppose him. Gonsalvo, "the Great Captain," by a series of brilliant military successes and political perfidies of the deepest dye, in the end secured the kingdom of Naples for his master, Ferdinand. The legitimate heir, and last descendant of the family of Alphonso, "the Magnanimous," was brought a prisoner to Spain, and died there after a captivity of fifty years.

Isabella, meantime, in the interior of her palace, was occupied by interests and feelings nearer and dearer to her heart than the conquest of kingdoms or the discovery of worlds; and, during the last few years of her life, she was gradually crushed to the earth by a series of domestic calamities, which no human wisdom could have averted, and for which no earthly prosperity could afford consolation.

In 1496, her mother, the queen-dowager of Castile, died in her arms. In 1497, just before Columbus sailed on his third voyage, a double family arrangement had been made between the houses of Spain and Austria, which bade fair to consolidate the power of both. The Infanta Joanna was betrothed to the Archduke Philip, son and heir of the Emperor Maximilian; and the same splendid and gallant fleet which bore her from the shores of Spain brought back Margaret of Austria, the destined wife of Prince Juan, the only son of Isabella and Ferdinand. In the spring of 1497, Juan and Margaret, then both in the bloom of youth, were united at Burgos, with all befitting pomp and revelry.

The queen's most beloved daughter, the Princess Isabella, had lost her young husband, Alphonso of Portugal; within four months after his marriage he was killed by a fall from his horse, and she retired to a convent, where, from an excess of grief or

10

piety, she gave herself up to a course of religious abstinence and austerities which undermined her constitution. Several years after the death of Alphonso she was induced to bestow her hand ou his cousin and heir, Don Emanuel, who had just ascended the throne of Portugal. While yet the customary festivities were going forward upon the occasion of this royal marriage, the young Prince Juan died of a fever, within five months after his marriage with Margaret, and her infant perished ere it saw the light. Isabella, though struck to the heart by this cruel disappointment of her best hopes and affections, found strength in her habitual piety to bear the blow, and was beginning to recover from the first bitterness of grief, when a stroke, even more lastingly and deeply felt, bowed her almost to the grave with sorrow. Her daughter, the Queen of Portugal, whom she appears to have loved and trusted beyond every human being, died in childbirth at Toledo, bequeathing to her mother's care a beautiful but feeble infant, the heir to Castile, Arragon, and Granada, to Portugal, Navarre, Naples, Sicily, and to all the opening glories of the eastern and western worlds. As if crushed beneath the burden of such magnificent destinies, the child pined away and died. These successive losses followed so quick upon one another, that it seemed as if the hand of Heaven had doomed the house of Ferdinand and Isabella to desolation.

The reader need hardly be reminded of the ignominious and ungrateful treatment of Columbus, nor of the manner in which he was sent home after his third voyage, loaded with fetters, from the world he had discovered, to the sovereigns he had enriched and aggrandized by his discoveries. In justice to Isabella, it is fit to account for her share in this revolting transaction ; and it cannot be done better or more succinctly than in the very words of the historian of Columbus :—

"The queen, having taken a maternal interest in the welfare of the natives, had been repeatedly offended by what appeared to her pertinacity on the part of Columbus, in continuing to make slaves of those taken in warfare, in contradiction to her known wishes. The same ships which brought home the companions of Roldan brought likewise a great number of slaves. Some Columbus had been obliged to grant to these men by articles of capitulation—others they had brought away clandestinely ; among them were several daughters of caciques, who had been seduced away from their families and their native island by these profligates. The gifts and transfers of these unhappy beings were all ascribed to the will of Columbus, and represented to Isabella in their darkest colors. Her sensibility as a woman and her dignity as a queen were instantly in arms. 'What power,' she exclaimed, indignantly, 'has the admiral to give away my vassals ?' She determined, by one decided and peremptory act, to show her abhorrence of these outrages upon humanity ; she ordered all the Indians to be restored to their country and friends. Nay, more, her measure was retrospective. She commanded that those who had formerly been sent home by the admiral should be sought out, and sent back to Hispaniola. Unfortunately for Columbus, at this very juncture, in one of his letters he had advised the continuance of Indian slavery for some time longer, as a measure important for the welfare of the colony. This contributed to heighten the indignation of Isabella, and induced her no longer to oppose the sending out of a commission to investigate his conduct, and, if necessary, to supersede his commission."

When Columbus had sailed on his first voyage of discovery, Isabella had given a strong proof of her kindly feeling toward him, by appointing his sons pages to Don Juan ; thus providing for their education, and opening to them a path to the highest offices in the court. Hence, perhaps, arose the friendship which existed between Columbus and Donna Joanna de Torres, who had been nurse or *gouvernante* of the young prince, and was high in the confidence and favor of Isabella. Too proud, perhaps, to address himself immediately to those who had injured him, Columbus wrote to Donna Joanna a detailed account of the disgraceful treatment he had met, and justified his own conduct. The court was then at Granada, and Joanna de Torres in attendance on the queen. No sooner had she received the letter than she carried it to her mistress, and read aloud this solemn and affecting appeal against the injustice and ingratitude with which his services had been recompensed. Isabella, who had never contemplated such an extremity, was filled with mingled astonishment, indignation, and sorrow. She immediately wrote to Columbus, expressing her grief for all he had endured, apologizing for the conduct of Bovadilla, and inviting him in affectionate terms to visit the court. He came accordingly, " not as one in disgrace, but richly dressed, and with all the marks of rank and distinction. Isabella received him in the Alhambra, and when he entered her apartment she was so overpowered that she burst into tears, and could only extend her hand to him. Columbus himself, who had borne up firmly against the stern conflicts of the world, and had endured with a lofty scorn the injuries and insults of ignoble men, when he beheld the queen's emotion, could no longer suppress his own. He threw himself at her feet, and for some time was unable to utter a word, for the violence of his tears and sobbings."* There can be no doubt that, had it depended on Isabella, Columbus would never more have had reason to complain of injustice or ingrati-

* Vide Life and Voyages of Columbus.

tude on the part of the sovereigns ; he had won her entire esteem and her implicit confidence, and all her intentions towards
him were sincerely kind and upright.* It was owing to the
interference of Ferdinand and his ministers that the vice-royalty
of the New World was taken from him and given to Ovando,
as a temporary measure ; but it was under Isabella's peculiar
patronage and protection that he sailed on his fourth voyage of
discovery, in 1502.

Isabella did not live to see him return from this eventful and
disastrous voyage. A dark cloud had gathered over her latter
years, and domestic griefs and cares pressed heavily upon her
affectionate heart. The Princess Joanna, now her heiress, had
married the Archduke Philip of Austria, who was remarkable
for his gay manners and captivating person—the marriage had
been one of mere policy on his part. But the poor princess,
who, unhappily for herself, united to a plain person and infirm
health, strong passions and great sensibility, had centered all
her affections in her husband, whom she regarded with a fond
and exclusive idolatry, while he returned her attachment with
the most negligent coolness. It does not appear that the imbecility of Joanna was natural, but rather the effect of accident
and disease, for occasionally she displayed glimpses of strong
sense, generous pride, and high feeling, which rendered the
derangement of her faculties more intensely painful and affecting. Though Isabella had the satisfaction of seeing Joanna a
mother—though she pressed in her arms a grandson,† whose
splendid destinies, if she could have beheld them through the
long lapse of years, might in part have consoled her ; yet the
feeble health of this infant, and the sight of her daughter's
misery, embittered her days. At length, on the departure of

* Vide Life and Voyages of Columbus   † Afterward the Emperor Charles V.

Philip for the Low Countries, the unhappy Joanna gave way to such transports of grief, that it ended in the complete bereavement of her senses.   To this terrible blow was added another— for, about the same time, the news arrived that Catherine of Arragon had lost her young husband, Prince Arthur, after a union of only five months.   Isabella's maternal heart, wounded in the early death or protracted sorrows of her children, had no hope, no consolation, but in her deep sense of religion.   Ximenes was at this time her confessor.   In his strong and upright, but somewhat harsh and severe mind, she found that support and counsel which might aid her in grappling with the cares of empire, but not the comfort which could soothe her affliction as a mother.   Ferdinand was so engrossed by the Italian wars and in weaving subtle webs of policy either to ensnare his neighbors or veil his own deep-laid plans, that he had little thought or care for domestic sorrows.   So Isabella pined away lonely in her grandeur, till the deep melancholy of her mind seized on her constitution, and threw her into a rapid decline.   While on her death-bed, she received intelligence of Ovando's tyrannical government at Hispaniola, and of the barbarities which had been exercised upon the unhappy Indians, her horror and indignation hastened the effects of her disease.   With her dying breath, she exacted from Ferdinand a solemn promise that he would instantly recall Ovando, redress the grievances of the poor Indians, and protect them from all future oppression. Ferdinand gave the required promise, and how he kept it is recorded in traces of blood and guilt in the history of the New World.   Soon after this conversation Isabella expired at Medina del Campo, after a lingering illness of four months; she died on the 25th of November, 1505, in the fifty-fourth year of her age, having reigned thirty-one years.   In her last will she expressed a wish to be buried in the Alhambra—" in a low sepulchre, without any monument, unless the king, her lord, should desire that his body after death should rest in any other spot. In that case, she willed that her body should be removed, and laid beside that of the king, wherever it might be deposited; in order," adds this affecting document of her piety, tenderness, and humility—" in order that the union we have enjoyed while living, and which (through the mercy of God) we hope our souls will experience in heaven, may be represented by our bodies in the earth."

The character of Isabella as a woman and a queen, though not free from the failings incidental to humanity, is certainly the most splendid, and at the same time the most interesting and blameless, which history has recorded. She had all the talents, the strength of mind, and the royal pride of Queen Elizabeth, without her harshness, her despotism, and her arrogance; and she possessed the personal grace, the gentleness, and feminine accomplishments of Mary Stuart, without her weakness. Her virtues were truly her own—her faults and errors were the result of external circumstances, and belonged to the times and the situation in which she was placed. What is most striking and singular in the character of Isabella, is the union of excessive pride—Castilian pride—amounting at times to haughtiness, and even willfulness, whenever her dignity as a queen was concerned, with extreme sensibility and softness of deportment as a woman. She adored her husband, and yet would never suffer him to interfere with her authority as an independent sovereign; and she was as jealous of her prerogative as Elizabeth herself When the cortes of Arragon hesitated to acknowledge her daughter Joanna the heiress to Arragon as well as to Castile, Isabella exclaimed, with all the willfulness of a proud woman.

"Another time it were a shorter way to assemble an army instead of assembling the states!"

Although exposed in early life to all the contagion of a depraved court, Isabella preserved a reputation unsullied, even by the breath of calumny. The women who formed her court and habitual society were generally estimable. The men, who owed their rise to her particular favor and patronage, were all distinguished either for worth or talent. The most illustrious were Columbus and Ximenes, certainly the two greatest men of that time, in point of original capacity, boldness of strength, and integrity of purpose. Ferdinand hated and oppressed the former, and hated and feared the latter. Both would have been distinguished in any age or under any circumstances, but, next to themselves, they owed their rise and their fame to Isabella. It was in the reign of Isabella that the Spanish language and literature began to assume a polished and regular form. The two most celebrated poets of her time were the Marquis de Santillana and Juan de Encina. She patronized the newly-invented art of printing, and the first printing-press set up in Spain was established at Burgos under her auspices, and printed books; and foreign classical works were imported free of duty. Through her zeal and patronage the University of Salamanca rose to that eminence which it assumed among the learned institutions of that period. She prepared the way for that golden age of Spanish literature which immediately succeeded.

"Isabella de la paz y bontad :"—Isabella of peace and goodness—was the simple, but beautiful designation bestowed upon her by her people; and the universal regret and enthusiastic eulogies with which they have embalmed her memory have been ratified by history and posterity.

Beatrice Cenci.

BEATRICE CENCI.

In an obscure part of Rome, near the Ghetto, or quarter of the Jews, stands a large gloomly pile, which, though partially modernized, retains all the characteristics of a feudal palace Its foundations are seated upon the ruins of an ancient amphitheatre, and its walls were probably raised, like most of the palaces in the Christian capital, at the expense of some noble monument of antiquity. A darkly tragic history, involving the fate of one of the oldest Patrician families of Rome, and ending in its extinction, is connected with this building. It is a tale of suffering and of blood—one in which the most monstrous perversity distorts the best and gentlest feelings of human nature, and converts a mild and lovely woman into a parricide.

The record of such crimes, though it raises a thrill of breathless horror, conveys at the same time a useful lesson. To watch the effects of a continued career of vice, or to trace the warping of an ardent but virtuous mind under the pressure of accumulated and unheard-of injuries, is to study a most important page in the book of mankind. Precept is powerful, no doubt; but when a terrific picture is placed before us, and the fearful reality brought home to the senses, it leaves a much more lasting impression.

Such is my object in relating the events which follow; as well as to show, that even the production of a positive good is not only no justification for crime, but that such crime leads to

certain and irreparable evil. Here we have a daughter inflict
ing death upon an iniquitous father ; and while a deep and soul-
stirring interest is awakened by the sorrows and sufferings of
Beatrice Cenci, a horror of the crime she committed will ever
couple her name with infamy.

Count Nicolo Cenci was the last living descendant of an
ancient and noble house. In early life he had entered the
ecclesiastical state, risen to the prelacy, and held, under the
Pontificate of Pius V., the office of Treasurer to the Apostolio
chamber. Being at length the sole survivor of his race, he
resolved, though somewhat advanced in years, to return to
secular life and marry—a practice not uncommon in the six-
teenth century. At his death he left an only son, the inheritor
of his honors and immense wealth.

This son, the child of his old age and of his ambition, was
Francesco Cenci, the father of Beatrice. The curse of iniquity
seemed entailed upon him from his cradle. He was one of
those human monsters which, bad as man may be, are the ano
malies of the species ; woe and despair were the ministers to his
enjoyments, and the very atmosphere tainted with his breath
was pregnant with death or misfortune to all who came within
its influence. Before he had reached his twentieth year, he
married a woman of great beauty and noble birth, who, after
bearing him seven children, and while still young, died a
violent and mysterious death. Very soon after, he married
Lucrezia Strozzi, by whom he had no family.

Count Francesco Cenci was a stranger to every redeeming
virtue of the human heart. His whole life was spent in
debauchery, and in the commission of crimes of the most un-
speakable kind. He had several times incurred the penalty of
death, but had purchased his pardon from the papal govern

ment at the cost of a hundred thousand Roman crowns for each offence. As he advanced in years, he conceived a most implacable hatred towards his children. To get rid of his three eldest sons, he sent them to Spain, where he kept them without even the common necessaries of life. They contrived, however, to return to Rome, and throw themselves at the feet of the Pope, who compelled their unnatural father to make them an allowance suitable to their rank. Their eldest sister, cruelly tortured at home, likewise succeeded, though with great difficulty, in making an appeal to the Pontiff, and was removed from her father's roof. She died a few years after.

When these victims of Count Cenci's hatred were thus placed beyond his reach, the vindictive old man became almost frantic with passion. But his wife, his daughter Beatrice, his son Bernardino, and a boy still younger, were yet in his power; and upon them he resolved to wreak his vengeance by the infliction of tenfold wretchedness.

To prevent Beatrice from following her sister's example, he shut her up in a remote and unfrequented room of his palace, no longer the seat of princely magnificence and hospitality, but a gloomy and appalling solitude, the silence of which was never disturbed, except by shouts of loose revelry, or shrieks of despair.

So long as Beatrice remained a child, her father treated her with extreme cruelty. But years sped on; the ill-used child grew up into a woman of surpassing loveliness, and the hand raised to fell her to the earth, became gradually relaxed, and at last fell powerless. The soul of the stern father had melted before her matchless beauty, and his ferocious nature seemed subdued But it was only the deceitful calm that precedes the tempest.

Just before this change took place, Beatrice's two brothers, Cristoforo and Vocio, were found murdered in the neighborhood of Rome. The crime was ascribed to banditti, but it was generally believed that a parent's hand had directed the assassin's dagger. Be that as it may, the wicked old Count refused the money necessary to bury his sons, alleging that he would wait until the other members of his hated family were cut off, and then spend the whole of his fortune in giving them all a magnificent funeral.

Count Cenci's unusual mildness toward his daughter, seemed at first to have its origin in a redeeming virtue which had imperceptibly stolen into his heart. Beatrice received the marks of his assumed kindness as a blessing of Providence; they called forth the kindliest emotions of her nature, and her heart overflowed with gratitude. But the real cause of the Count's change of conduct was soon revealed. He had indeed been moved by his daughter's beauty, though not by paternal affection. The wretched man had dared to contemplate the most unhallowed crime that ever blackened the annals of human depravity; and when this became manifest to Beatrice, she shrank back in horror and affright, her features were convulsed with agony, and the most appalling thoughts shot through her brain. Now began that mental struggle which ended in the perversion of her nature, and led to the frightful catastrophe that ensued. Beatrice Cenci, though the most gentle and affectionate of her sex, had nevertheless a firm and energetic soul. With all the attributes of feminine loveliness, with endowments that rendered her the ornament of society, she had a resoluteness of purpose, and an energy of courage, which nothing could shake. To this may be added a keen sense of injury. A mind of such a stamp, goaded by years of the most revolting cruelty, and recently outraged by a loathsome and unutterable attempt, was the more likely, upon taking a wrong bias, to advance recklessly on to crime. Beatrice was, besides, excited by a powerful and all-absorbing idea. Strongly imbued with the religious fanaticism of the age in which she lived, she imagined that, if hei father persevered in his monstrous course, her soul would be forever contaminated, and both parent and child excluded from eternal salvation. Hence despair fixed its fangs upon her heart, and smothered her better feelings. She at first contemplated the possibility of her father's death as the only chance of averting the threatened evil; and as her mind became familiarized with this idea, she gradually brought herself to think that she was called upon, if not to anticipate the will of Providence, at least to act as its instrument. It is probable that her resolution was strengthened, by witnessing the cruelties daily inflicted upon her step-mother and her two youngest brothers.

Ever since Count Cenci's hatred of Beatrice had yielded to a more atrocious sentiment, she had enjoyed greater freedom, and the fame of her beauty soon spread through Rome. Numerous suitors offered themselves to her notice; but she beheld them all with indifference, except Monsignore Guerra, an intimate friend of Giacomo, her eldest brother. This young man was handsome, valiant, accomplished, and her equal in rank. He had entered the church, and was then a prelate; but he intended o obtain a dispensation to marry, as Beatrice's grandfather had done. He loved Beatrice with the most devoted affection, which she as warmly returned. Count Cenci was jealous of all who approached his daughter, and the lovers could only converse in private when the Count was from home. For some months, he had seldom left his palace, and the cause of this sedentary life was but too apparent, not only to Beatrice, but to the Countess.

Lucrezia was a kind step-mother. There is a bond in the fellowship of suffering which begets affection, and Beatrice had always found sympathy and consolation in her father's wife. Into the bosom of the Countess she now poured the tale of her despair, forcibly directed her attention to the abyss upon the brink of which they all stood, and ultimately succeeded in making her mother-in-law a convert to her views and purposes. For the first time, perhaps, a wife and her step-daughter conspired the death of a husband and father. Trembling for their safety, and dreading the most fearful violence—led, moreover, by the superstitious fanaticism with which, in those days of blindness, Christianity was debased, to take a false view of futurity—two feeble women dared to conceive a crime that would have appalled the stoutest-hearted villain.

The lover of Beatrice was made the depository of this dreadful secret, and his assistance solicited. Guerra loved his beautiful mistress too ardently to question the propriety of anything she resolved upon, and, as her blind slave, he readily assumed the management of the plot. Having first communicated the matter to Giacomo, and wrung from him a perhaps reluctant concurrence, he next undertook to provide the murderers. These were soon found. The vassals of Count Cenci abhorred him as an insufferable tyrant; among them were Marzio and Olimpio, both of whom burned with Italian vindictiveness and hatred of their feudal lord. Marzio, besides, madly and hopelessly loved Beatrice. He was sent for to the Cenci palace, where, after a few gentle words from the syren, and the promise of a princely reward, he accepted the bloody mission; and Olimpio was induced to join him, from a desire of avenging some personal wrongs.

The first plan fixed upon by the conspirators was one likely to escape detection ; nevertheless, from some cause now unknown it was abandoned.   Count Cenci intended spending a year at Rocca-di-Petrella, a castle situated among the Apulian Apennines.   It belonged to his friend Marzio Colunna, who had placed it at his disposal.   A number of banditti, posted in the woods near the castle, were to have attacked the Count on his way thither, seized his person, and demanded so heavy a ransom that he could not possibly have the sum with him.   His sons were to propose fetching the money, and, after remaining some time absent, to return and declare that they had been unable to raise so large an amount.   The Count was then to be put to death.

The difficulties which arose to prevent the adoption of this plan, certainly offering the best chances of escape from the consequences of the crime, are involved in obscurity ; but the hand of Providence is here apparent.   The murder was adjourned to some more convenient opportunity, and Count Cenci set out with his wife, his daughter, and his two youngest sons, for Rocca-di-Petrella.

It raises feelings of horror and disgust, as we follow this family party in their slow progress across the Pontine marshes, meditating against each other, as they journeyed on, crimes the most revolting to human nature.   They moved forward like a funeral procession.   On reaching Rocca-di-Petrella, the Count immediately began to carry his designs against Beatrice into execution.

Day after day, the most violent scenes took place, and they but strengthened Beatrice in her desperate resolution.   At length she could hold out no longer ; and the rage of madness took possession of her mind.   One day—it was the 4th of

11

September, 1598—after a most trying interview with her father, she threw herself, in an agony of horror, into the arms of Lucrezia, and exclaimed in a hoarse, broken voice,—

" We can delay no longer—he must die !"

An express was that instant dispatched to Monsignore Guerra ; the murderers received immediate instructions, and on the evening of the 8th, reached Rocca-di-Petrella. Beatrice turned pale on hearing the signal which announced their arrival.

" This is the Nativity of the Virgin," said she to the Countess—" we must wait till to-morrow ; for why should we commit a double crime ?"

Thus was a most heinous offence, no less than the murder of a father and a husband, deferred, because the Church prohibited *all kind of work* on the day of the Virgin Mary's nativity Such were the feelings of these two women ; and such, I may safely aver, were the feelings of every desperate villain in Italy, at that period. Even Francesco Cenci, whose atrocities have found no parallel in ancient or modern times, built a chapel and established masses for the repose of his soul. Religion was no check—it was only a refuge or sanctuary against punishment ; and it served but to convince the dying criminal who had strictly observed its outward forms, of his certain passport to heaven.

On the following evening, Beatrice and Lucrezia administered an opiate to Count Cenci of sufficient strength to prevent him from defending his life. A short time after he had taken it, he fell into a heavy sleep.

When all was silent in the castle, the murderers were admitted by Beatrice, who conducted them into a long gallery, leading to the Count's bed-room. The women were soon left to themselves ; and strong as was their determination, and deep the sense of their wrongs, this moment must have been appalling to both. They listened in breathless anxiety—not a sound was audible. At length the door of the Count's room was opened, and the murderers rushed out horror-stricken.

"Oh God!" said Marzio, in dreadful agitation, "I cannot kill that old man. His peaceful sleep—his venerable white locks—Oh! I cannot do it!"

The cheeks of Beatrice became of an ashy paleness, and she trembled with anger. Her eyes flashed with fury, as her color returned, and the passions which shook her whole frame served but to give additional lustre to her beauty.

"Coward!" she exclaimed with bitterness, seizing Marzio by the arm; "thy valor lies only in words. Base murderer! thou hast sold thy soul to the devil, and yet thou lackest energy to fulfill thy hellish contract. Return to that room, vile slave, and do thy duty; or, by the seven pains of our Lady—" and as she said this, she drew a dagger from under the folds of her dress—"thy dastardly soul shall go prematurely to its long account."

The men shrank beneath the scowl of this girl. Completely abashed, they returned to their work of death, followed by Beatrice and Lucrezia. The Count had not been disturbed from his sleep. His head appeared above the coverlid; it was surrounded by flowing white hair, which, reflecting the moon-beams as they fell upon it through the large painted window, formed a silvery halo round his brow. Marzio shuddered as he approached the bed—the passage from sleep to eternity was brief.

The crime being consummated, Beatrice herself paid the promised reward, and presented Marzio with a cloak richly trimmed with gold lace. Th. murderers immediately left the castle through a ruined postern long·out of use, and partly walled up.

Beatrice and Lucrezia then returned to the murdered Count, and drawing the weapon from the wound—for the old man had been deprived of life by means of a long and sharply-pointed piece of iron, driven into the brain through the corner of the right eye—clothed the body in a dressing-gown, and dragging it to the further end of the gallery, precipitated it from a window then under repair, the balcony of which had been taken down. Beneath stood a huge mulberry-tree with strong and luxuriant branches, which so dreadfully mutilated the corpse in its fall, that, when found in the morning, it presented every appearance of accidental death. It is probable that no suspicion would ever have been excited, had not Beatrice, with strict injunctions to secrecy, given the blood-stained sheets and coverlid to a woman of the village for the purpose of being washed.

Rocca-di-Petrella being situated in the Neapolitan territory, the Court of Naples received the first intimation of the suspected crime. An inquiry was immediately set on foot; but, notwithstanding every search, the deposition of the woman who had washed the bed-clothes was the only evidence that could be obtained.

Meantime, Giacomo had assumed the title of Count Cenci; and his step-mother and sister, accompanied by Bernardino—for the youngest boy had died soon after the murder—had quitted Rocca-di-Petrella, and taken up their abode at the Cenci palace, there to enjoy the few peaceful months which Providence allowed to intervene betwixt the crime and its punishment. Here they received the first intelligence of the inquiry instituted by the Neapolitan Government; and they trembled at the thought of being betrayed by their accomplices.

Monsignore Guerra, equally interested in the concealment of the crime, resolved to make sure of the discretion of Marzio and Olimpio, and hired a bravo to dispatch them. Olimpio was accordingly murdered near Turin; but Marzio, being arrested at Naples for a fresh crime, declared himself guilty of Count Cenci's death, and had related every particular. This new evidence being instantly forwarded to the papal government by that of Naples, Beatrice and Lucrezia were put under arrest in the Cenci palace, and Giacomo and Bernardino imprisoned at Corte-Savella. Marzio was soon after brought to Rome and confronted with the members of the Cenci family. But when he beheld that Beatrice, whom he so fondly loved, standing before him as a prisoner—her fate hanging upon the words he should utter—he retracted his confession, and boldly declared that his former statement at Naples was totally false. He was put to the most cruel torture; but he persisted in his denial, and expired upon the rack.

The Cenci now seemed absolved from the accusation. But the murderer of Olimpio being arrested, as Marzio had been, for a different offence, voluntarily accused himself of this murder, which he had perpetrated, he said, in obedience to the commands of Monsignore Guerra. As Olimpio had also made some disclosures before he died, the confession of his assassin was considered so conclusive, that the whole of the prisoners were conveyed to the castle of St. Angelo. Guerra, seriously alarmed at the declaration of the bravo, fled from Rome in disguise, and, after encountering many perils, succeeded in leaving Italy. His flight was a confirmation of the evidence, and proceeding against the Cenci family were immediately commenced.

Criminal process in those days, as in the two succeeding centuries, was the mere application of physical torture to extort an

avowal of the crime imputed; for the law had *humanely* pro
vided that no criminal could be convicted but upon his own
confession.　The rack was, therefore, termed *the question*, and
was, in fact, the only form of interrogatory.　Thus, if an accused was innocent, and had the energy of soul to brave the
torture, he must bear it till he died; but if nature was subdued
by pain, he accused himself falsely, and was put to death on
the scaffold.　Such was the justice administered by men calling
themselves Christian prelates!

The question was applied to the Cenci.　Lucrezia, Giacomo,
and Bernardino, unable to bear the agony, made a full confession;
but Beatrice strenuously persisted in the denial of the murder.
Her beautiful limbs were torn by the instruments of torture;
but by her eloquence and address she completely foiled the tribunal.　The judges were greatly embarrassed—they dared not
pronounce judgment, and their president, Ulisse Moscatino, reported the state of the proceedings to the Pope, then Clement
VIII.

The Pontiff, fearing that Moscatino had been touched by the
extreme beauty of Beatrice, appointed a new president, and the
question was again applied.　The unhappy girl bore the most
intense agony without flinching; nothing could be elicited from
her but a denial of the crime with which she was charged.　At
length the judges ordered her hair to be cut off.　This last indignity broke her spirit, and her resolution gave way.　She now
declared that she was ready to confess, but only in the presence
of her family.　Lucrezia and Giacomo were immediately introduced; and when they saw her stretched upon the rack, pale
and exhausted, her delicate limbs mangled and bleeding, they
threw themselves beside her, and wept bitterly.

"Dear sister!" said Giacomo, "we committed the crime, and

have confessed it. There is now no further use in your allowing yourself to be so cruelly tortured."

"It is not of sufferiugs such as these, that we ought to complain," Beatrice replied, in a faint voice. "I felt much greater anguish on the day I first saw a foul stain cast upon our ancient and honorable house. As you must die, would it not have been better to have died under the most acute tortures, than to endure the disgrace of a public execution!"

This idea threw her into strong convulsions. She soon, however, recovered, and thus resumed—"God's will be done! It is your wish that I should confess—well! be it so." Then turning to the tribunal, "Read me," said she, "the confession of my family, and I will add what is necessary."

She was now unbound, and the whole proceedings read to her. She, however, signed the confession without adding a word.

The four prisoners were now conveyed to Corte-Savella, where a room had been prepared for their reception. Here they were allowed to dine together, and in the evening the two brothers were removed to the prison of Tardinova.

The Pope condemned the Cenci to be dragged through the streets of Rome by wild horses. This was a cruel sentence—more especially as it emanated from the head of the Catholic Church, and was quite arbitrary. The prelates and Roman nobility were struck with pity and indignation. A species of sophistry which did much more honor to their humanity than to their judgment, led them to urge in extenuation, nay, almost in justification of the crime, the provocation received, and the series of monstrous attrocities committed by the late Count Cenci They made the most energetic remonstrances to the Pope, who much against his will, granted a respite of three days and a caring by counsel.

The most celebrated advocates at Rome offered their services on this occasion, and Nicolo di Angeli, the most eloquent among them, pleaded the cause of the Cenci so powerfully, that Clement was roused to anger.

" What !" he exclaimed indignantly, " shall children murder their parent, and a Christian advocate attempt to justify such a crime, before the Head of the Church ?"

The counsel were intimidated; but Farinacci, another advocate, rose and addressing the Pope—

" Holy Father !" said he, with firmness, " we come not hither to employ our talents in making so odious a crime appear a virtue, but to defend the innocent, if it please your Holiness to give us a hearing."

The Pope made no reply, but listened to Farinacci with great patience, during four hours.   He then dismissed the advocates, and withdrew with Cardinal Marcello, to reconsider the case.

Doubtless, the parricide can find no extenuation of his crime ; nevertheless the circumstances between Beatrice and her father were so monstrous—the latter was such a fiend upon earth, and each of the prisoners had been so cruelly tortured by him, that the Pope determined to mitigate the severity of his sentence. He was about to commute it into imprisonment for life, when news reached Rome that the princess Costanza di Santa-Croce had been murdered at Subiaco by her son, because she had refused to make a will in his favor. This event again roused Clement's severity, and on the 10th of September, 1599, he directed Monsignore Taberna, governor of Rome, to resume proceedings against the Cenci, and let the law take its course.

The whole family were to be publicly beheaded in three days Farinacci again came forward and pleaded the cause of Bernardino, who had not been an accomplice or even privy to the crime, and succeeded in obtaining his pardon ; but on the horrible condition that he should attend the execution of the others.

The day before the execution, at five o'clock in the afternoon, the ministers of justice arrived at Corte-Savella, to read the sentence of the law to the wife and daughter of the murdered Count Cenci. Beatrice was in a sound sleep ; the judges surrounded her in silence, and the solemn voice of the *segretario* roused her from her last slumber in this world.

The idea of a public exposure upon the scaffold threw her into an agony of grief; but her mind soon recovered its tone, and she calmly prepared for death.

She began by making her will, in which she directed that her body should be buried in the church of San-Pietro in Montorio She bequeathed three hundred Roman crowns to the congregation of the Sante-Piaghe, and her own dower as a marriage portion to fifty portionless girls.

There is a strange serenity in this contemplation of conjugal life from the brink of the grave, especially by a young girl about to expiate, on the scaffold, the murder of her father. But the history of Beatrice Cenci is still involved in mystery, and it is therefore difficult to trace the workings of her mind.

"Now," said she to Lucrezia, "let us prepare to meet death with decency."

The fatal hour struck, and the nuns of the congregation of the Sette-Dolori came to conduct the prisoners to the place of death. They found Beatrice at prayers, but firm and resolute.

Meanwhile, her two brothers had left Tardinova, escorted by the congregation of Penitents. The celebrated picture of Piety, presented by Michael Angelo for the sole use of dying criminals, was borne before them. They were thus taken before a judge,

who, after reading Giacomo's sentence to him, turned to Bernar
dino,—

"Signor Cenci," he said, "our most Holy Father grants you
your life. Return thanks for his clemency. *You are condemned
to proceed to the place of execution, and witness the death of your
family!*"

The moment the judge had done speaking, the Penitents struck
up a hymn of thanksgiving, and withdrew the picture from before Bernardino, who was now placed in a separate cart, and the
procession again moved forward. During the whole of the
route, Giacomo was tortured with red-hot pincers. He bore the
pain with marvelous fortitude—not a sigh escaped him.

They stopped at the gate of Corte-Savella to take Beatrice
and Lucrezia, who came forth covered with their veils. That
of Beatrice was of gray muslin, embroidered with silver. She
wore a purple petticoat, white shoes, and a very high dress of
gray silk, with wide sleeves, which she had made during the
night. Both held a crucifix in one hand and a white pocket
handkerchief in the other; for though their arms were lightly
bound with cords, their hands were perfectly free. Beatrice
had just entered her twentieth year—never had she appeared
more lovely. There was, in her suffering countenance, an expression of resignation and fortitude, a calmness of religious
hope, that drew tears from the spectators. She kept up her
step-mother's courage, as they proceeded, and whenever they
passed a church or a Madonna, she prayed aloud with great
fervency.

On reaching the Ponte St. Angelo, near which the scaffold
was erected, the prisoners were placed in a small temporary
chapel prepared for them, where they spent a short time in
prayer. Giacomo, though the last executed, was the first to

ascend the scaffold, and Bernardino was placed by his side
The unhappy youth fainted, and was firmly bound to a chair.
Beatrice and Lucrezia were then led forth from the chapel.
An immense concourse of people had assembled, and each
bosom throbbed with painful interest.

At this moment three guns were fired from the castle of
St. Angelo. It was a signal to inform the Pope that the prisoners were ready for execution. On hearing it, Clement became
agitated, and wept; then falling on his knees, he gave the
Cenci full absolution, which was communicated to them in his
name. The assembled spectators knelt, and prayed aloud; and
thousands of hands were lifted up in deprecation of God's wrath
upon the blood-stained criminals about to appear before his
eternal throne. .

Lucrezia was the first led forward for execution. The
minister of the law stripped her to the waist. The unfortunate
woman trembled excessively—not indeed from fear, but from
the gross violation of decency, in thus exposing her to the gaze
of the multitude.

"Great God!" she cried, "spare me this. Oh! mercy,
mercy!"

The particulars of Lucrezia's execution are disgusting and
horrible; for the sake of human nature, such atrocities should
be buried in eternal silence. When her head fell, it made three
bounds, as if appealing against such cruelty. The *boja*, after holding it up to the terrified spectators, covered it with a silk veil,
and placed it in the coffin with her body. He then reset the axe
for Beatrice, who was on her knees in fervent prayer. Having
prepared the instrument of death, he rudely seized her arm, with
hands besmeared with the blood of her step-mother. She instantly arose, and said, in a firm and strongly accentuated voice:

"O my divine Saviour, who didst die upon the cross for me and for all mankind ; grant, I beseech thee, that one drop of thy precious blood may insure my salvation, and that, guilty as I am, thou wilt admit me into thy heavenly paradise."

Then presenting her arms for the *boja* to bind them,—

"Thou art about," she said, "to bind my body for its punishment ; mayest thou likewise unbind my soul for its eternal salvation !"

She walked to the block with a firm step, and, as she knelt, took every precaution that female delicacy could suggest ; then calmly laying down her head, it was severed by a single stroke.

Bernardino was two years younger than his sister Beatrice, whom he tenderly loved. When he saw her head roll upon the scaffold, he again fainted. But cruelty is ever active ; and he was recalled to life, that he might witness the death of his brother.

Giacomo was covered with a mourning cloak. Upon its removal, a cry of horror issued from the spectators, at the sight of his mangled and bleeding body. He approached Bernardino—

"Dear brother," said he, "if, on the rack, I said anything to criminate you, it was drawn from me by the intense agony I endured ; and, although I have already contradicted it, I here solemnly declare that you are entirely innocent, and that your being brought hither to witness our execution, is a wanton and atrocious piece of cruelty. Pardon me, my brother, and pray for us all."

He then knelt upon the scaffold, and began to pray. The *boja* placed a bandage over his eyes, and struck him a violen blow across the right temple, with a bar of iron. He fell without a groan, and his body was divided into four parts.

The congregation of Sante-Piaghe conveyed Bernardino back to his prison, where, during four days, he remained in dreadful convulsions ; and for a long time after both his reason and his life were despaired of. The bodies of Beatrice and Lucrezia, together with the severed quarters of Giacomo, were exposed till the evening, at the foot of Saint Paul's statue, on the Ponte St. Angelo. The congregations then took them away. The body of Beatrice was received by venerable matrons, who, after washing and perfuming it, clothed it in white, and surrounded it with flowers, consecrated candles, and vases of incense. It was ultimately placed in a magnificent coffin, conveyed to the church of San Pietro in Montorio, by the light of more than five hundred torches, and there buried, at the foot of the great altar, under the celebrated transfiguration by Raphael.

Bernardino was the only survivor of this unhappy family, and the last male heir of his race. He married a Bologuetti, and left an only daughter, who changed the name of the Cenci palace ; and from this marriage, the building came into the possession of the Bologuetti family, to whom it still belongs.

The old Cenci palace is in the most gloomy and obscure quarter of Rome. Its massive and sullen architecture, and its neglected and deserted appearance, accord perfectly with the tragical associations connected with it. One window, which is fronted with an open-work balcony, may have belonged to the very chamber of Beatrice ; and a dark and lofty archway, built of immense stones, may have been that through which she went out to the prison which she left only for the scaffold.

In the old Barberini palace is Guido's portrait of Beatrice, taken, according to the family tradition, on the night before her execution. Shelly's tragedy has made her sad story familiar to English readers, and his description of this picture leaves nothing to be added ; though no words, nor even copies, can give any idea of her touching loveliness, her expression of patient suffering, her quivering, half-parted lips, and tender hazel eyes of a beauty unattained on any other canvas in the world ; but her half-turned head, with its golden locks escaping from the folds of its white drapery, haunts yuor memory, as if you, too, like Guido, had caught a last glimpse of her as she mounted the scaffold.

Ann Boleyn.

ANN BOLEYN.

WHEN the sister of Henry VIII., a young and blooming girl of sixteen, arrived in France to wed Louis XII., a monarch old enough to be her grandfather, she was attended by several young ladies belonging to the noblest families of England. Among them was Ann Boleyn, celebrated not only by her misfortunes and untimely end, but on account of her being the immediate cause of the reformation, or establishment of the Protestant religiou in England. Hers is an eventful history

Ann was the daughter of Sir Thomas Boleyn, a gentleman allied to the noblest houses in the kingdom. His mother was of the house of Ormond, and his grandfather, when mayor of London, had married one of the daughters of Lord Hastings. Lady Boleyn, Ann's mother, was a daughter of the Duke of Norfolk. Sir Thomas Boleyn being a man of talent, had been employed by the king in several diplomatic missions, which he had successfully executed. When the Princess Mary left England to wear, for three short months, the crown of Queen Consort of France, Ann was very young; she therefore finished her education at the French Court, where her beauty and accomplishments were highly valued. After the death of Louis XII., his young widow having married Brandon, Duke of Suffolk, and returned to England, Ann entered the service of Claude, wife of Francis I. On the death of this queen, she had an appointment in the household of the Duchess of Alen-

12

çon, a very distinguished princess; but she retained it only a few months, and then returned to her native country.

The precise period of her arrival in England is not accurately known; but it was a fatal day for Catherine of Arragon, to whom she was soon after appointed maid of honor. In this situation she had frequent opportunities of conversing with the king; he was not proof against her fascinations, and became deeply enamored of her. But Henry's was the love of the sensualist—its only aim was self-gratification—and wherever it fell, it withered or destroyed.

Until Henry beheld Ann Boleyn, he had never expressed any dissatisfaction at his marriage with Catherine. On a sudden he conceived scruples with regard to this union. It was monstrous—it was incestuous, he said; and he could not reconcile it to his conscience to consider his brother's widow any longer his wife. It is true, that Catherine had gone through a ceremony at the altar, with Arthur, Prince of Wales, Henry's elder brother; but the prince had died soon after, being then only seventeen years of age. And when political reasons subsequently led to the marriage between Catherine and Henry, the new Prince of Wales felt no scruples—nay, his conscience slumbered twenty years before it was awakened to a sense of the enormity which now afflicted him.

But awakened at length it was; and it appeared to him under the form of a young girl beaming with beauty, wit, and loveliness. The conversation and manners of Ann Boleyn had a peculiar charm, which threw all the other English ladies into the shade. She had acquired it at the most polished and elegant, but perhaps the most licentious, court in Europe; and when Henry, fascinated by her wit, gazed with rapture on her fair form—when he listened with intense delight to her thoughtless sallies, and madly loved on, little did she think that, while her conduct was pure, this very thoughtlessness of speech would one day be expiated by a public and disgraceful death.

Ann refused to become the king's mistress; for she very justly thought, that the more elevated dishonor is, the more clearly it is perceived.

"My birth is noble enough," she said, "to entitle me to become your wife. If it be true, as you assert, that your marriage with the queen is incestuous, let a divorce be publicly pronounced, and I am yours."

This sealed the fate of Catherine of Arragon. Henry immediately directed Cardinal Wolsey, his prime minister and favorite, to write to Rome, and obtain a brief from the Pope, annulling his marriage. Knight, the king's secretary, was likewise dispatched thither to hasten the conclusion of this business.

Clement VII. then filled the pontiff's throne. Timid and irresolute, he dreaded the anger of the Emperor Charles V., Catherine's nephew, who kept him almost a prisoner, and would naturally avenge any insult offered to his aunt. Clement, therefore, eluded giving a definitive answer. But being pressed by the King of France, who was the more ready, from his hatred of the emperor, to advocate Henry's cause on this occasion, the Pope at length consented to acknowledge that Julius II. had no power to issue a bull authorizing Catherine's marriage with her brother-in-law. This declaration was a serious attack upon the infallibility of the popes; but Clement's situation was perilous, and the only chance he had of freeing himself from the thraldom of Charles V. was by conciliating the King's of England and France. But, on the other hand, he was anxious to bring about the re-establishment of his house at Florence, which he thought the emperor alone could effect. Moreover

Charles had a large army in Italy, constantly threatening Rome. The pontiff had likewise some other grounds of alarm. It is known that illegitimate children are excluded from the papal throne, and Clement was the natural son of Julian de Medicis; for though, if we believe the authority of Leo X., a promise of marriage had existed between his parents, it did not efface the stain. Nor was this all: in defiance of the severe laws of Julius II. against simony, Clement had been guilty of that crime, and Cardinal Colonna had a note of hand in his possession, subscribed by the Pope, and applied to facilitate his accession to the chair of St. Peter. The emperor was aware of both these facts; and taking advantage of Clement's timidity of character, constantly threatened to assemble a general council and have him deposed.

Thus was the pontiff urged to opposite acts by the rival monarchs; and his struggle between such contending interests led to that long ambiguity of conduct and ultimate decision which severed England from the Church of Rome.

Meanwhile, a secret marriage, it is said, had taken place between Henry VIII. and Ann Boleyn; and what seems to confirm this, is the activity Ann displayed in pressing Cardinal Wolsey, and Stephen Gardiner, his secretary, to bring the divorce to a conclusion. The following is a letter which she wrote to the cardinal, at a time when a contagious disease raged in London, and she had retired to a country residence with the king. It is a good specimen of her mind and character :—

" My Lord,

" In my most humblest wise that my heart can think, I desire you to pardon me that I am so bold to trouble you with my simple and rude writing, esteeming it to proceed from her that is much desirous to know that your grace does weil, as I perceive by this bearer that you do. The which I pray God long to continue, as I am most bound to pray; for I do know the great pains and troubles that you have taken for me both day and night, is never like to be recompensed on my part, but alonely in loving you next unto the king's grace, above all creatures living. And I do not doubt but the daily proofs of my deeds shall manifestly declare and affirm my writing to be true, and I do trust that you do think the same. My Lord, I do assure you I do long to hear from you news of the legate; for I do hope and they come from you they shall be very good; and I am sure you desire it as much as I, and more, and it were possible, as I know it is not; and thus remaining in a steadfast hope, I make an end of my letter, written with the hand of her that is bound to be,

" Your humble servant,

" ANN BOLEYN."

Underneath the King had added :—

" The writer of this letter would not cease till she had caused me likewise to set my hand; desiring you, though it be short, to take it in good part. I insure you there is neither of us but that greatly desireth to see you, and much more joyous to hear that you have escaped this plague so well, trusting the fury thereof to be passed, specially with them that keepeth good diet, as I trust you do. The not hearing of the legate's arrival in France, causeth us somewhat to muse; notwithstanding, we trust, by your diligence and vigilancy (with the assistance of Almighty God) shortly to be eased out of that trouble. No more to you at this time; but that I pray God send you as good health and prosperity as the writer would. By your

" Loving Sovereign and Friend,   HENRY K."

Though the king had fled from the contagion with Ann Boleyn, he had given no orders to enable Catherine to leave London; and she remained there exposed to the danger of the plague. No doubt the possibility of her death had occurred to Henry's mind, and the reckless attrocity of his character may justify the inference, that he had left her in London for the express purpose of exposing her to die of the disease, and thus at once settling the divorce question.

Just as the Pope's brief for the divorce was about to be issued, the sacking of Rome took place, and the Pontiff remained during a whole year imprisoned in the castle of St. Angelo. On being set at liberty by the Emperor, he was afraid to pronounce the dishonor of Charles's aunt, whose complaints resounded throughout Europe. At length, to temporize with all parties, and not lose sight of his own interest, he appointed Cardinal Campeggio, his legate in England, for the purpose of trying the question, but gave him secret orders to proceed as slowly as possible. The new legate was old and afflicted with gout, severe attacks of which were his ever-ready excuse for procrastination; and it took him ten months to travel from Rome to London.

Ann Boleyn, on hearing that the legate was at last on his way to England, again wrote to Wolsey, expressing her gratitude in strong terms.

"And as for the coming of the legate," she said, in this letter, "I desire that much, and if it be God's pleasure, I pray him to send this matter shortly to a good end, and then I trust, my lord, to recompense part of your great pains. In the which I must require you in the meantime to accept my good will, in the stead of the power, the which must proceed partly from you, as our Lord knoweth; to whom I beseech to send you long life, with continuance in honor."

But Catherine was by no means so grateful as Ann for the pains that Wolsey took to constitute an arbitrary and iniquitous tribunal, and she called him a heretic and abettor of adultery. This the cardinal-minister little heeded, for he had the king and the king's mistress on his side ; and the host of flatterers by whom he was surrounded made him believe that his power was too firmly established ever to be shaken.

Wolsey had greatly contributed to bring about Henry's connection with Ann Boleyn, because he thought that such a passion would absorb the king's time, and make him careless of business, by which the minister would become master of the kingdom. Queen Catherine, with her oratory, her rosary, and her religious austerity, was not the queen that suited Wolsey's views. She had nothing to attract the king from the cares and business of his kingdom. Ann Boleyn, on the contrary, was a creature formed of love ; she was always gay, happy, and endearing when in Henry's company. The king, therefore, overcome by a fascination which he could not resist, bent his neck to her yoke, and left the governance of his dominions in the hands of his ambitious minister.

When once the flowery chain had encircled Henry, Wolsey little cared whether it was sanctified or not by religion. In his corrupt mind, he perhaps thought it might be more durable, if it did not obtain the sanction of the Church. But he at length received the Pope's commission, and Campeggio arrived in England ; he, therefore, took his measures with the legate, and they opened their tribunal. To keep up an appearance of propriety, Ann immediately left London.

The two cardinals, having opened their court in London, cited the king and queen to appear before them. Both obeyed ; and when Henry's name was called, he rose and answered to it.

The queen was dressed in mourning ; her countenance was calm, though it but ill disguised the anguish of her mind. When the legate pronounced the words " Most·high, most powerful, and most illustrious Lady and Princess," Catherine, without looking at him, or making any reply, rose and threw herself at the king's feet, embracing his knees, and suffusing them with her tears She urged, she entreated, she conjured him by all that is most sacred to man, not to cast her off; but she sought in vain to soften a heart absorbed by love for another. She did not, however, thus humble herself for her own sake ; she was supplicating for her daughter, whom the decision of the legates might stamp with illegitimacy and dishonor.

" Sir," said she, " what is this tribunal ? Have you convoked it to try me ? And wherefore ? Have I committed any crime ? No : I am innocent, and you alone have authority over me. You are my only support, my sole protector. I am but a poor weak woman, alone, defenceless, and ready to fall under the attacks of my enemies. When I left my family and my country, it was because I relied on English good faith ; and now, in this foreign land, am I cut off from my friends and kindred, and deserted by those who once basked in the sunshine of my favor. I have, and desire to have, none but you for my support and protection—you, and your honor. Henry, do you wish to destroy your daughter's fame ? Consider, she is your first-born ! And would you suffer her to be disgraced, when I, her mother, am innocent, and you, her father, a powerful sovereign ?"

She then arose from her kneeling posture, and looking at the court with dignity—

" Is this the tribunal," said she, " that would try a Queen of England ? It consists of none but enemies, and not a single judge. They cannot pronounce an equitable judgment; I therefore decline their jurisdiction, and must be excused from heeding any further citations in this matter, until I hear from Spain."

Having made a profound obeisance to the king, she left the court. After her departure, the king protested he had no cause of complaint against her, and that *remorse of conscience* was his only reason for demanding a divorce.

The legates again cited the queen; and as she refused to appear, they declared her contumacious. There was a solemn mockery in the whole of these iniquitous proceedings, that rendered them frightful. At length they were drawing to a close; for Ann Boleyn, who had returned to London, was urging Wolsey forward with the full power of her charms, and the cardinal was by no means insensible to her flatteries. But when Henry was every moment expecting the judgment which would allow him to have Ann crowned, Cardinal Campeggio announced that the Pope had reserved to himself the ultimate examination of the case, which he had evoked to Rome before his own tribunal.

Henry at first raved and blasphemed, denouncing vengeance against the pontiff; but he soon became calmer, and set about finding a means of overcoming this new obstacle, and hurling his own thunders in defiance of those of the church. Ann wept bitterly at finding herself as far from the throne as ever. But how powerful were her tears! Henry vowed he would avenge each of them with an ocean of blood. Then it was that he threw off his allegiance to the Church of Rome, and ultimately united both Church and State under his sole governance.

Meanwhile, Ann's harassed mind thirsted for vengeance upon some one, for the annihilation of her hopes. She saw not yet the means of destroying the barrier which now stood betwixt her and the throne; and she had need of a victim. She found one in Cardinal Wolsey   It appeared to her unlikely that this man, influential as he was in the college of cardinals—for his hand had once touched the tiara—should require months and years to do that which he might have finished in a single day. Henry was not a man who required to be told, a second time, not to love: Wolsey had been his favorite, and this was more than sufficient to effect his ruin; for the king's friendship, like his love, proved a withering curse wherever it fell.

Wolsey gave an entertainment at York House, a palace which the most magnificent monarchs of Europe and Asia might have looked upon with envious admiration. There he sat, free from care, and joyously wearing away life, quaffing the choicest wines of Italy and France in cups of gold enchased with jewels and precious enamels. Richly sculptured buffets were loaded with dishes of massive gold, sparkling with precious gems. A hundred servants wearing their master's arms emblazoned on their liveries, circulated round the vast and fantastically sumptuous hall. Young girls, crowned with flowers, burned perfumes and embalmed the air, whilst in an upper gallery a band of the most skillful musicians of Italy and Germany produced a ravishing and voluptuous harmony.

Suddenly two men stood before the cardinal. Both were powerful in the kingdom; and on their appearance, the upstart minister was for a moment awed into respect. One was the Duke of Suffolk, the king's brother-in-law—the other was the Duke of Norfolk. They had come with orders from the king to demand the great seal from Wolsey.

"I will not deliver it up on a mere verbal order," replied the haughty priest.

The two noblemen withdrew, and returned on the following day with a letter from the king. Wolsey then delivered the seal into their hands, and it was given to Sir Thomas More Soon after, York House, now Whitehall, together with all the costly furniture it contained, was seized in the name of the king.

The fallen cardinal was ordered to retire to Asher, a country-seat he possessed near Hampton Court. He was pitied by nobody; for the manner in which he had borne his honors, and the general meanness of his conduct, had rendered him extremely unpopular. He wept like a child at his disgrace, and the least appearance of a return to favor threw him into raptures. One day, Henry sent him a kind message, with a ring in token of regard. The cardinal was on horseback when he met the king's messenger; he immediately alighted, and falling on his knees in the mud, kissed the ring with tears in his eyes.

This was hypocrisy of the meanest kind; for it was impossible he could have loved Henry VIII.

After the fall of Wolsey, a chance-remark make by Dr. Thomas Cranmer, Fellow of Jesus College, Cambridge, gave the king his cue as to the line of conduct he should adopt.

" Oh !" cried Henry in his gross joy, " that man has taken the right sow by the ear."

It was deemed expedient to get opinions on the divorce question from all the universities in Europe, and to lay these opinions before the Pope. This was done; but Clement, like all timid men, thinking to conciliate the nearest, and, as he thought, the most dangerous of his enemies, remained inexorable, and a decision was given against Henry. The Reformation immediately followed, and the new ecclesiastical authority in England was more obedient to Henry's wishes.

The marriage of the king and Ann Boleyn was now formally solemnized; and the woman on whose account the whole of

Europe had been embroiled for the last four years, ascended that throne destined to be only a passage to a premature grave.

Sir Thomas Eliot had been sent to Rome with an answer to a message from the Pope to Henry, and on his departure Ann Boleyn had given him a number of valuable diamonds to be employed in bribing those whose aid it was necessary to obtain. But nothing could avert the definitive rupture; and when Eliot was about to return to England, Sixtus V., then only a monk, shrugged up his shoulders, and lifting his eyes to Heaven, exclaimed,

"Great God! is it not the same to thee, whether Catherine of Arragon, or Ann Boleyn, be the wife of Henry VIII.?"

Ann Boleyn was now at the summit of her wishes. She was at length Queen of England, a title which had cost her too great anxiety of mind for her not to appreciate it far beyond its worth. But one thing embittered the joys it brought her—this was the idea that the same title was still retained by the unhappy Catherine. She, therefore, resolved to work her will with Henry, and deprive her late rival of this last remnant of the honors she had enjoyed, without reproach, during a period of more than twenty years, and until Ann's beauty had estranged the king's affection. Henry could not resist the tears and entreaties of his new queen, whose influence over him was strengthened by the birth of the Princess Elizabeth, and he sent Lord Montjoy to apprize Catherine that she was in future to bear no other title than that of Dowager Princess of Wales.

"I am still Queen of England," she replied with dignity; "and I cannot be deprived of that title except by death, or by a sentence of my divorce from the king, pronounced by the Pope."

The thunders of the Church were at length brought into play

against Henry. Paul III. had succeeded to the papal throne, and though, whilst cardinal, he had always favored Henry's pretensions, perceiving now that a final breach had been effected with the English Church, he declared that the King of England had incurred the penalty of major excommunication. A bull was, therefore, sent forth declaring Henry's throne forfeited, and the issue of his marriage with Ann Boleyn incapable of succeeding to the crown of England. No person, under pain of excommunication, was to acknowledge him king; and the nobility of England were enjoined, under the same penalty, to take up arms against him as a rebel and traitor to the church and to Christ. All the archbishops, bishops, and curates of England, were commanded to excommunicate him every holiday after the Gospel at mass, and the Emperor Charles V. was exhorted, as protector of the Church, to enforce these orders with his armies. The King of France, as the most Christian king, was likewise enjoined to break off all intercourse with Henry VIII. To make the insult the more bitter, the Pope ordered all the curates in the neighborhood of Calais to read the bull of excommunication in their several churches, and proclaim it from the pulpit.

Henry felt but little concern at this noisy but powerless attack. Having assembled a parliament, an act was passed investing him with all the powers of the Pope in England. But he had also an eye to the temporalities of the church; and upon the strength of the spiritual authority he had acquired, he abolished the monasteries, and confiscated the ecclesiastical possessions. To gratify his own avarice and reward his favorites at no cost to himself, he robbed the clergy of the property bestowed upon them, by pious founders, for their support and that of the poor. Though three centuries have since elapsed, the effects of these measures are still felt in England. The overgrown revenues of some of the bishoprics, the enormous wealth of the deans and chapters, the inadequate stipends of the inferior clergy, the system of the poor's rates so inefficient and yet so burthensome, the lay impropriations despoiling both the clergy and the poor—nay, the very unpopularity of tithes, which are principally claimed by pluralists and seculars, are all fruits, not of the reformation itself, but of the system of spoiliation pursued by Henry VIII. the moment he had converted the worship of Almighty God into a political engine.

Ann Boleyn has been accused of prompting the king to these measures; but I apprehend that the charge proceeds solely from the blind vindictiveness of the Catholic party. Ann was thoughtless, giddy, and fond of admiration; but her mind was as incapable of preconceiving as of pursuing a cold and pre-meditated system of vengeance. Her anger was easily roused when her vanity was wounded or her interests opposed, but it evaporated as easily. It is true, that she felt a bitterness of hostility almost foreign to her nature towards Catherine; but that unhappy princess stood in her way and endangered the inheritance of her daughter. This is certainly the most un-amiable part of Ann's character, and nothing can be said in its justification.

The dignity and propriety of Catherine's conduct, joined to her misfortunes, called forth the pity of the whole Christian world. Henry again ordered her, under the severest penalties, to forego the title of Queen; and the persons in her service were commanded to call her the Princess of Wales. Catherine refused the services of those of her officers who obeyed this mandate, and for a few days she was wholly without attendants. So many persecutions, and a deep sense of the injuries she had received, preyed upon her health, and she fell dangerously ill. The king gave orders that the greatest care should be taken of her, and everything done that could contribute to her comfort; as if, after he had stricken his victim to death, he would fain heal the wound.

Ann was alarmed at this seeming return of the king's tenderness for Catherine. The clamors raised by the Catholic party also gave her strong apprehensions that the claims of her daughter would be disallowed. She therefore again exerted her influence over Henry, and the Princess Elizabeth was proclaimed, by sound of trumpet, heir to the throne of England, to the exclusion of her sister Mary.

Catherine died on the 6th of January, 1536, at Kimbolton, in the county of Huntingdon, in the fiftieth year of her age. Before she expired, she wrote a very affecting letter to the king, in which she recommended her daughter to his fatherly care. The last sentence of this letter is deserving of notice, and could have been written only by a woman :—

" I make this vow, that mine eyes desire you above all things."

Henry's stern nature was overcome by these simple words, written at the moment of death, when the illusions of the world disappear before the awful view of eternity. He wept over this letter, penned by a hand already cold and stiff—he wept at this ast address of his victim, at this last proof of fond affection which he had so basely repaid.

Ann evinced the most indecent joy on receiving the news of Catherine's death. When the messenger arrived, she was washing her hands in a splendid vermeil basin, beside which stood a ewer of the same metal. She immediately took both, and thrusting them into his hands—

" Receive this present," said she, " for your good news."

The same day her parents came to see her at Whitehall
She ran and embraced them in a delirium of joy.

"Rejoice!" she cried; "now is your daughter truly a
Queen."

A few days after this event, Ann was delivered of a still-born
son, which the Catholic party attributed to the effect of the excommunication. Henry's passion for her now began to subside,
and he soon loved her no more. Inconstancy was as much a
part of his nature as cruelty. The possession of Ann, purchased at such immense sacrifices, divested of the excitement
which, during six years, had kept it alive, had no longer any
charms for him. If the austerity of Catherine's temper had
estranged him from her, the excessive gayety of her successor
produced the same effect. Ann's lively sallies, to which Henry
had once listened as if spell-bound, now threw him into fits of
ill-humor of several hours' duration; for his heart had so many
moving folds that its vulnerable side one day was impenetrable
the next. Courtiers are keen-sighted, and those about the king
soon perceived that he was absorbed by a new passion. Jane
Seymour had replaced Ann Boleyn in Henry's love, just as Ann
had replaced Catherine of Arragon. But to indulge in this new
passion, and elevate its object to the throne, it was necessary
to convict the queen of a crime; and there was no want of
accusers the moment the tide of Ann's favor had begun to ebb.

The queen had many enemies beside the Catholic party.
Her extreme gayety and powers of ridicule, the mere effects of
exuberant spirits in a young and sprightly woman, had drawn
upon her much greater resentment than serious insult would
have done Thus, the moment the decline of Henry's affection was perceived, accusations poured in, the least of which
was sufficient to insure Ann's disgrace and death.

But to avoid giving umbrage to the nation, whose discontent had already been manifested on other occasions, an offence of more than usual enormity was requisite. Ann had a brother, the Viscount of Rocheford, to whom she was tenderly attached. The Viscountess of Rocheford, his wife, a woman of the most profligate character, was the first to instill the poison of jealousy into the king's ear, and to insinuate calumnies of the blackest dye, which also implicated her husband. Henry Norris, groom of the stole, Weston and Brereton, gentlemen of the privy chamber, and Mark Smeton, a musician of the king's band, were faithfully devoted to Ann, and had won her friendship and confidence. They were also included in the plot, as accomplices of her alleged profligacy. She had herself facilitated the plans of her accusers by her general thoughtlessness and levity of demeanor, as well as by some silly speeches.

Ann was more vain than proud; and her vanity was applied principally to the charms of her person. To obtain admiration, she spared neither her smiles nor her powers of pleasing. Her education at the French court had tainted her with that spirit of gallantry, more in conversation than in actions, which distinguished the first years of the reign of Francis I. But her conduct was strictly virtuous, and her soul pure and innocent. Inferences were, however, drawn from things perfectly harmless in themselves, but certainly unbecoming in a young female; and these, coupled with the infamous tales of her sister-in-law, had roused all the malignant feelings of Henry's nature.

On the 1st of May, 1536, there was a tilting-match at Greenwich, and the queen had never appeared in better spirits. Henry thought that she looked at Rocheford with something more than brotherly affection. Norris, who had just been tilting, having approached her, she greeted him with a smilo
13

and dropped her handkerchief. Though this was probably accidental, Henry attributed it to an improper feeling towards the groom of the stole, and, uttering a dreadful oath, immediately left Greenwich. When his departure was communicated to Ann, she only laughed and said,

"He will return."

But he did not return, and a few hours after, those accused of being her accomplices in adultery were arrested and sent to the Tower, while she was confined to her room. She now saw her impending fate.

"I am lost!" said she, in tears, to her mother and to Miss Methley, one of her maids of honor; "I am forever lost."

Next morning she was placed in a litter and conveyed to the Tower, where she was closely imprisoned, and not allowed to communicate with anybody, even in writing. Her uncle's wife, Lady Boleyn, was appointed to sleep in the same room with her, in order to extort admissions from her which might be turned to her disadvantage. The lady hated the queen, and therefore made no scruple to accept so odious a mission.

Henry was always in a hurry to consummate a crime when he had once conceived it. He therefore lost not an instant in constituting a tribunal of peers for the trial of the brother and sister. The Duke of Norfolk, forgetful of the ties of blood between himself and Ann, and prompted by his ambition, became her most dangerous enemy. He presided at this tribunal as Lord High Steward, and twenty-five peers were appointed to sit with him. They opened their court on the 15th of May, and the queen having appeared before them, declared that she was innocent, and throwing herself upon her knees, appealed to God for the truth of her statement. She confessed certain instances of perhaps unbecoming levity, but the sum of her offences would not have tainted the reputation of a young girl. She defended herself with admirable ability and address. But she was doomed beforehand, and she and her brother were condemned to die. The sentence bore, that she should be beheaded or burnt, according to the king's good pleasure; but Henry spared her the pile.

Ann's benevolence of character had led her to confer obligations on all around her; but when the wheel of fortune turned, not a voice was raised in her favor except that of Cranmer, who remained faithful to her, but unhappily had no means of averting her fate.

No one can doubt the queen's innocence; and if her conduct, during the few fleeting years of her greatness, was sometimes marked with thoughtless imprudence, she met her death with noble dignity and fortitude. There is often a strength of heroism in woman quite beyond the feeble and helpless condition of her sex; and this was displayed by Ann to an extent which will always combine the highest admiration with the pity awakened by her mirfortunes. A short time before her trial, she wrote the king a letter, which, says a celebrated English historian, "contains so much nature and even elegance, that it deserves to be transmitted to posterity." I therefore give it a place here.

"Sir,—Your Grace's displeasure and my imprisonment are things so strange unto me, as what to write or what to excuse, I am altogether ignorant. Whereas you send unto me (willing me to confess a truth and so obtain your favor) by such an one whom you know to be mine ancient professed enemy, I no sooner received this message by him, than I rightly conceived your meaning; and if, as you say, confessing a truth indeed may procure my safety, I shall with all willingness and duty perform your command.

" But let not your Grace ever imagine that your poor wife will ever be brought to acknowledge a fault where not so much as a thought thereof proceeded. And to speak a truth, never prince had wife more loyal in all duty and in all true affection, than you have ever found in Ann Boleyn, with which name and place I could willingly have contented myself, if God and your Grace's pleasure had been so pleased. Neither did I at any time so far forget myself in my exaltation or received queenship, but that I always looked for such an alteration as I now find ; for the ground of my preferment being on no surer foundation than your Grace's fancy, the least alteration, I knew, was fit and sufficient to draw that fancy to some other subject. You have chosen me, from a low estate, to be your queen and companion, far beyond my desert or desire. If then you found me worthy of such honor, good your Grace let not any light fancy, or bad counsel of mine enemies, withdraw your princely favor from me ; neither let that stain, that unworthy stain of a disloyal heart towards your good Grace, ever cast so foul a blot on your most dutiful wife, and the infant-princess, your daughter. Try me, good king, but let me have a lawful trial, and let not my sworn enemies sit as my accusers and judges ; yea, let me receive an open trial, for my truth shall fear no shame ; then shall you see, either mine innocency declared, your suspicion and conscience satisfied, the ignominy and slander of the world stopped, or my guilt openly declared : So that whatsoever God or you may determine of me, your Grace may be freed from an open censure ; and mine offence being so lawfully proved, your Grace is at liberty, both before God and man, not only to execute worthy punishment on me as an unlawful wife, but to follow your affection, already settled on that party, for whose sake I am now as I am, whose name I could some good while since have pointed unto—your Grace being not ignorant of my suspicion therein.

"But if you have already determined of me, and that not only my death, but an infamous slander must bring you the enjoying of your desired happiness; then I desire of God that he will pardon your great sin therein, and likewise mine enemies, the instruments thereof; and that he will not call you to a strict account for your unprincely and cruel usage of me, at his general judgment-seat, where both you and myself must shortly appear, and in whose judgment I doubt not (whatsoever the world may think of me) mine innocence shall be openly known and sufficiently declared.

"My last and only request shall be, that myself may only bear the burthen of your Grace's displeasure, and that it may not touch the innocent souls of those poor gentlemen, who (as I understand) are likewise in strait imprisonment for my sake. If ever I have found favor in your sight, if ever the name of Ann Boleyn hath been pleasing in your ears, then let me obtain this request; and I will so leave to trouble your Grace any further, with mine earnest prayers to the Trinity to have your Grace in his good keeping, and to direct you in all your actions. From my doleful prison in the Tower this 6th of May.

"Your most loyal and ever faithful wife,

"ANN BOLEYN."

This letter produced no other effect than to hasten the trial. It is said that the decision of the peers was at first in favor of the queen and her brother, but that the Duke of Norfolk having compelled them to reconsider a verdict so contrary to the king's expectations, both were condemned to death.

Ann with resignation prepared to meet her fate. The day

before her execution, she forced the wife of the Lieutenant of the Tower to sit in the chair of state, and bending her knee, entreated this lady, in the name of God to go to the Princess Mary and entreat forgiveness for all the affronts her Highness had received from her, hoping they would not be punished in the person of her daughter Elizabeth, to whom she trusted Mary would prove a good sister.

Next morning she dressed herself with royal magnificence.

" I must be bravely attired," she said, " to appear as becomes the queen of the feast."

She sent the king a last message before she died, not to solicit any favor, but to thank him for the care he took of her elevation.

" Tell him," she said, " that he made me a marchioness, then a queen, and is now about to make me a saint—for I die innocent."

When the Lieutenant of the Tower came to inform her that all was ready, she received him not only with firmness, but with gayety.

" The executioner," she observed with a smile, " is skillful, and my neck is slender." And she measured her neck with her hands.

She walked to the scaffold with a firm step. Having ascended it, she prayed devoutly for the king, praised him highly, and termed him " a gentle and most merciful prince." But these exaggerated praises can be attributed only to her fear that her daughter Elizabeth might suffer, on her account, the same indignities that Catherine of Arragon, through her obstinacy, had brought upon the princess Mary. Ann Boleyn was beheaded on the 29th of May, 1536, by the executioner of Calais, who had been sent for as the most expert in Henry's dominions.

Her body was carelessly placed into a common elm chest, and buried in the Tower.

· Henry's subsequent conduct is a complete justification of Ann Boleyn. The very day after her execution, he married Jane Seymour, who did not live long enough to be sacrificed to a new attachment; for she died, little more than two years after her marriage, in giving birth to Edward VI.

The character of Ann Boleyn has been basely calumniated by party historians, especially by Sanderus, or Sanders, "who," says Bishop Burnet, "did so impudently deliver falsehoods, that from his own book many of them may be disproved." Though never calculated to become a great queen, Ann Boleyn had nevertheless many good and amiable qualities, which more than compensate for the silly vanity and thoughtlessness of a young and beautiful woman, conscious of her personal attractions, and continually beset by flatterers. She was high-minded, benevolent to a fault, and strictly virtuous; and though her history is remarkable only from the influence it had upon the affairs of Europe during several years, and from its having led to a reformation of religion in England, yet the moment her young and innocent life was doomed to be offered up a sacrifice to the brutal passions of Henry VIII., she displayed the fortitude and elevation of mind which preceded her death, and won a right to the admiration of posterity, and to a high seat in that temple which the celebrated women of all countries have raised to their own fame.

Lady Jane Gray.

Lady Jane Gray.

LADY JANE GRAY.

AMBITION punished, seldom excites pity; but can a tribute of commiseration be refused to a beautiful woman, only seventeen years of age, who laid her head upon the block to expiate the ambition of another? Such was the fate of Lady Jane Gray! A crown had no attractions for her—she had no desire to reign! It seemed as if this unfortunate and lovely young creature felt her feet slip on the very steps of that throne which the Duke of Northumberland forced her to ascend. A warning presentiment told her that a life of quiet seclusion was the only means she had of escaping a violent death. She long resisted the fatal counsel of her father-in-law; but she was dragged on by her evil destiny.

Lady Jane Gray, born in 1537, was the granddaughter of Mary Tudor, sister of Henry VIII. This princess, being left a widow by the death of her husband, Louis XII., King of France, and having no children by this marriage, returned to England and married Brandon, Duke of Suffolk, whom she had long loved, and who was Lady Jane's grandfather. The subject of this memoir, when she was scarcely sixteen, married Lord Guildford Dudley, fourth son of John Dudley, Duke of Northumberland. Lady Jane Gray was beyond measure lovely; her features were beautifully regular, and her large and mild eyes were the reflection of a pure and energetic soul, though peaceful and unambitious. She had a strong passion for study, especially that of abstruse science. Though young, she had acquired vast learning, and was deeply read in the ancients; she was very familiar with Greek and extremely partial to Plato. Living at one of her country-seats, she divided her time between her books and her husband, until political events of high importance troubled her peaceful life and destroyed her happiness.

Edward Seymour, Duke of Somerset, Protector of England, exercised over that kingdom a despotic sway to which the nobles would no longer submit. The latter, equally disgusted with the pride of Thomas Lord Seymour, the Protector's brother, applauded the Duke of Northumberland when he succeeded in successively removing these two favorites from the king's person; and Northumberland thought himself popular, when he was only loved on account of his hatred towards the Seymours. Edward VI., a weak and sickly child, who could ill bear the weight of the crown that encircled his pallid brow, always bestowed his favor upon those near his person, and Northumberland succeeded Somerset. But the new favorite, fearing, and with good reason, that he should not long retain this station, as the king might die, and was indeed then dying, though only sixteen years of age, employed, with considerable address, the prejudices of religion to gain his ends. He described to Edward, in hideous colors, the character of his sister, Mary, the Catholic; and represented in an equally unfavorable light, Elizabeth, daughter of that Ann Boleyn who was condemned and executed for adultery. Could then the crown of England, he asked, be placed upon a dishonored brow, or the welfare of the English nation be intrusted to an intolerant fanatic? Northumberland was a man of ability; he shook the timid conscience of Edward, who, fearing Mary's violence, and prejudiced against Elizabeth, changed the order of succession, and designated as his successor, Jane Gray, the eldest daughter of Henry Gray.

At the period of Edward's death, there were four female claimants to the crown of England. Two of them were daughters of Henry VIII.,—Mary the Catholic, born of a repudiated wife—Elizabeth the Protestant, born of a wife beheaded as an adulteress. The two others, descended from Henry VII., were Lady Jane Gray, and Mary Stuart, Queen of Scotland— the one a Protestant, like Elizabeth, and claiming by the last will of Edward VI.; the other a Catholic, like Mary, and having not a very clear right, nor the means of enforcing it, even if it were established.

Lady Jane Gray, in the innocence of her heart, was unacquainted with her own claims, and was, besides, unambitious to change her lot. But an ambitious father-in-law forced her upon a throne, to reign only a few days, and then die by the hand of the public executioner. In vain did the lovely young creature entreat her father-in-law to allow her to retain her freedom. The obstinate duke, always at the head of intrigues, determined to gain his point with her whom he deemed a child. "Shall it be for nothing," said he, "that I have caused the daughters of two queens to be declared illegitimate in order to place the crown upon the head of my daughter-in-law? No, indeed!"

Northumberland, not trusting solely to the will of Edward VI. to get Lady Jane Gray acknowledged queen after the king's death, was anxious, before he made the attempt, to have the two daughters of Henry VIII. in his power. He, therefore, a short time before Edward's death, prevailed on the council to write to Mary and Elizabeth, requesting their presence to afford assistance and consolation to a dying brother. They accordingly set out for London; but Edward having expired before their arrival, Northumberland concealed his death, in order that the princesses might continue their journey, and fall into the snare he had laid for them.   Mary had already reached Hoddesdon, about seventeen miles from London, when the Earl of Arundel sent her an express to inform her of her brother's death, and warn her of the projects of Northumberland.   She immediately retired in all haste, and reached Kenninghall in Norfolk, whence she proceeded to Framlingham in Suffolk. She wrote to all the principal nobility and gentry in the kingdom, calling upon them to take up arms in defence of the crown and its legitimate heir; she also sent to the council to announce that she was aware of her brother's death, and commanded them to take the necessary steps for her being proclaimed.   Dissimulation being no longer of any use, Northumberland boldly declared his plan, and, attended by several of the great nobles of England, proceeded to Zion House, where he did homage to Lady Jane Gray as Queen of England.   It was then only that this lovely and unfortunate young woman was made acquainted with the intentions of her father-in-law. She rejected the proffered crown, and urged the priority of right possessed by the daughters of Henry VIII.   For a long time she persisted in her refusal; and her resistance was at length overcome, more by the persuasion of her husband, Lord Guildford Dudley, than by the entreaties of her father-in-law. She was immediately conducted to the Tower of London, where it was customary for the sovereigns of England to spend the first days of their accession to the throne; and she went thither rather as a beautiful victim to be offered up in sacrifice, than as the new sovereign of a great nation.

In vain she was proclaimed Queen of England; not a sign

of rejoicing was heard, and the people maintained a sullen silence. There was no feeling against Lady Jane Gray; but the unpopularity of the Dudleys was excessive, and it was easily seen that, under the name of Jane, they would be the real rulers of England. This made the nation look toward Mary, and the promises of religious toleration which she held out, induced them to support her cause.

Meanwhile Mary was obtaining the submission of the people of Suffolk. All the inhabitants of this county professed the reformed religion, and the moment she pledged herself that they should freely exercise their faith, they attached themselves to her cause. The most powerful of the nobility flocked to her standard, and Sir Edward Hastings, who had received a commission from the council to levy troops in the county of Buckingham for Lady Jane Gray, brought these troops to Mary. A fleet also which Northumberland had sent to cruise off the coast of Suffolk, entered Yarmouth, and declared for the daughter of Henry VIII. Soon after, the ministers of Jane's government, who considered themselves little better than Northumberland's prisoners, left the Tower in a body, and with the Mayor and Aldermen of London proceeded to do homage to her whom they deemed their legitimate sovereign.

Success attended Mary's arms, and she was universally acknowledged queen. At first she appeared mild and clement, assuming an expression of benevolence, and talking only of pardon. But such a word from her was a cruel mockery. If there was pardon, there must have been injury; and it was in Mary's nature never to forget an offence. This seeming mildness was only the slumber of vengeance, which was soon to awake and throw mourning and desolation over the land. Northumberland was at first the only individual she seemed desirous of sacrificing to her resentment. Lady Jane Gray and her husband were imprisoned in the Tower, and the Queen of England was proclaimed most just and merciful, because she had taken only a single life.

In a very short time, however, cries of sedition were heard. The people, alarmed at having a religion forced upon them in which they had no belief, showed symptoms of disaffection. Mary gave no heed to the promises she had solemnly made whilst struggling for her rights. She reinstated the Catholic bishops, and brow-beat the inhabitants of Suffolk when they urged her pledge to them.

Mary was alarmed at the cries of sedition uttered by the people. Lady Jane and her husband were brought before an iniquitous council, who condemned them both to die; and the Mayor of London having begged that a public example might be made, obtained that Lord Guildford Dudley should be executed in public. The unfortunate nobleman, on his sentence being communicated to him, requested an interview with his wife. She refused to see him, but wrote him a letter to the following purport:—

" Do not let us meet, Guildford—we must see each other no more until we are united in a better world. We must forget our joys so sweet, Guildford, our loves so tender and so happy. You must now devote yourself to none but serious thoughts. No more love, no more happiness here upon earth !—we must now think of nothing but death ! Remember, my Guildford, that the people are waiting for you, to see how a man can die. Show no weakness as you approach the scaffold; your fortitude would be overcome, perhaps, were you to see me. You could not quit your poor Jane without tears; and tears and weakness must be left to us women. Adieu, my Guildford, adieu !

Be a man—be firm at the last hour—let me be proud of you."

Guildford died like a hero, and Jane was proud of him. Ah! it was not from weakness that this noble-minded creature refused the crown; she was happy with her books, her affection, and her beloved husband, under her arbors of flowers. It was the absence of happiness in a crown, not its weight that alarmed her.

She saw her husband leave the Tower and proceed to the place of execution. She prayed a long time for him; her own turn then came, and she prepared for death. Mary, desirous of increasing her sufferings, pretended to convert her, and offered to pardon her if she would abjure the reformed religion. But, with a sweet smile of sadness, she refused. For, at that time, what was life to her?—nothing but a vast solitude, through which she would have to wander alone and deserted. She preferred death!

For three days she was assailed by the importunities of Catholic priests, who thought they had shaken her faith. Jane made them no reply, but continued her prayers. Having written a last letter of adieu* to her sister, the Countess of Pembroke, she took off her mourning, dressed herself in white, had her long and beautiful hair cut off by her female attendants, and walked boldy to the place of execution. When, however, she saw the sparkling of the steel axe, she turned pale. She knelt, prayed again, lifted up her eyes and looked at the heavens!—then placing her head upon the block, she received the stroke that conferred upon her a crown of which no human passions could deprive her—the crown of martyrdom!

* This letter was written in Greek. A good translation of it into French may be found in Larrey's History of England.

14

This was the third time in London, within a period of twenty years, that the blood of a queen had stained the scaffold. The reign of Elizabeth was to present a fourth act of the same tragedy.

Catherine Gray, Countess of Pembroke, was more to be pitied than her sister Jane; for, after all, what is death to one who has lost everything that makes life valuable? But Catherine, separated from a world in which the man she loved still lived, must often have prayed to God to give her the sleep of the grave.

Catherine Gray had married the Earl of Pembroke; but their union was so unhappy that both demanded a separation, and their marriage was dissolved by a judicial act. She then became the wife of the Earl of Hertford, who set out for France, leaving her pregnant. Catherine Gray being of the royal blood of Tudor, her marriage without the consent of her sovereign was imputed to her as a crime; and on ascending the throne, Mary, as happy in having to inflict punishment as another would have been to show clemency, condemned her to imprisonment for life. The Earl of Hertford, on his return from France, was also sentenced to imprisonment, and the Archbishop of Canterbury declared the marriage null and void. Nevertheless, the Earl protested against the sentence of the Archbishop, as well as against that of his other judges. He loved Catherine with the tenderest affection; and still looking upon her as his wife, bribed the keeper of the Tower, and obtained access to her prison. Catherine became a mother a second time; and Mary persecuted the Earl of Hertford with all the vindictive hatred of a queen whose authority is despised, and of a woman already past the age of inspiring love, who cannot forgive young people for their superiority in this respect. The Earl's accusation consisted of three counts :—First, of having seduced a princess of the royal blood ; secondly, of having violated a state prison ; and thirdly, of having approached a woman from whom the law had separated him. He was condemned to a fine of five thousand pounds sterling for each offence. He paid the fifteen thousand pounds, and, after a long confinement, consented to sign a voluntary act of separation from Catherine ; but not till after a long struggle, and a resistance which bore ample testimony of the strength of his attachment.

The unfortunate Catherine Gray died in prison, in 1562, after a long and painful captivity. Like her sister Jane, she was learned and fond of study. Both were young and lovely, and the fate of both showed that royal birth is no security against misfortune Tears are shed in the palaces of kings as well as the peasant s hovel ; and arms loaded with jewels often bear the chains of captivity. Poison is sometimes drank in a cup of gold, and the crowned head severed by the executioner's axe !

Leonora d'Este.

LEONORA D'ESTE.

Of all the heaven-bestowed privileges of the poet, the highest, the dearest, the most enviable, is the power of immortalizing the object of his love ; of dividing with her his wreath of glory, and repaying the inspiration caught from her eyes with a crown of everlasting fame. It is not enough, that in his imagination he has deïfied her—that he has consecrated his faculties to her honor—that he has burned his heart in incense upon the altar of her perfections ; the divinity, thus decked out in richest and loveliest hues, he places on high, and calls upon all ages and all nations to bow down before her, and all ages and all nations obey ! worshiping the beauty thus enshrined in imperishable verse, when others, not less fair, have gone down unsung, " to dust and endless darkness." How many women, who would otherwise have stolen through the shade of domestic life, their charms, virtues, and affections buried with them, have become objects of eternal interest and admiration, because their memory is linked with the brightest monuments of human genius.

Leonora D' Este, a princess of the proudest house in Europe, might have wedded an emperor and have been forgotten. The idea, true or false, that she it was who frenzied the brain and broke the heart of Tasso, has glorified her to future ages—has given her a fame something like that of the Greek of old, who bequeathed his name to posterity by firing the grandest temple in the universe.

No poet, perhaps, ever owed so much to female influence as Tasso, or wrote so much under the intoxicating inspiration of love and beauty. The high tone of sentiment, the tenderness and the delicacy which pervade all his poems, which prevail even in his most voluptuous descriptions, may be traced to the adoration he cherished for Leonora.

When Tasso was first introduced to Leonora, in her brother's court at Ferrara, in 1565, she was in her thirtieth year—still eminently lovely—in that soft, artless, unobtrusive style of beauty, which is charming in itself, and in a princess irresistible, from its contrast with the loftiness of her station and the trappings of her rank. Her complexion was extremely fair; her features small and regular; and the form of her head peculiarly graceful. Her eyes were blue, and her exquisitely beautiful mouth, Tasso styles "a crimson shell"—

> Purpurea conca, in cui si nutre
> Candor di perle elette e pellegrine.

Ill health, and her early acquaintance with the sorrows of her unfortunate mother,* had given to her countenance a languid and pensive cast, and destroyed all the natural bloom of her complexion; but "*Paleur qui marque une ame tendre, a bien son prix :*" so Tasso thought; and this pallor which " vanquishes the rose, and makes the dawn ashamed of her blushes," he has frequently and beautifully celebrated.

When Tasso first visited Ferrara he was just one-and-twenty with all the advantages which a fine countenance, a majestic figure, noble birth, and exceeding talents could bestow. He was already distinguished as the author of the Rinaldo, his

* Renée of France, the daughter of Louis XII. She was closely imprisoned during twelve years, on suspicion of favoring the early reformers.

earliest poem, in which he had celebrated (as if prophetically)
the Princess D'Este—and chiefly Leonora. Tasso, from his
boyish years, had been a sworn servant of beauty. Refined,
even to fastidiousness, in his intercourse with women, he had
formed, in his own poetical mind, the most exalted idea of
what a female ought to be, and, unfortunately, she who first
realized all his dreams of perfection was a princess—" there
seated where he durst not soar."

Although Leonora was his senior by several years, disparity
of age is certainly no argument against the passion she inspired
For a young man, at his first entrance into life, to fall in love
ambitiously—with a woman, for instance, who is older than
himself, or with one who is, or ought to be, unattainable—is a
common occurrence. Leonora was not unworthy of her illustrious conquest. She was of studious and retired habits—seldom joining in the amusements of her brother's Court, then the
gayest and most magnificent in Italy. Her mother, Reneé of
France, had early instilled into her mind a love of literature,
and especially of poetry. She was passionately fond of music,
and sang admirably; and, to a sweet-toned voice, added a gift,
which, unless thus accompanied, loses half its value and almost
all its charm. She spoke well; and her eloquence was so per-
suasive, that we are told she had power to move her brother
Alphonso, when none else could. Tasso says most poetically,

> " E l' aura del parlar cortese e saggio,
>   Fra le rose spirar, s'udia sovente;"

—meaning—for to translate literally is scarcely possible—that
"eloquence played round her lips like the zephyr breathing
over roses."

With what emotions must a young and ardent poet have

listened to his own praises from a beautiful mouth, thus sweetly gifted! He says, "My heart was touched through my ears; her gentle wisdom penetrated deeper than hei beauty could reach."

To be summoned daily into the presence of a princess thus beautiful and amiable—to read aloud his verses to her, to hear his own praises from her lips, to bask in her approving smiles, to associate with her in her retirement, to behold her in all the graceful simplicity of her familiar life—was a dangerous situation for Tasso, and surely not less so for Leonora herself. That she was aware of his admiration and perfectly understood his sentiments, and that a mysterious intelligence existed between them, consistent with the utmost reverence on his part, and the most perfect delicacy and dignity on hers, is apparent from the meaning and tendency of innumerable passages scattered through his minor poems—too significant to be mistaken. Without multiplying quotations which would extend this sketch from pages into volumes, it is sufficient that we may trace through Tasso's verses the little incidents which varied this romantic intercourse. The frequent indisposition of Leonora, and her absence when she went to visit her brother, the Cardinal d'Este, at Tivoli, form the subjects of several beautiful little poems. He relates, in a beautiful little madrigal, that, standing alone with her in a balcony, he chanced, perhaps in the eagerness of conversation, to extend his arm on hers. He asks pardon for the freedom, and she replies with sweetness, "You offended not by placing your arm there, but by withdrawing it." This little speech in a coquette would have been *sans consequence*. From such a woman as Leonora it spoke volumes, and her lover felt it so. But Leonora knew, as well as her lover, that a princess "was no love-mate for a bard." She knew far better than her lover, until *he* too had been taught by wretched experience, the haughty and implacable temper of her bi >ther Alphonso, who never was known to brook an injury or forgive an offender. She must have remembered the twelve years' imprisonment, and the narrow escape from death, of her unfortunate mother, for a less cause. She was of a timid and reserved nature, increased by the extreme delicacy of her constitution. Her hand had frequently been sought by princes and nobles, whom she had uniformly rejected at the risk of displeasing her brother, and the eyes of a jealous court were upon her. Tasso, on the other hand, was imprudent, hot-headed, fearless, ardently attached. For both their sakes, it was necessary for Leonora to be guarded and reserved, unless she would have made herself the fable of all Italy. And in what glowing verse has Tasso described all the delicious pain of such a situation! now proud of his fetters—now execrating them in despair.

Then came a cloud, but whether of temper or jealousy, we know not; and Tasso, withdrawing himself from the object of devotion, accompanied Lucrezia d'Este, then Duchess of Urbino, to her villa of Castel Durante, where he remained for some time, partaking in all the amusements of her gay court, without once seeing Leonora. He then wrote to her, and the letter, fortunately, has been preserved entire. Though guarded in expression, it is throughout in the tone of a lover piqued, and yet conscious that he has himself offended; and seeking, with a sort of proud humility, the reconciliation on which his happiness depends.

In the meanwhile, there was a report that Leonora was about to be united to a foreign prince. Her hand had been demanded of her brother with the usual formalities, and the anguish and jealous pain which her lover suffered at this period, is finely expressed in the Canzone,

> " Amor tu vedi, e non hai duolo o sdegno," &o.

and in the sonnet,

> " Io sparso, ed altri miete !" &c.

This dreaded marriage never took place ; and Tasso, relieved from his fears and restored to the confidence of Leonora, was again comparatively blessed.

* * * * * * * *

About two years after the completion of the " Jerusalem Delivered," while all Europe rung with the poet's fame, Tasso fled from the court of Ferrara in a fit of distraction. His frenzy was caused partly by religious horrors and scruples ; partly by the petty but accumulated injuries which malignity and tyranny had heaped upon him ; partly by a long-indulged and hopeless passion. He fled, to hide himself and his sorrows in the arms of his sister Cornelia. The brother and sister had not met since their childish years ; and Tasso, wild with misery, forlorn and penniless, knew not what reception he was to meet with. When arrived within a league of his birth-place, Sorrento, near Naples, he changed clothes with a shepherd, and in this disguise appeared before his sister, as one sent with tidings of her brother's misfortunes. The recital, we may believe, was not coldly given. Cornelia was so violently agitated by the eloquence of the feigned messenger, that she fainted away, and Tasso was obliged to hasten the denouement by discovering himself. In the same moment he was clasped in her affectionate arms, and bathed with her tears.

And how was it with her, whose life was a weary, a per

petual sacrifice to her exalted position ? Through her the world had opened upon him with a diviner beauty ; she was the source of the high imaginations, the glorious fancies, the heaven-ward aspirations, which raised him above the herd of vulgar men ; yet, while for glory she gave a heart, it was forever denied to her to make her lover happy. While, through love for her he suffered ignominy, and wrong, and madness, was it not hers, in silence and in secret, to mourn over the hopeless bitter-ness of that love, and of her own undying affection ? Was he not her thought, her dream, her supplication ?

Tasso resided for three years with his sister, the object of her unwearied and tender attention. And now, recalled, it is said, by the letters of Leonora, the poet returned to Ferrara. Still, hate pursued him—and he was taken, and imprisoned as a lunatic at St. Anne's. They show travelers the cell in which he was confined. Over the entrance-gallery leading to it, is written up in large letters, " *Ingresso alla Prigione di Tor-quato Tasso,*" as if to blazon, in the eye of the stranger, what is at once the renown and disgrace of that fallen city. The cell itself is small, dark, and low. The abhorred grate is a semicircular window, strongly cross-barred with iron, which looks into a court-yard, so built up that the noon-day sun scarcely reaches it.

A cruel, a most unjust imputation rests on the memory of Leonora. She is accused of cold-heartedness in suffering Tasso to remain so long imprisoned, without interceding in his favor, or even vouchsafing a reply to his affecting supplications for release, and for her mediation in his behalf. It was from this cell that Tasso addressed that affecting Canzone to Leonora, and her sister Lucrezia, which begins, " Figlie di Renata"— " Daughters of Renée !" Thus, in the very commencement,

by this tender and delicate apostrophe, bespeaking their com-
passion, by awakening the remembrance of their mother, like
him so long a wretched prisoner.

Although there exists, we suppose, no *written* proof that Leonora pleaded the cause of Tasso, or sought to mitigate his sufferings; neither is there any proof of the contrary. If then,
we do not find her publicly appearing as his benefactress, and
using her influence over her brother in his behalf, is it not a presumption that she was implicated in his punishment? We know
little, or rather nothing of the private intrigues of Alphonso's
palace; we have no " memories secretès " of that day—no dia-
ries kept by prying courtiers, to enlighten us on what passed in
the recesses of the royal apartments. No woman ever loses all
interest in a lover, even though she have ceased to regard him
as such, unless he has destroyed that interest through unkind-
ness, or brutality towards herself; and Leonora, who appears
on every other occasion so blameless, so tender-hearted, so
beneficent, would have been incapable of selfishness, or cruelty,
or even of indifference, to a lover like Tasso. What comfort
or kindness she could have granted, must, under the circumstances, have been bestowed with infinite precaution; and, from
gratitude and discretion, carefully concealed. We know that
after the first year of his confinement, Tasso was removed to a
less gloomy prison; and we know that Leonora died a few weeks
afterwards; but what share she might have had in procuring
this mitigation of his suffering, we do not know, nor how far
the fate of Tasso might have affected her so as to hasten her
own death.

After the removal of Tasso to this larger cell, he made a collection of his smaller poems lately written, and dedicated them
to the two Princesses. But Leonora was no longer in a state to

be charmed by the verses, or flattered or touched by the admir
ing devotion of her lover—her poet—her faithful servant: she
was dying. A slow and cureless disease preyed on her delicate
frame, and she expired in the second year of Tasso's imprisonment. When the news of her danger was brought to him, he
requested his friend Pignarola to kiss her hand in his name, and
to ask her whether there was anything which, in his sad state,
he could do for her ease or pleasure? We do not know how
this tender message was received or answered; but it was too
late. Leonora died in February, 1581, after lingering from the
November previous.

Thus perished, of a premature decay, the woman who had
been for seventeen years the idol of a poet's imagination—the
worship of a poet's heart; she who was not unworthy of being
enshrined in the rich tracery-work of sweet thoughts and bright
fancies she had herself suggested. The love of Tasso for the
Princess Leonora might have appeared, in his own time, something like the " desire of the moth for the star;" but what is it
now ?—what was it *then* in the eyes of her whom he adored?
How far was it permitted, encouraged, and repaid in secret?
This we cannot know; and perhaps had we lived in the time—
in the very Court, and looked daily into her own soft eyes, practiced to conceal—we had been no wiser

When Leonora died, all the poets of Ferrara pressed forward
with the usual tribute of elegy and eulogium; but the voice of
Tasso was not heard among the rest. He alone flung no garland
on the bier of her whose living brow he had wreathed with the
brightest flowers of song. This is adduced by Serassi as a proof
that he had never loved her. Ginguiné himself can only account
for it, by the presumption that he was piqued by that coldness
and neglect, which, we have seen, was merely suppositious.

Strange reasoning! as if Tasso, while his heart bled over his loss, in his solitary cell, could have deigned to join this crowd of courtly mourners!—as if, under such circumstances, in such a moment, the greatness of his grief could have burst forth in any terms that must not have exposed him to fresh rigors, and the fame, at least the discretion of her he had loved, to suspicion No: nothing remained to him but silence—and he was silent.

Catherine Alexiewna.

15

CATHERINE ALEXIEWNA

EMPRESS OF RUSSIA

On the morning of the 20th of August, 1702, the Russian can
non began to batter in breach of the old ramparts of Marienburg.
Shermetoff commanded the besieging army.   He had been sent
by Peter the Great to avenge the humiliations inflicted upon the
Russians, during the preceding year, at Narva, and in Poland ;
and about a month before the period at which this narrative
commences, he had defeated the Swedish army under the command of Slippenbach.   Marienburg surrendered at discretion
in a few hours, and the Russians, exasperated at the store-houses
and magazines having been set on fire, put the Swedish garrison
to the sword, and made the inhabitants prisoners—a lot much
worse in those days than death ; for it was a condition of
slavery.   Among the captives, all of whom were casting a lingering look at the homes from which they were now driven, was a
Lutheran minister, attended by three young girls.   One of
these was strikingly handsome.   She had just been discovered
by the Russian soldiers concealed in an oven, in which her fright
had led her to seek refuge.   The family was brought before
General Bauër, Sheremetoff's lieutenant, who was surprised at
the beauty of the eldest girl.

" Thy name ?" said he; in a harsh voice to the minister.

" Gluck."

" Thy religion ?"

" Lutheran."

" Why did thy daughter hide herself ? Thinkest thou that
we refuse our protection to the weak and innocent ?"

" The young girl of whom you speak," the trembling minis
ter replied, " is not a member of my family. I love her as my
child ; but she is a stranger to my blood."

" Oh ! oh !" muttered the general, with an expressive look.
" Who is she then ?"

" The daughter of poor peasants, who dwelt in the neighborhood of Derpt, in Livonia. I took charge of her when her
mother died, and have taught her the little I know. Her name
is Martha Alfendey."

" 'Tis well ! You may retire. As for you," said the general, addressing the young girl, " remain here."

Instead of obeying this command, she clung to the arm of her
protector.

" General," said the minister, " Martha was married this
morning ; the ceremony had just been performed when the firing
began."

Bauër laughed, and repeated his order. Resistance was impossible. The pastor withdrew, and the poor girl remained
with her future master ; for she was now a slave, and the slave
too of a man who in a few years was to become her subject.

This young female, as the reader may have already anticipated,
was Catherine—a name she afterwards assumed, together with
that of Alexiewna, when she embraced the tenets of the Greek
Church. In the present narrative, I shall give her no other.

Catherine was eminently beautiful ; and there was an extreme
fascination in her look and smile. After a short period of service, Bauër thought he might advance his own interests by
making a present of his fair slave to Sheremetoff. He accordingly
dressed her after the Russian fashion, and presented her to the

marshal, with whom she remained some time. But Menzicoff, then all powerful with the Czar, having seen her by chance, offered to purchase her ; and Sheremetoff, whether from indifference, or because he was desirous of making a merit of his compliance, sent her as a free offering to the prince. Thus, in less than two years, Catherine became the property of three different masters.

Menzicoff, one day, had to entertain the Czar. Peter loved to give such marks of his royal favor ; that cost him nothing, and, in a country like Russia, were highly prized. Seated at a table loaded with a profusion of gold plate, sparkling crystal, and the finest linen of Holland and Saxony, trimmed with Brussels lace, the Czar was in that joyous mood to which he sometimes yielded when the thorns of his diadem tore his brow or the weight of his sceptre tired his arm. He wore on that day a coat of very coarse cloth, cut after his own fashion ; for he affected a simplicity of attire very much out of keeping with the oriental magnificence he was fond of displaying. His mirth was always boisterous ; and in the midst of a loud peal of laughter he suddenly stopped, replaced upon the table the chased goblet he held in his hand, and followed with his eyes a young, beautiful and elegantly-dressed female, who had just poured wine into his cup, smiling with respectful modesty as she performed the office. Peter thought he never beheld so fascinating a creature.

" Who is that woman ?" said he to the favorite.

" My slave, dread lord," replied the trembling prince.

" Thy slave !" cried Peter, in a voice of thunder ; then in a mild tone, almost in a whisper, he added, " I will purchase thy slave. What is her price ?"

" I shall consider myself most fortunate," Menzicoff replied " if your majesty will vouchsafe to accept her."

The same day, Catherine was taken to a house in a remote part of Moscow. Menzicoff was in hopes that the Czar would take but little notice of his new acquisition, and that his slave would ultimately be sent back to him; but the fair captive had caught a glimpse of her future greatness, and soon brought into play that energy of genius which ultimately placed the imperial crown upon her head. The powers of her mind and her extraordinary talents became known throughout Russia, long before she appeared as the savior, not only of the empire, but of the honor of Peter's throne. At first the Czar visited her only occasionally; soon, however, not a day passed without his seeing her; and ultimately he took his ministers to her house, and transacted all the business of the state in her presence, frequently consulting her and taking her advice upon the most knotty difficulties. Her cheerfulness, her mildness of temper, and especially her energy of mind, so congenial with his own, filled up the void left in his heart by former disappointments. His first wife, Eudocia Lapoukin, had proved faithless, and he had repudiated her. He afterwards wished to wed the beautiful Anne Moëns, who refused the proffered honor, because she still considered him the husband of another. In his intercourse with Catherine, he therefore yielded to a deep and overwhelming passion, which seemed likely to compensate for former sufferings. It was not long before he contracted a secret marriage with his lovely slave, and in the enjoyment of her affection his heart recovered its tone, and he was happy.

In this almost unknown retreat, Catherine bore him two daughters—Anna, born in 1708, and Elizabeth, born in 1709. From this time the power of the fair captive of Marienburg was acknowledged throughout the empire, and she found herself strong enough to show Russia that she was indeed its sovereign.

She was aware that the Czarowitz Alexis, Peter's son by Eudocia, hated her; yet she never attempted to widen the breach between him and the Czar. She also knew that Eudocia was intriguing against her, but she never thought of revenge; for she had a soul worthy of her high destiny—a soul truly great, and standing out in such prominent relief as to throw many of her errors into the shade.

Her power over the Czar was greatly strengthened by her having become necessary to his existence. From his infancy, Peter had been subject to convulsions, which often endangered his life; this complaint was attributed to the effects of poison administered by an ambitious sister. During these attacks, his sufferings were intense; and before and after they came on, he was seized with mental uneasiness and throbbing of the heart, which threw him into a state of the most gloomy despondency. Catherine found means, by her attentions, to assuage his sufferings; she had also magic words at command to soothe-his mind. Whenever, therefore, he found one of his attacks coming on, he sought the society of the sorceress, whose voice and look charmed away his pain; and he ever found her kind and affectionate, ready to minister to his comfort, and pour balm upon his anguish.

Hitherto Catherine had appeared to Peter only as a fond and fascinating woman; but the time was near at hand when he found that she had a soul of the most dauntless heroism.

The battle of Pultawa had been fought, and Charles XII. defeated, abandoned, and almost unattended, was in rapid flight toward Turkey. The Swedish monarch had left Saxony at the head of forty-five thousand men, and was afterwards joined by the Livonian army under Lewenhaupt, amounting to sixteen thousand more. But the Russians were superior in numbers

The slaughter on this memorable day was dreadful. The Swedes seemed panic-struck ; they lost nine thousand killed, and sixteen thousand prisoners. Lewenhaupt, with fourteen thousand men, laid down his arms to ten thousand Russians.

Peter followed up his victory ; but, like a great and generous monarch, wrote to Charles XII., entreating him not to go to Turkey in search of assistance from the enemies of Christianity, but to trust him, and he would prove a good brother. This letter, it is said, concluding with an offer of peace, was dictated by Catherine. But it was dispatched too late—Charles had already crossed the Dnieper.

The Czar soon seized upon the advantages which this success of his arms placed at his disposal. He concluded a treaty with Prussia, laid siege to Riga, restored the kingdom of Poland to the Elector of Saxony, and ratified the treaty with Denmark. Having at length completed his measure for the further humiliation of Sweden, he returned to Moscow, to make preparations for the triumphal entry of his army into that capital.

The year 1710 was opened with this solemnity. It was truly a noble sight, and calculated to give the Russian people an exalted idea of their strength as a nation. The greatest magnificence was displayed in the ceremony. Seven splendid triumphal arches were erected for the vanquished to pass under ; and as *an act of presence*, and to prove the defeat not only of a rival monarch but of a whole nation, the Swedish artillery and standards, and the litter of the fugitive king, appeared in the procession. The Swedish ministers and troops who had been made prisoners, advanced on foot, followed by the most favored troops of Peter's army, on horseback, the generals each according to his rank, and the Czar in his place as major-general. A deputation from the different bodies of the state was stationed at each triumphal arch, and at the last came a troop of young noblemen, the sons of the principal boyards, clad in Roman dresses, who presented crowns of laurel to the emperor.

At this period war was extending its miseries throughout Europe. Denmark was preparing to invade Sweden; whilst France, Holland, Italy, Portugal, Germany, and England, had drawn the sword to contend for the inheritance of Charles II. of Spain. The whole of the North was in arms against Charles XII. Nothing now remained, but a war with Turkey, to involve every province in Europe in strife and bloodshed; and this soon occurred.

Peter's glory was at its zenith when Achmet III. commenced hostilities against him. Charles flattered himself that the Sultan had decided upon this course to avenge the defeat of the Swedes; but Achmet was actuated solely by his own interest.

The Czar lost no time in taking his measures. Having dispatched Appraxin to Asoph to take the command of the fleet and land forces, he constituted a senate of regency, made an appeal to the loyalty of the young nobles of Russia, and sent forward the four regiments of his guards. When all was ready, he issued a proclamation, calling upon the Russian nation to acknowledge a new Czarian. This was no other than Catherine, the orphan, brought up by the Lutheran minister, and the captive of Marienburg. He now declared his marriage, and designated her as his consort. She set out with the Czar on his expedition against the Turks; and, being constantly near his person, redoubled her soothing attentions on the march, during which Peter had several severe returns of his complaint. He was soon in the presence of Baltagi-Mohammed, having advanced by the frontiers of Poland, and crossed the Dnieper in order to disengage

Sheremetoff. On reaching the river he entreated Catherine not to follow him to the opposite bank.

" Our two destinies form but one life," she replied. " Where you are, there must I be also."

Ever-pleasing, good-humored, and affable, she became the delight and pride of the soldiers. She seldom used her carriage, but was generally on horseback by Peter's side ; and she endured the same privations as the lowest officer in the army. Though frequently overcome with fatigue, her attentions and kindness to the sick officers and men were unremitting. She sent them assistance, paid them visits, and then returned to the Czar, dissipating by her smiles the clouds that gathered on his brow as his danger became greater and more imminent. In this way they reached the banks of the Pruth.

The situation of the Russian army at length became so critical as to call forth all the resources of Peter's skill and energy. His communications with General Renne were cut off, and his provisions exhausted. Prodigious swarms of locusts alighted and destroyed all traces of vegetation ; and water was so scarce that none could be obtained, except by drawing it from the river under a heavy fire from the Turkish artillery.

Peter, in despair at finding himself in a situation even worse perhaps than that to which he had reduced Charles XII. at Pultawa, determined upon a retreat. But Baltagi-Mohammed having come up with him, Peter's regiment of the Preobasinski guards sustained the attack of the whole Turkish army, which lasted for several hours. Night came on, and the Russians, overcome with fatigue, were unable to continue their retreat.

Two Swedish generals were employed in the grand vizier's army—Count Poniatowski, father of him who was afterwards king of Poland, and the Count of Sparre.   The former advised that Peter's supplies should be cut off, and the Russian army be thus compelled to surrender or die of starvation ; the latter urged an immediate attack upon the Czar's discouraged troops, who might easily be cut to pieces.

On the following day, the Russians were surrounded on all sides.   The hostile armies were engaged several hours, during which eight thousand Russians withstood the attack of a hundred and fifty thousand Turks, killing seven thousand of them, and ultimately forcing them back.   The armies then intrenched themselves for the night.   The Russians suffered dreadfully for want of water ; the men who were sent to fetch it, fell dead upon the banks of the river under the grape-shot of the Turkish artillery.   Meantime, Peter was striding with hurried steps within the space which his soldiers had intrenched with all the wagons they could muster.   Discouragement was but too evident upon every brow, and the Czar clearly perceived that the noble army of which he was so proud, and upon which his fortunes now depended, had no other prospect than starvation or slavery.

He returned to his tent in an agony of grief difficult to describe, and gave orders that no one should be allowed to enter.   His reason was all but gone ; for he was at this moment under one of those attacks to which he was subject whenever his mind was greatly excited.   Seated at a table upon which he had laid his sword, he seemed overcome by the weight of his misfortunes.   On a sudden he started—he had heard his name called ; a gentle hand pressed his—Catherine stood by his side.

"I had given orders that nobody should enter," said Peter angrily · "why have you presumed to disobey them ?"

" Such orders cannot surely extend to me," replied Catherine
with mildness. " Can you deprive the woman, who ever since
the opening of the campaign has shared all your dangers, of the
right to talk to you about your army, composed of your subjects,
of which she is one ?"

The words uttered with solemnity, and in that *sotte voce*
which woman alone can assume, made a strong impression upon
the Czar. He threw his arms round Catherine, and placing his
head upon her bosom, moaned piteously.

" Why, Catherine, hast thou come hither to see me die ?—for
to die I am resolved ; I will never submit to be dragged along
in triumph by those unbelievers."

" Thou hast no right to die, Peter," said Catherine, in the
same mild and solemn tone, though her heart throbbed violently—and she had great difficulty to restrain her tears ; " thy
life is not thine own. Wouldst thou, moreover, leave the road
to Moscow open, so that Mahommed may proceed thither and
take thy daughters to grace his master's harem ?"

" Great God !" exclaimed the Czar, starting back.

" Or wouldst thou let him go to Petersburg, thy well-beloved
city, and himself execute that which he requires of thee ?"

" No !" said Peter, seizing his sword ; " he shall not go
thither—I am still alive to prevent it."

" Thou art beside thyself, Peter," Catherine continued ;
" thou knowest not what thou dost. I am but a woman—a
simple ignorant woman ; but I love thee, not only because thou
hast raised me from the lowly state of a peasant and a slave to
the dignity of thy consort, but for thine own glory. I also love
the Russian people, and am resolved to save you both. Hear
me !"

Subjugated by Catherine's manner and the greatness of soul

which beamed from her countenance, the Czar gazed upon her in astonishment. Already calmed by her words of mingled tenderness and energy, he placed her by his side and prepared to listen to her. She immediately began, and with great precision and clearness developed the plan she had formed ever since the critical situation of the army had led her to suppose that every ordinary resource would fail. Peter assented to all she proposed, and Catherine lost not an instant in carrying her project into execution. She collected together the few jewels she had brought with her on an expedition free from all unnecessary splendor of attire, and selected an officer, upon whose talents and presence of mind she could depend, to carry them as a present to the grand-vizier; she likewise added, for the Kiaja, all the ready money she could collect. These preparations being made, she sent for Sheremetoff, and made him write a letter to Baltagi-Mohammed. Norberg, chaplain to Charles XII., has stated, in his history of that monarch, that the letter was written by the Czar himself, and couched in the most abject terms. This is untrue; it was written by Sheremetoff, in his own name, and not only with becoming dignity, but each expression was so measured as to prevent the grand-vizier from forming a suspicion of the extreme state to which the Russian army was reduced. Sheremetoff wrote under the dictation of Catherine, herself unable to write, but whose instinctive genius —the real fountain of science—rendered her as superior in counsel, as she was in energy of mind.

For some hours Mohammed made no reply, and the Turkish artillery continued to scatter its missiles along the banks of the river. As the sun sank towards the horizon, the anxiety in the Russian camp became intense. Catherine, ever active, was almost at the same time soothing and encouraging Peter and scattering her magic words of heroism among the officers and men of his army. She seemed every where at once, and all were animated by her presence. She pointed out to the troops their sovereign, as he passed along, sorrowing at their sorrow, and unhappy at their misfortunes ; she urged them to assuage his grief, by showing him that their courage remained unshaken. Her words were electrical : the ministers and generals soon surrounded Peter, and, in the name of the whole army, demanded to cross the Pruth immediately. Ten of the oldest generals held a council of war, at which Catherine presided, and the following resolution, proposed by her, was signed and presented to the Czar :—

"Should the enemy refuse the conditions proposed by Marshal Sheremetoff, and dare to call upon us to lay down our arms, it is the unanimous opinion of the army, its generals, and the imperial ministers of state, that we should cut our way through them."

In consequence of this resolution, the baggage was surrounded by an intrenchment, and the Russians had already advanced within a hundred yards of the Turkish army, when the grand-vizier published a suspension of arms. Vice-Chancellor Schaffiroff was immediately dispatched to the Turkish camp, negotiations were begun, and the honor of the Russian arms remained without a blemish   A treaty of peace was soon after concluded at Falksen, a village on the banks of the Pruth. A disagreement about a clause of the treaty led to an answer from Peter which may efface many blood-stained lines in his history.

Prince Cantemir, a subject of the Ottoman Porte, was under the protection of Russia, and Mohammed insisted upon his being given up. In reply to Schaffiroff, Peter wrote as follows :—

"I would rather give up to the Turks all the country as far

as Zurzka, because I should have hopes of being able to recover it; but the loss of my faith would be irretrievable. We sovereigns have nothing we can properly call our own, except our honor, and were I to forfeit that, I should cease to be a king.''

Cantemir was therefore not given up.

Just as the treaty was ready for signature, Charles XII. arrived at the Turkish camp, and vented bitter reproaches on Mohammed, who treated him with the most cutting indifference.

" If I had taken the Czar prisoner," said the viceroy of Stamboul, with a smile of bitter irony, " who would there be to govern in his stead ? It is not right that every sovereign should quit his dominions."

Charles, forgetful of the dignity not only of the monarch but of the man, tore the vizier's robe with his spurs, which Mohammed, in his superiority over the royal adventurer, feigned not to perceive. He left it to Providence to inflict its will upon Charles's brilliant and tumultuous life, and to complete that lesson of adversity which had begun at Pultawa, where the Swedish king was vanquished by Menzicoff, originally a pastry-cook's boy, and continued on the banks of the Pruth, where Baltagi-Mohammed, once a slave and a hewer of wood, decided on the fate of three empires.

Subsequently, the revenge of the man of the seraglio was more characteristic. He withdrew the pension which the Porte allowed its royal guest, and gave him orders, couched in the form of advice, to quit the Turkish empire. This led to the well-known affair at Bender.

Charles XII. has accused the grand-vizier of incapacity. This is an error grafted on the prejudice of hatred; for Mahommed was a man of high talents, and to every reflecting mind the sound policy of his conduct on this occasion is evident. All the

writers of the Swedish party accuse him of having received a
bribe to betray his trust.   This is equally absurd.   The jewels
sent him by Catherine were a mere compliance with an eastern
custom, which requires that a present should always precede the
demand of an audience, and were not of sufficient value to tempt
him to become a traitor, even were he so disposed.   The charge
is as devoid of foundation as that, in 1805, General Mack
received a large sum for his surrender at Ulm.   A minister of
state or an eminent general has the eyes of the whole world fixed
upon him, and if he descend to such an act of baseness, they are
sure to be discovered.   When, therefore, no positive evidence
is adduced, such imputations ought to be disregarded.   In the
present case, the charge is impossible ; for Peter had no means
of raising a sum adequate to tempt the cupidity of the grand-
vizier.

Peace being concluded, the Czar retired by Jassy, and prepared for the execution of the treaty.   Peter's life was now less
agitated, but his complaint returned so frequently, and with such
aggravated symptoms, that he began to think his life was drawing to a close.   Then it was that the Czarina seemed to him as
a consoling angel.   A secret melancholy preyed upon his mind,
occasioned by the check his ambition had received, and made
dreadful ravages upon his health ; he, therefore, set out for
Carlsbad, accompanied by Catherine, who now never quitted him.
On his return, the marriage took place between the Czarowitz
Alexis and the Princess of Wolfenbuttel.   The nuptial ceremony was performed at Torgau, on the 9th of January, 1712.

Catherine has been accused of exciting Peter's hatred towards
his son—an odious imputation, which nothing appears to justify.
The Prince Alexis Petrowitz had always been an object of dislike to his father, and this feeling was greatly aggravated by the

prince's own conduct. The time of these scenes has long been past, and we may now dispassionately weigh the conduct of both father and son. But it is cruelly unjust to impute these dissensions to the Czarina, without a single fact to substantiate the charge. Catherine was not at Torgau when the prince's marriage took place, but at Thorn, in Polish Prussia. An excuse had been made to prevent her from being present at the ceremony, but it was in no wise connected with her feelings as a step-mother. Though Czarina of Russia, she had, nevertheless, at that period not been formally acknowledged, and had only the title of Highness which rendered her rank too equivocal for her name to appear in the marriage contract, or for the rigidity of German etiquette to assign her a place in the ceremony suitable to the wife of the Czar. On the conclusion of the marriage Peter sent the young couple to Wolfenbuttel, and proceeded to Thorn to fetch Catherine, whom he conducted to Petersburg with the dispatch and simplicity that always characterized his mode of traveling.

Some weeks after, and without Catherine having manifested the slightest wish on the subject, Peter again formally declared his marriage, and on the 19th of February, 1712, she was regularly proclaimed Czarina. Though in consequence of the disasters of the late war, the ceremony on this occasion was less magnificent than it would otherwise have been ; it bore, nevertheless, a character of splendor which no other monarch than Peter could have imparted to it, especially at that period. This was the philosophy displayed by the chief of a great empire, who at the very time he had obtained a princely alliance for the heir to his throne—for that Czarowitz whose birth was the only advantage he possessed—placed as his own consort upon that throne an obscure female, a slave captured during the sacking

16

of a town, but in whom he had found a noble mind and a generous heart. There is in his action a real respect for high genius —there is, moreover, a grateful sense of kind and useful services which does the greatest honor to the human heart.

Catherine again became pregnant, and in 1713 gave birth to another daughter. She had hoped for a son, as Peter made no secret of his wish to have one ; and the disappointment affected her so much that she became seriously ill. At length a fresh pregnancy was announced, on which occasion Peter instituted the order of St. Catherine, and celebrated the event by a triumphal entry.

Of all the sights which Peter could give his subjects, this was the most pleasing to them. On the present occasion, the officers of the Swedish navy, whom the Czar had made prisoners, with Rear-admiral Erenschild at their head, were made to pass under a triumphal arch which Peter had himself designed, and do homage to a half-savage, named Romodanowski, upon whom the Czar, in one of his jovial fits, had had conferred the mock-title of Czar of Moscow, treating him in public as if he were really master of that city, and ordering almost all his decrees to be followed. This man, the most rude and brutal of Russians, was Peter's court-fool, kept in imitation of the practice in the middle ages. Romodanowski had always a frightful bear by his side, which he had made his favorite, as he was himself the favorite of his imperial master.

The Czarina was at length delivered of a son. But the Czar's pleasure at this event was embittered by the Czarowitz Alexis having also a son ; and this rekindled in his bosom those stormy passions often so dreadful, even to the objects of his fondest affection.

Catherine's confinement interrupted for a time her excursions with the Czar through his dominions, sometimes upon the lakes, and sometimes at sea, even during violent storms ; but they were resumed on her recovery. Peter had visited every part of Europe, like a man anxious to acquire knowledge, and to study the manners of different nations. He now resolved to make a second tour, and study the manners of courts. Catherine accompanied him to Copenhagen, Prussia, and several of the German principalities. At length Peter saw Amsterdam once more, and visited the cottage at Sardam, in which he had long resided as a simple shipwright. He, however, reached the Dutch capital alone, the Czarina having remained at Schwerin, unwell, and far advanced in pregnancy. Some hours after he had left her, she was informed that, during his residence at Sardam, he had passionately loved a young girl of that place. In alarm at this information, she immediately left Schwerin to follow him, notwithstanding the intense cold—it being then the month of January. On reaching Vesel, the pains of labor came on unexpectedly, and she was delivered of a male child, which died soon after. In less than twenty-four hours after, she resumed her journey, and on the tenth day arrived at Amsterdam. Peter at first received her with anger ; but moved by this proof of her affection, in which she had risked her life to follow him, he soon forgave her. They visited together the cottage at Sardam, which had been converted into an elegant and commodious little dwelling ; thence they proceeded to the house of a rich shipbuilder named Kalf, where they dined. Kalf was the first foreigner who had traded with Petersburg, and had thereby won the Czar's gratitude. Catherine took great notice of this family, because she knew that Peter was pleased at the attentions she bestowed upon foreigners of talent in general, and especially upon Kalf, to whom he considered himself so greatly indebted.

The Czar remained three months in Holland, where he was detained by matters of great 'moment. The European conspiracy of Goëtz and Alberoni, in favor of the Stuarts, had already extended its ramifications far and wide, and Peter deemed it necessary to go to Paris in order to see more clearly into the plot. But a too rigorous etiquette would have been required for the Czarina, at the French court; and, being apprehensive of the trifling and sarcastic wit of the French courtiers, he was unwilling to expose his consort to that which the Livonian peasant and the slave of Menzicoff might have been forced to endure. Catherine, therefore, remained in Holland during his absence. On his return, he listened very attentively to her remarks on the plan of Goëtz and Alberoni, and it was by her advice that he kept in such perfect measure with all the conspirators, leaving them to place their batteries, and reserving to himself the power of either using or rendering them nugatory, as it might suit his purpose

Catherine, at this period, was only thirty-three years of age, and as beautiful as on the day when Peter first beheld her. The strong feeling then inspired by the young and artless girl, had ripened into a sentiment of deep affection identic with his existence ; it had become a passion which, in a man like Peter the Great, was necessarily exclusive and suspicious. In him, jealousy was like a raging fiend—its effects were appalling. But I must not anticipate. He continued to travel with Catherine by his side, happy at seeing her share his fatigues, not only without repining, but with the same smile upon her lips, the same sparkle in her eye. Yet the life they both led was as simple and as full of privations as that of Charles XII. or the King of Prussia. The train of a German bishop was more magnificent than that of the sovereigns of Russia. During this journey to Holland, Catherine, to avoid a short separation from the Czar, made an excursion with him which lasted ten days, during which she had not a single female attendant. It was by such attentions that she secured her power over Peter's heart.

The Czar had originally intended to prolong his journey, and proceed to Vienna, whither he had been invited by the Emperor of Austria, his son's brother-in-law. But important news from Russia induced him to alter his intention, and return in all haste to Petersburg, where the noble qualities of a great monarch were soon to disappear, and leave in their room nothing but the ferocity of a savage and blood-thirsty Scythian.

His son, he said, was conspiring against him. But the unhappy prince was a mere tool in the hands of the monks, and of the old disaffected boyards who had resisted Peter's measures for the civilization of his country.

Eudocia Theodorowna Lapaukin, Peter's first wife, had been educated in the prejudices and superstitions of her age and country. Unable to comprehend the great designs of the Czar, she had always endeavored to impede them. Her son had been allowed constantly to visit her in her retirement, and had imbibed from her the same feelings against his father's innovations. He considered them sacrilegious and abominable, and was led to suppose that his opinions were shared by the whole nation. Thus was the bitterest animosity excited between the Czar and his son, and attended with those lamentable effects which always ensue when the bonds of nature are burst asunder by hatred. This feeling, when it exists between a parent and his child, ought to have a separate name.

The Czar's marriage with Catherine had completed the disaffection of the prince, who considered himself a victim destined to be sacrificed in order to leave the throne free for the children of this new marriage. Haunted by these feelings, and by a dread of his father's ultimate projects with regard to himself, he sought refuge in debauchery of the lowest and most debasing kind, to which indeed he had always been addicted. His life was now most brutal and degrading. His marriage, far from reclaiming him, had rather increased his evil propensities. His wife died from ill-usage, aggravated by the want of even the common necessaries, four years after their union, leaving him an only son.

It was at this period that Peter began to be alarmed at the future prospects of Russia. If the nation, scarcely emancipated from its savage state, fell under the rule of his son, he foresaw the annihilation of all his plans of improvement, and that his successor would become the slave of those old boyards with long beards, who could not elevate their minds above the rude and barbarous customs of their ancestors. This induced him, before he set out for Germany, to write to the Czarowitz, offering him his choice of a change of conduct or a cloister.

The Czar was in Denmark when he heard that his son had clandestinely left Russia, and he immediately returned to Moscow. Alexis, betrayed by his mistress, was arrested at Naples, and conducted back to Moscow. On appearing before his irritated parent, he trembled for his life, and tendered a voluntary renunciation of his claims to the throne.

It has been urged by some writers that the influence of a step-mother was but too apparent in the bitterness of Peter's feelings toward the Czarowitz. Catherine had a son just born; she had also two daughters, and it was but reasonable that she should entertain fears on their account, if Alexis succeeded to the throne. And was it natural, they ask, that a father should offer his first-born as a sacrifice to fears that might never be realized ?—that he should use the blood of his child as a cement to join the stones of his political edifice ?

But Peter had real grounds of apprehension for the safety of the establishments he had created, and was justified in supposing that the plans he might leave to be executed by his successor, would never be carried into execution. He had spent his life in emancipating his country from the lowest state of moral degradation, and he anticipated the glory to which his empire would rise after his death. He, therefore, discarded the feelings of the father to assume those of the stern legislator; and perhaps he felt less difficulty in doing so from the brutalized condition of his son, whom he had never beheld with affection.

On the 14th of February, 1718, the great bell of Moscow vibrated its hollow death-knell through the city. The privy councillors and boyards were assembled in the Kremlin; the archimandrites, the bishops, and the monks of St. Basil, in the cathedral. A vast multitude circulated, in silent consternation, through the city, and it went from mouth to mouth that the Czarowitz was about to be condemned on the accusation of his father.

Alexis still clung to life, and, in the hope that he might yet be allowed to live, tendered a second renunciation of his claims to the throne, expressly in favor of Catherine's children. When he had signed it, he thought himself safe. How little did he know his stern father! He was conducted to the cathedral, there again to hear the act of his exheredation read; and when he had drained the cup of anguish prepared for him, it was filled again and again. But the debased heart of the wretched man would not break; he was unable to feel the full weight of infamy heaped upon him.

On his return, sentence of death was passed upon him, and

he fell into dreadful convulsions, which terminated in apoplexy
Before he received the sacrament, he requested to see his father.
Peter went to his bed-side—unmoved at the groans of the son
whom his words had stricken with death. For a time the symptoms became milder, but they soon after returned with greater
violence, and in the evening the prince expired.

Catherine attended the funeral; perhaps she did so in compliance with the Czar's wish; but it has been imputed to her as
a sort of savage triumph over the remains of him who was now
unable ever to come forward and say to her son, " Give me back
my crown."

Those anxious to divest her of all blame in this tragical event,
pretend that she had entreated the Czar to shut up the prince
in a monastery. But this defence is more injurious than useful;
as it shows that, at all events, she advised shutting out from the
world him whom God had placed upon the steps of the throne
before her son. On the other hand it is said, that Catherine,
if she interfered at all, should have used her exertions, even to
the braving of Peter's wrath, to prevent the condemnation of
Alexis, for whose life she was more accountable than his own
mother; and that she, whose influence over the Czar was unbounded, who could at all times awaken the kindliest emotions
of his nature, must have succeeded, had she seriously made the
attempt, in obtaining the prince's pardon.

But this is mere hypothetical reasoning. Nobody either
knew, or could know, what passed in private between the Czar
and his consort, and it is but just to give Catherine the benefit
of her conduct throughout her whole previous life, no one act
of which can justify such an imputation.

I have, however, seen a manuscript, in which it is positively
asserted, that Catherine was by no means guiltless of the death

of Alexis; and in support of this statement, it is urged, that hei power over the Czar was so great as to eradicate the hatred he had so long entertained toward Charles XII. Certain it is, that Peter followed her advice in most of his great political measures; and it was much more through her exertions, than those of Messrs. Goëtz and Alberoni, that the famous treaty was concluded to restore the Stuarts to the throne of England. But is this alone sufficient to stamp her memory with so foul a stain?—and was not the case of the Czarowitz one calculated to call forth, with a violence which no influence could repress, all the savage ferocity of Peter's character?

Scarcely was the treaty concluded against the reigning family in England, ere a chance-ball from a culverin killed Charles XII. in Frederickshall. This event was soon succeeded by other disasters—the Spanish fleet was burned; the conspiracy of Cellamarre was discovered in France; Goëtz was beheaded at Stockholm, and Alberoni banished from Italy. And of this formidable league the Czar alone remained—having committed himself with none of the conspirators, and yet being master of the whole. It was Catherine who had communicated with Goëtz in Holland, because, though the Czar wished to avoid speaking to him, he was nevertheless anxious to treat. She it was who managed the whole business, and in truth she displayed wonderful address and diplomatic tact. Soon after the failure of the conspiracy, she again rendered the Czar a service almost as ignal as that on the banks of the Pruth. On the death of Charles XII., tne negotiations with Sweden were again broken off. Though the congress of Aland was not dissolved, the English and Swedish fleets had united, and hostilities were again threatened. The new Queen of Sweden, however, being desirous of peace, had the Czarina privately spoken to; and

Catherine communicated this to Peter, who, acting upon her advice, consented to the holding of a congress at Neustadt, in Finland, where peace was concluded on the 10th of September, 1721. The exertions of Catherine contributed much more to bring about this event, than the united talents of the statesmen composing the congress.

Peter was overjoyed at this peace. He was now able to employ his numerous armies in cutting roads and canals through Russia, and in such other works as formed part of his plans for the improvement of his country. The triumphal entries which I have before mentioned, were nothing in comparison to the rejoicings which took place on this occasion. The prisons were thrown open, and all criminals pardoned, except those guilty of high treason, to whom the Czar could not consistently extend his clemency, after having condemned his son to death for the same crime.

Russia now conferred upon Peter the titles of Father of his Country, Great, and Emperor. The Chancellor Goloffkin, at the head of the senate and synod, and speaking in the name of all the bodies of the state, saluted him by these titles, in the great cathedral. On the same day, the ambassadors of France, Germany, England, Denmark, and Sweden, complimented him by the same titles. He was now acknowledged Emperor throughout Europe ; and strong among the strong, the prosperity of his dominions doubled his power.

"It is my wish," said he one day, to the Archbishop of Novogorod, "to acknowledge by a striking public ceremony all the services which Catherine has rendered me. It is she who has maintained me in the place I now occupy. She is not only my tutelary angel, but that of the Russian empire. She shall be anointed and crowned Empress ; and as you are primate

of Russia, you shall perform the ceremony of her consecra
tion."

The archbishop bowed. He had long been anxious that Peter should revive the patriarchate, and this opportunity seemed to him too good to be lost. He, therefore, observed to the emperor, that such a ceremony would derive additional splendor from being performed by the patriarch of Russia.

"Sir," replied Peter, with a frown, "had I required a patriarch in my dominions, I should long since have appointed Jotoff,* who would make a very good one. Catherine shall be crowned, and well crowned too—but without a patriarch."

The archbishop attempted to reply; but Peter having lifted a stick which he always carried, the prelate was silent.

On the 18th of May, 1724, the ceremony of Catherine's coronation took place in the cathedral at Moscow. The declaration made by the emperor on this occasion, after stating that several Christian princes, and among others Justinian, Leo the philosopher, and St. Heraclius, had crowned their wives in the same manner, contained the following words:—

"And being further desirous of acknowledging the eminent services she has rendered us, especially in our war with Turkey, when our army, reduced to twenty-two thousand men, had to contend with more than two hundred thousand, we crown and proclaim her Empress of Russia."

Peter, always simple in his dress, was pleased to see Catherine follow his example; but no man knew better how to use pomp and pageantry when the occasion required it. At this ceremony, Catherine appeared resplendent with gold and jewels, and her retinue was worthy of a great sovereign. One thing in it was remarkable—the emperor walked before her on foot,

* Jotoff was a half-witted old man, a sort of buffoon

as captain of a company of new body-guards, which he had
formed under the title of Knights of the Empress. When the
procession reached the church, he stationed himself by her side,
and remained there during the whole ceremony. He himself
placed the crown upon her head. She then attempted to em-
brace his knees; but he raised her before her knee had touched
the ground, and embraced her tenderly. On their return, he
ordered that the crown and sceptre should be borne before her.
Catherine had reason to be proud of such a triumph of genius
over the prejudices of society; but she was not long to enjoy
it, for a cruel reverse awaited her, and that reverse was brought
on by her own folly.

Catherine owed everything to the emperor, and the benefits
he had conferred upon her, claimed a strength of gratitude
never to be shaken. But an offence which she received, and
the conviction that the emperor had become indifferent to her,
made her for a moment lose sight of this feeling, and led to the
deplorable events which I have still to relate.

One day, whilst the empress was at her toilet, a vice-admiral,
named Villebois, a Frenchman in the service of Russia, arrived
with a message from the emperor. Villebois was a man of low
origin; he had left his country to avoid the gallows, and the
grossness of his habits was such as qualified him to be one of
Peter's pot-companions. He was completely intoxicated when
he entered the empress's apartment. This Catherine did not
at first perceive; but she made the discovery by receiving from
Villebois one of the grossest insults that can be offered to a
woman. She demanded vengeance of the emperor for this
affront; but Peter laughed at it, and merely condemned the
offender to six months' labor at the galleys.

The seeming indifference which dictated this sentence, cut

her to the soul. She imagined she had lost Peter's affection, for it was the only way in which she could account for his not punishing more severely the man who had offended her. On other occasions he would inflict death for an indiscreet word, and here, he had treated with ridicule a gross outrage offered to his wife—to that Catherine whom he had once so fondly loved. This unfortunate idea having once taken possession of her mind, daily gained strength.

Ever since her coronation, she had an establishment separate from that of the emperor. Her lady of the bed-chamber, Madame de Balk, was that same beautiful Anna Moëns to whom Peter had formerly been attached, and who had refused to become Czarina. She had first married the Prussian minister Kayserlingen, and after his death, Lieutenant-General Balk. Peter had placed her in her present station, and had also appointed her brother, Moëns de la Croix, chamberlain to the empress. Moëns was young, handsome, and highly accomplished. The admiration he at first felt for Catherine soon ripened into a warmer feeling, and, unhappily, he had but too frequent opportunities of seeing her in private. On the other hand, the mind of the empress was ill at ease, and needed consolation. This led to a most imprudent intimacy, which, if not connected with guilt in Catherine, was, to say the least of it, extremely improper.

By the care of Madame de Balk it remained for a long time unperceived. But at length, Jagouchinsky, a contemptible ruffian, then a favorite of Peter's, and one of the companions of his orgies, had a suspicion of it, and determined to watch the empress and her chamberlain. Having at length satisfied himself that his conjectures were not unfounded, he boldly declared to Peter that Catherine was faithless to his bed. On receiving this intimation, the emperor roared like a raging lion. His first idea was to put her and her supposed paramour to death, and then stab the informer to the heart, as being acquainted with his shame. But, on reflection, he resolved to do nothing till he had obtained full evidence of the crime. He, therefore, feigned to quit Petersburg, but only retired to his winter palace, whence he sent a confidential page to the empress that he should be absent two days.

At midnight he entered a secret gallery of Catherine's palace, of which he alone kept the key. Here he passed Madame de Balk unperceived, and entered a room where a page, who either did not know him or pretended not to know him, attempted to stop his progress. Peter knocked him down, and entering the next apartment found the empress in conversation with Moëns. Having approached them, he made an attempt to speak, but the violence of his emotion choked his utterance. Casting at the chamberlain, and at his sister, who had just entered the room, one of those withering glances which speak but too plainly, he turned towards Catherine, and struck her so violently with his cane that the blood gushed from her neck and shoulder. Then rushing out of the room, he ran like a mad-man to the house of Prince Repnin, and burst violently into his bed-room.

The Prince roused from his sleep, and seeing the emperor standing by his bed-side frantic with rage, gave himself up for lost.

" Get up," said Peter, in a hoarse voice, " and fear nothing. Don't tremble, man—thou hast nothing to fear."

Repnin rose and heard the emperor's tale. Meantime Peter was walking up and down the room, breaking everything within his reach.

" At day-break," said he, when he had finished his tale, " I will have this ungrateful wanton beheaded."

" No, sir," replied Repnin with firmness, " you will give no
such orders. You will take this matter into further consideration ; first, because you have been injured, and secondly, because you are the absolute master of your subjects. But why,
sir, should the circumstance be divulged ?—it can answer no
good purpose. You have revenged yourself upon the Strelitz ;
you have considered it your duty to condemn your own son to
death ; and if you now behead the empress, your fame will be
forever tarnished. Let not each phasis of your reign be marked
by blood. Let Moëns die ;—but the empress !—would you at
the very moment you have placed the imperial crown upon her
head, sever that head ? No, sir ! the crown you gave her ought
to be her safeguard."

Peter made no reply—he was fearfully agitated. For a considerable time he kept his eyes sternly fixed upon Repnin, then
left him without uttering another word. Moëns and his sister
were immediately arrested, and imprisoned in a room of the
winter-palace. Their food was taken to them by Peter himself, who allowed no other person to see them.

At length he interrogated Moëns in the presence of General
Uschakoff. Having fixed his eyes upon the chamberlain with a
disdainful look, he told him that he was accused, as was also his
sister, of having received presents, and thereby endangered the
reputation of the empress.

Moëns returned Peter's scowl, and replied :—

" Your victim is before you, sir. State as my confession
anything you please, and I will admit all."

The emperor smiled with convulsive bitterness. Proceedings
were immediately begun against the brother and sister. Moëns
was condemned to be beheaded—Madame de Balk to receive
eleven blows with the knout. This lady had two sons, one a

page, the other a chamberlain ; both were degraded from their rank, and sent to the Persian army to serve as common soldiers.

Catherine threw herself at the emperor's feet to obtain the pardon of Madame de Balk, reminding Peter how dearly he had once loved Anna Moëns. The emperor brutally pushed her back, and in his fury broke with a blow of his fist a large and beautiful Venitian looking-glass.

" There," said he, " it requires only a blow of my hand to reduce this glass to its original dust."

Catherine looked at him with the most profound anguish, and replied, in a melting accent,—

" It is true that you have destroyed one of the greatest ornaments of your palace, but do you think that your palace will be improved by it ?"

This remark rendered the emperor more calm, but he refused to grant the pardon. The only thing Catherine could obtain was, that the number of blows should be reduced to five. These Peter *inflicted with his own hand*.

Moëns died with great firmness. He had in his possession a miniature portrait of the empress set in a small diamond bracelet. It was not perceived when he was arrested, and he had preserved it till the last moment, concealed under his garter, whence he contrived to take it unperceived, and deliver it to the Lutheran minister who attended him and who exhorted him to return it to the empress.

Peter stationed himself at one of the windows of the senate-house, to behold the execution. When all was over, he ascended the scaffold, and seizing the head of Moëns by the hair, lifted it up with the ferocious delight of a savage exulting in successful revenge. Some hours after he entered the apart ment of the empress. He found her pale and care-worn, but her eyes were tearless, though her heart was bursting.

" Come and take a drive," said he, seizing her by the hand and dragging her towards an open carriage. When she had entered it, he drove her himself to the foot of the pole to which the head of her late chamberlain was nailed.

" Such is the end of traitors !" he exclaimed—fixing the most scrutinizing gaze upon Catherine's eyes, expecting to see them full of tears. But the empress was sufficiently mistress of her emotions to appear indifferent to this sight of horror. Peter conducted her back to the palace, and had scarcely left her when she fell fainting upon the floor.

From that time until the emperor's last illness, they never met except in public. It is said that Peter burnt a will he had made, appointing Catherine his successor ; but there is not the slightest proof that such a will ever existed. It is also said that he stated his determination of having her head shaved and confining her in a convent, immediately after the marriage of Elizabeth, her second daughter.

Catherine had a strong party at the Russian court, and was extremely popular throughout the empire. The army was wholly devoted to her ; both officers and men had seen her among them sharing their dangers and privations, and she was their idol. A measure of such extreme harshness would, perhaps, have endangered Peter's own power, and exposed him to great personal danger. Menzicoff, an able and clear-sighted statesman, in whom the empress had great confidence, was at the head of her party, and ready to support her in any measures she might take for her personal safety. But the violent agitation to which Peter had been lately a prey, and the shock he had received from supposing Catherine faithless to his bed, brought on one of those attacks which had often before placed his life in jeopardy. This time, the symptoms appeared so aggravated, that the physicians lost all hope. The convulsions succeeded each other with frightful rapidity, and the life of Peter the Great was soon beyond the power of human art. On receiving intimation of his illness, Catherine immediately hastened to his bed-side, which she no longer quitted. She sat up with him three successive nights, without taking any rest during the day, and on the 28th of January, 1725, he expired in her arms.

Peter had been unable to speak from the moment his complaint took a fatal turn. He, however, made several attempts to write, but unsuccessfully; and the following words alone could be made out :—

" Let everything be delivered to ——"

Meanwhile, Menzicoff had taken his measures to secure the throne for Catherine, whose son had died in 1719. He seized upon the treasury and the citadel, and the moment Peter's death was announced, he proclaimed the Empress under the name of Catherine I. He encountered but little opposition, and the great majority of the nation hailed her accession to the throne as a blessing.

The beginning of her reign was glorious, for she religiously followed the intentions of Peter. He had instituted the Order of St. Alexander Newski, and she conferred it; he had also formed the project of founding an academy, and she founded it. She suppressed the rebellion of the Cossacks, and there is no doubt that, if she had lived, her reign would have been remarkable. But a short time after her accession to the throne, she fell into a state of languor, arising from a serious derangement of her health. The complaint was aggravated by an immoderate use of Tokay wine, in which her physicians could not prevent her from indulging ; and she died on the 27th of May, 1727, aged thirty-eight years.

Catherine was one of the most extraordinary women the world has produced. She would have distinguished herself in any station. Her soul was great and noble ; her intellect quick and capacious. Her total want of education only serves to throw a stronger light upon her strength of mind and powerful genius. Doubtless there are some passages in her life, which might, with advantage, be expunged from her history ; but much has been imputed to her, of which she was guiltless. She has been taxed with hastening Peter's death, by giving him poison. This Voltaire has triumphantly refuted. The imputation was raised by a party who had espoused the interests of the Czarowitz, and were hostile to the improvements introduced by Peter More than a century had elapsed since these events took place, and the hatred and prejudices which attended them have gradually melted away. Any but a dispassionate examination of this heinous charge is now impossible, and it must lead to a complete acquittal of Catherine.

Maria Theresa.

MARIA THERESA,

Maria Theresa, of Austria—born on the 13th of May 1717—was the daughter of Charles the Sixth, Emperor of Germany, and Elizabeth Christina, of Brunswick, a lovely and amiable woman, who possessed and deserved her husband's entire confidence and affection.

Maria Theresa had beauty, spirit, and understanding. To her sister, Marianna, she was tenderly attached. The two arch-duchesses were brought up under the superintendence of their mother, and received an education in no respect different from that of other young ladies of rank of the same age and country. In those accomplishments to which her time was chiefly devoted, Maria Theresa made rapid progress. She inherited from her father a taste for music, which was highly cultivated, and re-mained to the end of her life one of her principal pleasures. She danced and moved with exquisite grace. Metastasio, who taught her Italian, and also presided over her musical studies, speaks of his pupil with delight and admiration, and in his letters he often alludes to her talent, her docility, and the sweet-ness of her manners. Of her progress in graver acquirements we do not hear. Much of her time was given to the strict ob-servance of the forms of the Roman Catholic faith ; and though she could not derive from the bigoted old women and ecclesias-tics around her any very enlarged and enlightened ideas of religion, her piety was at least sincere. She omitted no opportunities of obtaining information relative to the history and geography of her country; and she appears to have been early possessed with a most magnificent idea of the power and grandeur of her family, and of the lofty rank to which she was destined. This early impression of her own vast importance was only counterbalanced by her feelings and habits of devotion, and by the natural sweetness and benignity of her disposition.

Such was Maria Theresa at the age of sixteen or seventeen. She had been destined from her infancy to marry the young Duke of Lorraine, who was brought up in the court of Vienna, as her intended husband. It is very, very seldom that these political state-marriages terminate happily, or harmonize with the wishes and feelings of those principally concerned; but in the present case "the course of true love" was blended with that of policy. Francis Stephen of Lorraine was the son of Leopold, Duke of Lorraine, surnamed the Good and Benevolent. His grandmother, Leonora of Austria, was the eldest sister of Charles VI., and he was consequently the cousin of his intended bride. Francis was not possessed of shining talents, but he had a good understanding and an excellent heart; he was, besides, eminently handsome, indisputably brave, and accomplished in all the courtly exercises that became a prince and a gentleman. In other respects his education had been strangely neglected he could scarcely read or write. From childhood the two cousins had been fondly attached, and their attachment was perhaps increased, at least on the side of Maria Theresa, by those political obstacles which long deferred their union, and even threatened at one time a lasting separation. Towards the end of his reign the affairs of Charles VI., through his imbecility and misgovernment, fell into the most deplorable, the most inextricable confusion. Overwhelmed by his enemies, unaided by his friends and allies, he absolutely entertained the idea of entering into a treaty with Spain, and offering his daughter Maria Theresa, in marriage to Prince Charles, the heir of that monarchy.

But Maria Theresa was not of a temper to submit quietly to an arrangement of which she was to be made the victim ; she remonstrated, she wept, she threw herself for support and assistance into her mother's arms. The empress, who idolized her daughter and regarded the Duke of Lorraine as her son, incessantly pleaded against this sacrifice of her daughter's happiness. The English minister at Vienna* gives the following lively description of the state of affairs at this time, and of the feelings and deportment of the young archduchess :—" She is," says Mr. Robinson, " a princess of the highest spirit ; her father's losses are her own. She reasons already ; she enters into affairs ; she admires his virtues, but condemns his mismanagement ; and is of a temper so formed for rule and ambition, as to look upon him as little more than her administrator. Notwithstanding this lofty humor, she sighs and pines for her Duke of Lorraine. If she sleeps, it is only to dream of him— if she wakes, it is but to talk of him to the lady in waiting ; so that there is no more probability of her forgetting the very individual government and the very individual husband which she thinks herself born to, than of her forgiving the authors of her losing either."

Charles VI., distracted and perplexed by the difficulties of his situation, by the passionate grief of his daughter, by the remonstrances of his wife and the rest of his family, and without spirit, or abilities, or confidence in himself or others, became a pitiable object. During the day, and while transacting business

* Mr. Robinson, afterward the first Lord Grantham of his family.

with his ministers, he maintained his accustomed dignity and
formality ; but in the dead of the night, in the retirement of his
own chamber, and when alone with the empress, he gave way
to such paroxysms of affliction, that not his health only, but his
life was endangered, and his reason began to give way. A
peace with France had become necessary on any terms, and
almost at any sacrifice ; and a secret negotiation was commenced with Cardinal Fleury, then at the head of the French
government, under (or, more properly speaking, *over*) Louis the
Fifteenth. By one of the principal articles of this treaty, the
Duchy of Lorraine was to be given up to France, and annexed
to that kingdom ; and the Duke of Lorraine was to receive, in
lieu of his hereditary possessions, the whole of Tuscany. The
last Grand Duke of Tuscany of the family of the Medici, the
feeble and degenerate Cosmo III., was still alive, but in a state
of absolute dotage, and the claims of his heiress, Anna de'
Medici, were to be set aside. Neither the inhabitants of Lorraine nor the people of Tuscany were consulted in this arbitrary
exchange. A few diplomatic notes between Charles's secretary
Bartenstein and the crafty old cardinal, settled the matter. It
was in vain that the government of Tuscany remonstrated, and
in vain that Francis of Lorraine overwhelmed the Austrian
ministers with reproaches, and resisted, as far as he was able,
this impudent transfer of his own people and dominions to a
foreign power. Bartenstein had the insolence to say to him,
" Monseigneur, point de cession, point d'archiduchesse."

Putting love out of the question, Francis could not determine
to stake his little inheritance against the brilliant succession
which awaited him with Maria Theresa. The alternative, however, threw him into such agony and distress of mind, that even
his health was seriously affected. But peace was necessary to

the interests, and even to the preservation of the empire. Lorraine was given up, and the reversion of the grand-duchy of Tuscany settled upon Francis.* The preliminaries of this treaty being signed in 1735, the emperor was relieved from impending ruin, and his daughter from all her apprehensions of the Prince of Spain; and, no further obstacles intervening, the nuptials of Maria Theresa and Francis of Lorraine were celebrated at Vienna in February, 1736. By the marriage contract the Pragmatic Sanction was again signed and ratified, and the Duke of Lorraine solemnly bound himself never to assert any personal right to the Austrian dominions. The two great families of Hapsburgh and Lorraine, descended from a common ancestor, were by this marriage re-united in the same stock.

Prince Eugene, who had commanded the imperial armies for nearly forty years, died a few days after the marriage of Maria Theresa, at the age of seventy-three. His death was one of the greatest misfortunes that could have occurred at this period, both to the emperor and the nation.

A young princess, beautiful and amiable, the heiress of one of the greatest monarchies in Europe, married at the age of eighteen to the man whom she had long and deeply loved, and who returned her affection, and soon the happy mother of two fair infants, presents to the imagination as pretty a picture of splendor and felicity as ever was exhibited in romance or fairy tale; but when we turn over the pages of history, or look into real life, everywhere we behold the hand of a just Providence equalizing the destiny of mortals.

During the four years which elapsed between Maria Theresa's

---

* Tuscany has ever since remained in the family of Lorraine; the present Grand-duke Leopold II. is the great-grandson of Francis

marriage and her accession to the throne, her life was embittered by anxieties arising out of her political position. Her husband was appointed generalissimo of the imperial armies against the Turks, in a war which both himself and Maria Theresa disapproved. He left her in the first year of their marriage, to take the command of the army, and more than once too rashly exposed his life. Francis had more bravery than military skill. He was baffled and hampered in his designs by the weak jealousy of the emperor and the cabals of the ministers and generals. All the disasters of two unfortunate campaigns were imputed to him, and he returned to Vienna disgusted, irritated, sick at heart, and suffering from illness. The court looked coldly on him; he was unpopular with the nation and with the soldiery; but his wife received him with open arms, and, with a true woman's tenderness, " loved him for the dangers he had passed." She nursed him into health, she consoled him, she took part in all his wrongs and feelings, and was content to share with him the frowns of her father and the popular dislike. They were soon afterward sent into a kind of honorable exile into Tuscany, under pretence of going to take possession of their new dominions, and in their absence it was publicly reported that the emperor intended to give his second daughter to the Elector of Bavaria, to change the order of succession in her favor, and disinherit Maria Theresa. The archduchess and her husband were more annoyed than alarmed by these reports, but their sojourn at Florence was a period of constant and cruel anxiety.

Maria Theresa had no sympathies with her Italian subjects; she had no poetical or patriotic associations to render the " fair white walls of Florence" and its olive and vine-covered hills interesting or dear to her; she disliked the

heat of the climate; she wished herself at Vienna, whence
every post brought some fresh instance of her father's misgovernment, some new tidings of defeat or disgrace. She
mourned over the degradation of her house, and saw her magnificent and far-descended heritage crumbling away from her.
The imbecile emperor, without confidence in his generals, his
ministers, his family, or himself, exclaimed, in an agony, " Is
then the fortune of my empire departed with Eugene ?"
and he lamented hourly the absence of Maria Theresa, in
whose strength of mind he had ever found support when his
pride and jealousy allowed him to seek it. The archduchess
and her husband returned to Vienna in 1739, and soon afterward the disastrous war with the Turks was terminated by a
precipitate and dishonorable treaty, by which Belgrade was
ceded to the Ottoman Porte. The situation of the court of
Vienna at this period is thus described by the English minister,
Robinson :—" Everything in this court is running into the last
confusion and ruin, where there are as visible signs of folly and
madness as ever were inflicted on a people whom Heaven is
determined to destroy, no less by domestic divisions than by the
more public calamities of repeated defeats, defencelessness,
poverty, plague, and famine."

Such was the deplorable state in which Charles bequeathed
to his youthful heiress the dominions which had fallen to him
prosperous, powerful, and victorious, only thirty years before.
The agitation of his mind fevered and disordered his frame,
and one night after eating most voraciously of a favorite
dish,* he was seized with an indigestion, of which he expired
October 20th, 1740. Maria Theresa, who was then near her
confinement, was not allowed to enter her father's chamber.

* Mushrooms stewed in oil.

We are told that the grief she felt on hearing of his dissolu·
tion endangered her life for a few hours, but that the following
day she was sufficiently recovered to give audience to the
ministers.

Maria Theresa was in her twenty-fourth year when she
became in her own right Queen of Hungary and Bohemia,
Archduchess of Austria, Sovereign of the Netherlands, and
Duchess of Milan, of Parma, and Placentia ; in right of her ·
husband she was also Grand-duchess of Tuscany. Naples and
Sicily had indeed been wrested from her father, but she pretended to the right of those crowns, and long entertained the
hope and design of recovering them. She reigned over some
of the finest and fairest provinces of Europe ; over many nations speaking many different languages, governed by different
laws, divided by mutual antipathies, and held together by no
common link except that of acknowledging the same sovereign.
That sovereign was now a young inexperienced woman, who
had solemnly sworn to preserve inviolate and indivisible the vast
and heterogeneous empire transmitted to her feeble hand, as if
it had depended on her will to do so. Within the first few
months of her reign the Pragmatic Sanction, so frequently
guarantied was trampled under foot. France deferred, and at
length declined to acknowledge her title. The Elector of Bavaria, supported by France, laid claim to Austria, Hungary,
and Bohemia. The King of Spain also laid claim to the Austrian succession, and prepared to seize on the Italian states ;
the king of Sardinia claimed Milan ; the King of Prussia, not
satisfied with merely advancing pretensions, pounced like a
falcon on his prey,—

Spiegato il crudo sanguinoso artiglio,—

and seized upon the whole duchy of Silesia, which he laid waste and occupied with his armies.*

Like the hind of the forest when the hunters are abroad, who hears on every side the fierce baying of the hounds, and stands and gazes round with dilated eye and head erect, not knowing on which side the fury of the chase is to burst upon her—so stood the lovely majesty of Austria, defenceless, and trembling for her very existence, but not weak, nor irresolute, nor despairing.

Maria Theresa was by no means an extraordinary woman. In talents and strength of character she was inferior to Catherine of Russia and Elizabeth of England, but in moral qualities far superior to either; and it may be questioned whether the brilliant genius of the former, or the worldly wisdom and sagacity of the latter, could have done more to sustain a sinking throne, than the popular and feminine virtues, the magnanimous spirit, and unbending fortitude of Maria Theresa. She had something of the inflexible pride and hereditary obstinacy of her family; her understanding, naturally good, had been early tinged with bigotry and narrowed by illiberal prejudices; but in her early youth these qualities only showed on the fairer side, and served but to impart something fixed and serious to the vivacity of her disposition and the yielding tenderness of her heart. She had all the self-will and all the sensibility of her sex; she was full of kindly impulses and good intentions; she was not naturally ambitious, though circumstances afterward developed that passion in a strong degree; she could be roused to temper,

* The French government had secretly matured a plan of partition, by which the inheritance of Maria Theresa was to have been divided among the different claimants in the following manner :—Bohemia and Upper Austria were assigned to the Elector of Bavaria; Moravia and Upper Silesia to the Elector of Saxony; Lower Silesia to the King of Prussia; and Lombardy to the King of Spain.

but this was seldom, ánd never so far as to forget the dignity and propriety of her sex. It should be mentioned, (for in the situation in which she was placed is was by no means an unimportant advantage,) that at this period of her life few women could have excelled Maria Theresa in personal attractions. Her figure was tall, and formed with perfect elegance ; her deportment at once graceful and majestic ; her features were regular ; her eyes were gray, and full of lustre and expression ; she had the full Austrian lips, but her mouth and smile were beautiful ; her complexion was transparent ; she had a profusion of fine hair ; and, to complete her charms, the tone of her voice was peculiarly soft and sweet. Her strict religious principles, or her early and excessive love for her husband, or the pride of her royal station, or perhaps all these combined, had preserved her character from coquetry. She was not unconscious of her powers of captivation, but she used them, not as a woman, but as a queen—not to win lovers, but to gain over refractory subjects. The " fascinating manner" which the historian records, and for which she was so much admired, became later in life rather too courtly and too artificial ; but at four-and-twenty it was the result of kind feeling, natural grace, and youthful gayety.

The perils which surrounded Maria Theresa at her accession were such as would have appalled the strongest mind. She was not only encompassed by enemies without, but threatened with commotions within. She was without an army, without a treasury, and, in point of fact, without a ministry—for never was such a set of imbecile men collected together to direct the government of a kindom, as those who ccmposed the *conference* or state-council of Vienna, during this period. They agreed but in one thing—in jealousy of the duke of Lorraine, whom they considered as a foreigner, and who was content perforce to remain a mere cipher.

Maria Theresa began her reign by committing a mistake, very excusable at her age. Her father's confidential minister, Bartenstein, continued to direct the Government, though he had neither talents nor resources to meet the fearful exigencies in which they were placed. The young queen had sufficient sense to penetrate the characters of Sinzendorf and Staremberg; she had been disgusted by their attempts to take advantage of her sex and age, and to assume the whole power to themselves. She wished for instruction, but she was of a temper to resist any thing like dictation. Bartenstein discovered her foible; and by his affected submission to her judgment, and admiration of her abilities, he conciliated her good opinion. His knowledge of the forms of business, which extricated her out of many little embarrassments, she mistook for political sagacity—his presumption for genius; his volubility, his readiness with his pen, all conspired to dazzle the understanding and win the confidence of an inexperienced woman. It is generally allowed that he was a weak and superficial man; but he possessed two good qualities —he was sincerely attached to the interests of the house of Austria, and, as a minister, incorruptible.

In her husband Maria Theresa found ever a faithful friend, and comfort and sympathy, when she most needed them; but hardly advice, support, or aid. Francis was the soul of honor and affection, but he was illiterate, fond of pleasure, and unused to business. Much as his wife loved him, she either loved power more, or was conscious of his inability to yield it. Had he been an artful or ambitious man, Francis might easily have obtained over the mind of Maria Theresa that unbounded influence which a man of sense can always exercise over an affectionate woman;
18

but, humbled by her superiority of rank, and awed by her superiority of mind, he never made the slightest attempt to guide or control her, and was satisfied to hold all he possessed from her love or from her power.

The first war in which Maria Theresa was engaged was began in self-defence—never was the sword drawn in a fairer quarrel or a juster cause. Her great adversary was Frederick II. of Prussia, aided by France 'and Bavaria. On the side of tho young queen were England and Holland. Nothing could exceed the enthusiasm which her helpless situation had excited among the English of all ranks: The queen of Hungary was a favorite toast—her head a favorite sign. The parliament voted large subsidies to support her, and the ladies of England, with the old Duchess of Marlborough at their head, subscribed a sum of £100,000, which they offered to her acceptance. Maria Theresa, who had been so munificently aided by the king and parliament, either did not think it consistent with her dignity to accept of private gifts, or from some other reason, declined the proffered contribution.

The war of the Austrian succession lasted nearly eight years. The battles and the sieges, the victories and defeats, the treaties made and broken, the strange events and vicissitudes which marked its course, may be found duly chronicled and minutely detailed in histories of France, England, or Germany. It is more to our present purpose to trace the influence which the character of Maria Theresa exercised over passing events, and their reaction on the fate, feelings, and character of the woman.

Her situation in the commencement of the war appeared desperate. Frederick occupied Silesia, and in the first great battle in which the Austrians and Prussians were engaged, (the battle of Molw'tz), the former were entirely defeated Still the queen refused to yield up Silesia, at which price she might have purchased the friendship of her dangerous enemy. Indignant at his unprovoked and treacherous aggression, she disdainfully refused to negotiate while he had a regiment in Silesia, and re-jected all attempts to mediate between them. The birth of her first son, the archduke Joseph, in the midst of these distresses, confirmed her resolution. Maternal tenderness now united with her family pride and her royal spirit; and to alienate voluntarily any part of his inheritance appeared not only humiliation, but a crime. She addressed herself to all the powers which had guarantied the Pragmatic Sanction, and were therefore bound to support her. And first to France : To use her own words—"I wrote," said she, "to Cardinal Fleury; pressed by hard necessity, I descended from my royal dignity, and wrote to him in terms which would have softened stones !" But the old car-dinal was absolute *flint*. From age and long habit, he had become a kind of political machine, actuated by no other princi-ple than the interests of his government; he deceived the queen with delusive promises and diplomatic delays till all was ready; then the French armies poured across the Rhine, and joined the Elector of Bavaria. They advanced in concert within a few leagues of Vienna. The elector was declared Duke of Austria; and, having overrun Bohemia, he invested the city of Prague.

The young queen, still weak from her recent confinement, and threatened in her capital, looked round her in vain for aid and counsel. Her allies had not yet sent her the promised assistance ; her most sanguine friends drooped in despair; her ministers looked upon each other in blank dismay. At this crisis the spirit of a feeling and high-minded woman saved her-self, her capital, and her kingdom. Maria Theresa took alone

the resolution of throwing herself into the arms of her Hungarian subjects.

Who has not read of the scene which ensued, which has so
often been related, so often described ? and yet we all feel that
we cannot hear of it too often. When we first meet it on the
page of history, we are taken by surprise, as though it had no
business there ; it has the glory and the freshness of old romance.   Poetry never invented anything half so striking, or
that so completely fills the imagination.

The Hungarians had been oppressed, enslaved, insulted, by
Maria Theresa's predecessors. In the beginning of her reign,
she had abandoned the usurpations of her ancestors, and had
voluntarily taken the oath to preserve all their privileges entire.
This was partly from policy, but it was also partly from her own
just and kind nature. The hearts of the Hungarians were
already half-won when she arrived at Presburg, in June, 1741.
She was crowned Queen of Hungary on the 13th, with the peculiar national ceremonies. The iron crown of St. Stephen was
placed on her head, the tattered but sacred robe thrown over
her own rich habit, which was incrusted with gems, his scimitar
girded to her side. Thus attired, and mounted upon a superb
charger, she rode up the Royal Mount,* and according to the
antique custom, drew her sabre, and defied the four quarters of
the world, " in a manner that showed she had no occasion for
that weapon to conquer all who saw her."†   The crown of St.
Stephen, which had never before been placed on so small or so
lovely a head, had been lined with cushions to make it fit. It
was also very heavy, and its weight, added to the heat of the
weather, incommoded her ; when she sat down to dinner in the

* A rising ground near Presburg, so called from being consecrated to this ceremony.   † Mr. Robinson's Dispatches.

great hall of the castle, she expressed a wish to lay it aside. On lifting the diadem from her brow, her hair, loosened from confinement, fell down in luxuriant ringlets over her neck and shoulders; the glow which the heat and emotion had diffused over her complexion added to her natural beauty, and the assembled nobles, struck with admiration, could scarce forbear from shouting their applause.

The effect which her youthful grace and loveliness produced on this occasion had not yet subsided when she called together the Diet, or Senate of Hungary, in order to lay before them the situation of her affairs. She entered the hall of the castle, habited in the Hungarian costume, but still in deep mourning for her father; she traversed the apartment with a slow and majestic step, and ascended the throne, where she stood for a few minutes silent. The chancellor of the state first explained the situation to which she was reduced, and then the queen, coming forward, addressed the assembly in Latin, a language which she spoke fluently, and which is still in common use among the Hungarians.

"The disastrous state of our affairs," said she, "has moved us to lay before our dear and faithful states of Hungary the recent invasion of Austria, the danger now impending over this kingdom, and propose to them the consideration of a remedy. The very existence of the kingdom of Hungary, of our own person, of our children, of our crown, are now at stake, and, forsaken by all, we place our sole hope in the fidelity, arms, and long-tried valor of the Hungarians!"

She pronounced these simple words in a firm but melancholy tone. Her beauty, her magnanimity, and her distress, roused the Hungarian chiefs to the wildest enthusiasm; they drew their sabres half out of the scabbard, then flung them back to

the hilt with a martial sound, which re-echoed through the lofty
hall, and exclaimed with one accord, "Our swords and our
blood for your majesty—we will die for · our *king*, Maria
Theresa!" Overcome by sudden emotion, she burst into a
flood of tears. At this sight, the nobles became almost frantic
with enthusiasm. "We wept too," said a nobleman, who assisted
on this occasion, (Count Koller); "but they were tears of admiration, pity, and fury." They retired from her presence,
to vote supplies of men and money, which far exceeded all her
expectations.

Two or three days after this extraordinary scene, the deputies
again assembled, to receive the oath of Francis of Lorraine,
who had been appointed co-regent of Hungary. Francis, having
taken the required oath, waved his arm over his head and
exclaimed with enthusiasm, "My blood and life for the queen
and kingdom!" It was on this occasion that Maria Theresa
took up her infant son in her arms and presented him to the
deputies, and again they burst into the acclamation, "We will
die for Maria Theresa and her children!"*

The devoted loyalty of her Hungarian subjects changed the
aspect of her affairs. Tribes of wild warriors from the Turkish
frontiers—Croats, Pandours, and Sclavonians—never before seen
in the wars of civilized Europe, crowded round her standard,
and by their strange appearance and savage mode of warfare
struck terror into the disciplined soldiers of Germany. Vienna
was placed in a state of defence; and Frederick, fallen from his
"pitch of pride," began to show some desire for an accommo-

* September 21st, 1741. The Archduke Joseph was then about six months old.
It was not when Maria Theresa made her speech to the Diet on the 13th, that
she held up her son in her arms; for it appears that he was not brought to
Presburg till the 20th. Voltaire, whose account is generally read and copied,
is true in the main, but more eloquent than accurate.

dation. At length a truce was effected by the mediation of England; and the queen consented, with deep reluctance and an aching heart, to give up a part of Silesia, as a sop to this royal Cerberus. Hard necessity compelled her to this concession; for while she was defending herself against the Prussians on one side, the French and Bavarians were about to overwhelm her on the other. The Elector of Bavaria had seized on Bohemia, and was crowned King of Prague; and under the auspices and influence of France, he was soon afterward elected Emperor of Germany, and crowned at Frankfort by the title of Charles VII.

It had been the favorite object of Maria Theresa to place the imperial crown on the head of her husband. The election of Charles was, therefore, a deep mortification to her, and deeply she avenged it. Her armies, under the command of the Duke of Lorraine and General Kevenhuller, entered Bavaria, wasted the hereditary dominions of the new emperor with fire and sword, and on the very day on which he was proclaimed at Frankfort, his capital, Munich, surrendered to the Austrians, and the Duke of Lorraine entered the city in triumph. Such were the strange vicissitudes of war!

Within a few months afterward the French were everywhere beaten; they were obliged to evacuate Prague, and accomplished with great difficulty their retreat to Egra. So much was the queen's mind imbittered against them, that their escape at this time absolutely threw her into an agony. She had, however, sufficient self-command to conceal her indignation and disappointment from the public, and celebrated the surrender of Prague by a magnificent fête at Vienna. Among other entertainments there was a chariot-race, in imitation of th Greeks—in which, to exhibit the triumph of her sex, ladies alone were permitted to contend, and the queen herself and her sister entered the lists. It must have been a beautiful and gallant sight. Soon afterward Maria Theresa proceeded to Prague, where she was crowned Queen of Bohemia, May 12, 1743.

In Italy she was also victorious. Her principal opponent in that quarter was the high-spirited Elizabeth Farnese, the Queen of Spain.* This imperious woman, who thought she could manage a war as she managed her husband, commanded her general, on pain of instant dismissal, to fight the Austrians within three days ; he did so, and was defeated.

At the close of this eventful year, Maria Theresa had the pleasure of uniting her sister Marianna to Prince Charles of Lorraine, her husband's brother. They had been long attached to each other, and the archduchess was beautiful and amiable ; but a union which promised so much happiness was mournfully terminated by the death of Marianna, within a few months after her marriage.

The effect produced on the mind of Maria Theresa, by these sudden vicissitudes of fortune and extraordinary successes, was not altogether favorable. She had met dangers with fortitude— she had endured reverses with magnanimity; but she could not triumph with moderation. Sentiments of hatred, of vengeance, of ambition, had been awakened in her heart by the wrongs of her enemies and her own successes. She indulged a personal animosity against the Prussians and the French, which almost shut her heart, good and beneficent as Heaven had formed it, against humanity and the love of peace. She not only rejected with contempt all pacific overtures, and refused to acknowledge the new emperor, but she meditated vast

* Third wife of Philip V. Her story is very prettily told by Madame de Genlis in " La Princesse des Ursins."

schemes of conquest and retaliation. She not only resolved on recovering Silesia, and appropriating Bavaria, but she formed plans for crushing her great enemy, Frederick of Prussia, and partitioning his dominions, as he had conspired to ravage and dismember hers.

This excess of elation was severely chastised. In 1744 she lost Bavaria. Frederick suspected and anticipated her designs against him ; with his usual celerity he marched into Bohemia, besieged and captured Prague, and made even Vienna tremble. Maria Theresa had one trait of real greatness of mind—she was always greatest in adversity. She again had recourse to her brave Hungarians, and repairing to Presburg. she employed with such effect her powers of captivation, that she made every man who approached her a hero for her sake. The old palatine of Hungary, Count Palffy, unfurled the blood-red standard of the kingdom, and called on the magnates to summon their vassals and defend their queen ; 44,000 crowded round the national banner, and 30,000 more were ready to take the field. Maria Theresa, who knew as well as Mary Stuart herself, the power of a woman's smile, or word, or gift, bestowed apropos, sent to Count Palffy on this occasion her own charger, royally caparisoned, a sabre enriched with diamonds, and a ring, with these few words in her own hand-writing ;—

" Father Palffy, I send you this horse, worthy of being mounted by none but the most zealous of my faithful subjects ; receive at the same time this sword to defend me against my enemies, and this ring as a mark of my affection for you.

" MARIA THERESA."

The enthusiasm which her charms and her address excited in Hungary from the proudest palatine to the meanest peasant, again saved her.　In the following year Bohemia and Bavaria were recovered; and the unfortunate emperor, Charles the Seventh, driven from all his possessions, after playing for a while a miserable pageant of royalty in the hands of the French, died almost broken-hearted.　With his last breath he exhorted his successor to make peace with Austria, and reject the imperial dignity which had been so fatal to his family.　The new elector, Maximilian Joseph, obeyed these last commands, and no other competitor appearing, Maria Theresa was enabled to fulfill the ambition of her heart, by placing the imperial diadem on her husband's head.　Francis was proclaimed Emperor of Germany at Frankfort; and the queen, who witnessed from a balcony the ceremony of election, was the first who exclaimed " Vive l'emperor!"　From this time Maria Theresa, uniting in herself the titles of Empress of Germany and Queen of Hungary and Bohemia, is styled in history, the empress-queen.　This accession of dignity was the only compensation for a year of disasters and losses in Italy and the Netherlands.　Still she would not submit, nor bend her high spirit to an accommodation with Frederick on the terms he offered ; and still she rejected all mediation.　At length the native generosity of her disposition prevailed.　The Elector of Saxony,* who had been for some time her most faithful. and efficient ally, was about to become a sacrifice through his devotion to her cause, and only peace could save him and his people.　For his sake the queen stooped to what she never would have submitted to for any advantage to herself, and on Christmas-day, 1745, she signed the peace of Dresden, by which she finally ceded Silesia to Frederick, who, on this condition, withdrew his troops from Saxony, and acknow ledged Francis as Emperor.

* Augustus III.

The war with Louis XV. still continued with various changes
of fortune. In 1746 she lost nearly the whole of the Netherlands. The French were commanded by Marshal Saxe, the
Austrians by Charles of Lorraine. The former was flushed
with high spirits and repeated victories. The unfortunate Prince
Charles was half-distracted by the loss of his wife—the Archduchess Marianna had died in her first confinement; and her
husband, paralyzed by grief, could neither act himself, nor give
the necessary orders to his army.

By this time (1747) all the sovereigns of Europe began to
be wearied and exhausted by this sanguinary and burthensome
war; all, except Maria Theresa, whose pride, wounded by the
forced cession of Silesia and the reduction of her territories in
the Netherlands and in Italy, could not endure to leave off a
loser in this terrible game of life. It is rather painful to see
how the turmoils and vicissitudes of the last few years, the
habits of government and diplomacy, had acted on a disposition
naturally so generous and so just. In her conference with the
English minister she fairly got into a passion, exclaiming, with
the utmost indignation and disdain, "that rather than agree to
the terms of peace, she would lose her head"—raising her voice
as she spoke, and suiting the gesture to the words. With the
same warmth she had formerly declared, that before she would
give up Silesia she would *sell her shift!* In both cases she was
obliged to yield. When the plenipotentiaries of the various
powers of Europe met at Aix-la-Chapelle in 1748, her ministers,
acting by her instructions, threw every possible difficulty in the
way of the pacification; and when at length she was obliged to
accede, by the threat of her allies to sign without her, she did so
with obvious, with acknowledged reluctance, and never afterward
forgave England for having extorted her consent to this measure

The peace of Aix-la-Chapelle, which was one of the great events of the last century, was signed by the empress-queen on the 23d of October, 1748. " Thus," says the historian of Maria Theresa, " terminated a bloody and extensive war, which at the commencement threatened the very existence of the house of Austria ; but the magnanimity of Maria Theresa, the zeal of her subjects, and the support of Great Britain triumphed over her numerous enemies, and secured an honorable peace. She retained possession of all her vast inheritance except Silesia, Parma, Placentia, and Guastalla. She recovered the imperial dignity, which had been nearly wrested from the house of Austria, and obtained the guarantee of the Pragmatic Sanction from the principal powers of Europe. She was, however, so dissatisfied, that her chagrin broke out on many occasions, and on none more than when Mr. Keith requested an audience to offer his congratulations on the return of peace. Maria Theresa ordered her minister to observe that compliments of condolence would be more proper than compliments of congratulation, and insinuated that the British minister would oblige the empress by sparing a conversation which would be highly disagreeable to her, and no less unpleasing to him.*

Maria Theresa had made peace with reluctance. She was convinced—that is, she *felt*—that it could not be of long continuance ; but for the present she submitted. She directed her attention to the internal government of her dominions, and she resolved to place them in such a condition that she need not fear war whenever it was her interest to renew it.

She began by intrusting her military arrangements to the superintendence of Marshal Daun, one of the greatest generals of that time She concerted with him a new and better system

History of the House of Austria, vol. ii., p. 358

of discipline ; and was the first who instituted a military academy at Vienna. She maintained a standing army of one hundred and eight thousand men ; she visited her camps and garrisons, and animated her troops by her presence, her gracious speeches, and her bounties. - Her enemy, Frederick, tells us how well she understood and practiced the art of enhancing the value of those distinctions which, however trifling, are rendered important by the manner of bestowing them. He acknowledges that " the Austrian army acquired, under the auspices of Maria Theresa, such a degree of perfection as it had never attained under any of her predecessors, and that a woman accomplished designs worthy of a great man."

But Maria Theresa accomplished other designs far more worthy of herself and of her sex. She made some admirable regulations in the civil government of her kingdom ; she corrected many abuses which had hitherto existed in the administration of justice ; she abolished forever the use of torture throughout her dominions. The collection of the revenues was simplified ; the great number of tax-gatherers, which she justly considered as an engine of public oppression, was diminished. Her father had left her without a single florin in the treasury. In 1750, after eight years of war and the loss of several states, her revenues exceeded those of her predecessors by six millions. One of her benevolent projects failed, but not through any fault of her own. She conceived the idea of civilizing the numerous tribes of gipsies in Hungary and Bohemia ; but, after persevering for years, she was forced to abandon the design. Neither bribes nor punishment, neither mildness nor severity could subdue the wild spirit of freedom in these tameless, lawless outcasts of society, or bring them within the pale of civilization.

All the new laws and regulations, the changes and improvements which took place, emanated from Maria Theresa herself; and they were all more or less wisely and benevolently planned, and beneficial in their effect. We trace in Maria Theresa's public conduct two principles—a regard for the honor of her house, that is, her royal and family pride, and a love for her people ; but, from the prejudices in which she had been educated, it frequently happened that the latter consideration was sacrificed to the former. What she designed and performed for the good of her subjects was done quietly and effectually ; and what she wanted in genius was supplied by perseverance and good sense. Though peremptory in temper, jealous of her authority, and resisting the slightest attempt to lead or control her, Maria Theresa had no overweening confidence in her own abilities. She was at first almost painfully sensible of the deficiencies of her education and of her own inexperience. She eagerly sought advice and information, and gladly and gratefully accepted it from all persons ; and on every occasion she listened patiently to long and contradictory explanations. She read memorials and counter memorials, voluminous, immeasurable, perplexing. She was not satisfied with knowing or comprehending everything ; she was, perhaps, a little too anxious to do everything, see everything, manage everything herself. While in possession of health and strength she always rose at five in the morning, and often devoted ten or twelve hours together to the dispatch of business ; and, with all this close application to affairs, she found time to enter into society, to mingle in the amusements of her court, and to be the mother of sixteen children.

In her plans and wishes for the public good Maria Theresa had the sympathy, if not the co-operation, of her husband ; but she derived little or no aid from the ministry, or, as it was

termed, the conference, which was at this time (after the conclusion of the first war,) more inefficient than even at the period
of her accession. She had gradually become sensible of the incapacity and presumption of Bartenstein ; and, as he declined
in favor and confidence, Count (afterward Prince) Kaunitz rose
in her estimation. Kaunitz was ten years older than the empress. He had spent nearly his whole life in political affairs,
rising from one grade to another, through all the subaltern
offices of the state. He had been her minister at Aix-la-
Chapelle in 1748 ; in 1753 he was appointed chancellor of
state—in other words, prime minister—and from this time ruled
the councils of the empress-queen to the day of her death, a
period of nearly thirty years. Frederick of Prussia describes
Kaunitz as " un homme frivole dans ses gouts, profond dans
les affaires." From the descriptions of those who knew him
personally, he appears to have been a man of very extraordinary
talents, without any elevation of character ; a finical eccentric
coxcomb in his manners ; a bold, subtle, able statesman ; in-
ordinately vain, and, as his power increased, insolent and over-
bearing ; yet indefatigable in business, and incorruptible in his
fidelity to the interests of his sovereign.

Eight years of almost profound peace had now elapsed, and
Maria Theresa was neither sensible of the value of the blessing,
nor reconciled to the terms on which she had purchased it.
While Frederick existed—Frederick, who had injured, braved,
and humbled her—she was ready to exclaim, like Constance,
" War ! war !—no peace ! Peace is to me a war !" In vain was
she happy in her family, and literally adored by her subjects ;
she was not happy in herself. In her secret soul she nourished
an implacable resentment against the King of Prussia ; in the
privacy of her cabinet she revolved the means of his destruc-

tion. The loss of Silesia was still nearest her heart, and she never could think of it but with shame and anguish. Mingling the imagination and sensibility of a woman with the wounded pride of a sovereign, she never could hear the word " Silesia " without a blush—never turned her eyes on the map, where it was delineated as part of her territories, without visible emotion, and never beheld a native of that district without bursting into tears. She might have said of Silesia, as Mary of England said of Calais, that it would be found after death engraven on her heart. There were other circumstances which added to the bitterness of her resentment : Frederick, who, if not the most detestable, was certainly the most disagreeable monarch ever recorded in history, had indulged in coarse and cruel sarcasms against the empress and her husband ; they were repeated to her ; they were such as equally insulted her delicacy as a woman and her feelings as a wife ; and they sank deeper into her feminine mind than more real and more serious injuries   All Maria Theresa's passions, whether of love, grief, or resentment, partook of the hereditary obstinacy of her disposition. She could not bandy wit with her enemy—it was not in her nature ; but hatred filled her heart, and projects of vengeance occupied all her thoughts. She looked round her for the means to realize them ; there was no way but by an alliance with France—with France, the hereditary enemy of her family and her country !— with France, separated from Austria by three centuries of mutual injuries and almost constant hostility. The smaller states of Europe had long regarded their own safety as depending, in a great measure, on the mutual enmity and jealousy of these two great central powers ; a gulf seemed forever to divide them , but, instigated by the spirit of vengeance, Maria Theresa determined to leap that gulf.

Her plan was considered, matured, and executed in the profoundest secrecy; even her husband was kept in perfect ignorance of her designs. She was not of a temper to fear his opposition, but her strong affection for him made her shrink from his disapprobation. Prince Kaunitz was her only coadjutor; he alone was intrusted with this most delicate and intricate negotiation, which lasted nearly two years. It was found necessary to conciliate Madame de Pompadour, the mistress of Louis XV., who was at that time all-powerful. Kaunitz, in suggesting the expediency of this condescension, thought it necessary to make some apology. The empress merely answered, " Have I not flattered Farinelli ?"* and, taking up her pen, without further hesitation, this descendant of a hundred kings and emperors—the pious, chaste, and proud Maria Theresa—addressed the low-born profligate favorite as " ma chère amie," and " ma cousine." The step was sufficiently degrading, but it answered its purpose. The Pompadour was won to the Austrian interest; and through her influence this extraordinary alliance was finally arranged, in opposition to the policy of both courts, and the real interests and inveterate prejudices of both nations.

When this treaty was first divulged in the council of Vienna, the Emperor Francis was so utterly shocked and confounded, that, striking the table with his hand, he vowed he would never consent to it, and left the room. Maria Theresa was prepared for this burst of indignation; she affected, with that duplicity in which she had lately become an adept, to attribute the whole scheme to her minister, and to be as much astonished as Francis himself. But she represented the necessity of hear-

* She had sent compliments and presents to the singer Farinelli, when he was a favorite in the Spanish court.

19

ing and considering the whole of this new plan of policy before they decided against it. With a mixture of artifice, reason and tenderness, she gradually soothed the facile mind of her husband, and converted him to her own opinion, or at least convinced him that it was in vain to oppose it. When the report of a coalition between Austria and France was spread through Europe, it was regarded as something portentous. In England it was deemed incredible, or, as it was termed in parliament, unnatural and monstrous. The British minister at Vienna exclaimed, with astonishment, "Will you, the empress and archduchess, so far humble yourself as to throw yourself into the arms of France ?" "Not into the arms," she replied, with some haste and confusion, "but on the side of France. I have," she continued, "hitherto *signed* nothing with France, though I know not what may happen ; but whatever does happen, I promise, on my word of honor, not to sign anything contrary to the interests of your royal master, for whom I have a most sincere friendship and regard."

The immediate result of the alliance with France was " the seven years' war," in which Austria, France, Russia, Sweden, and Denmark, and afterward Spain, were confederated against the King of Prussia, who was assisted by Great Britain and Hanover, and only preserved from destruction by the enormous subsidies of England, and by his own consummate genius and intrepidity.

Until eclipsed by the great military events of the present century, this war stood unequaled for the skill, the bravery and the wonderful resources displayed on both sides—for the surprising vicissitudes of victory and defeat—for the number of great battles fought within so short a period—for the instances of individual heroism, and the tremendous waste of human life. In the former war our sympathies were all on the side of Maria Theresa. In the seven years' contest, we cannot refuse our admiration to the unshaken fortitude and perseverance with which Frederick defended himself against his enemies. He led his armies in person. The generals of Maria Theresa were Marshal Daun, Marshal Loudon, and Marshal Lacy—the first a Bohemian, the second of Scottish, and the third of Irish extraction. The empress, influenced equally by her tenderness and her prudence, would never allow her husband to take the field. Francis was personally brave, even to excess, but he had not the talents of a great commander, and his wife would neither risk his safety nor hazard the fate of her dominions by intrusting her armies to his guidance.

In this war Maria Theresa recovered, and again lost Silesia; at one time she was nearly overwhelmed and on the point of being driven from her capitol; again the tide of war rolled back, and her troops drove Frederick from Berlin.

When Marshal Daun gained the victory of Kolin, (June 18, 1757), by which the Austrian dominions were preserved from the most imminent danger, the empress-queen instituted the order of Maria Theresa, with which she decorated her victorious general and his principal officers. She loaded Daun with honors, and distributed rewards and gratuities to all the soldiers who had been present; medals were struck—Te Deums were sung; in short, she triumphed gratefully and gloriously. When a few years afterward, the same Marshal Daun lost a decisive battle,* after bravely contesting it, Maria Theresa received him with greater honors than after his former success; she even went out from her capital to meet him on his return, an honor never before conferred on any subject, and by the most flatter-

* The battle of Torgau.

ing expressions of kindness and confidence, she raised his spirits and reconciled him with himself; and this was in reality a more glorious triumph. The Roman senators, when they voted thanks to Fabius after his defeat, " because he had not despaired of the fate of Rome," displayed not more magnanimity than did this generous woman, acting merely from the impulse of her own feminine nature.

When Frederick of Prussia captured any of the Austrian officers, he treated them with coldness, rigor and sometimes insult; Maria Theresa never retaliated. When the Prince de Bevern was taken prisoner in Silesia, Frederick, like a mere heartless despot as he was, declined either to ransom or exchange him. He did not even deign to answer the prince's letters. The prince applied to Maria Theresa for permission to ransom himself, and she gave him his liberty at once, without ransom and without condition. These are things which never should be forgotten in estimating the character of Maria Theresa. Heaven had been so bountiful to her in mind and heart, that the possession of power could never entirely corrupt either; still and ever she was the benevolent and high-souled woman.

Next to France, her chief ally in this war, was the Empress Elizabeth of Russia, whose motives of enmity against Frederick were, like those of Maria Theresa, of a personal nature. Frederick had indulged in some severe jests, at the expense of that weak and vicious woman. She retorted with an army of 50,000 men. It appears a just retribution that this man, who disdained or derided all female society, who neglected and illtreated his wife, and tyrannized over his sisters,* should have been nearly destroyed through the influence of the sex he

---

* For one instance of his detestable tyranny, see the story of the poor Princess Amelia, in Thiebault.

despised. Of all his enemies, the two empresses were the most powerful, dangerous, and implacable. In seven terrible and sanguinary campaigns did Frederick make head against the confederated powers; but the struggle was too unequal. In 1762, Maria Theresa appeared everywhere triumphant; all her most sanguine hopes were on the point of being realized, and another campaign must have seen her detested adversary ruined, or at her feet. Such was the despondency of Frederick at this time, that he carried poison about him, firmly resolved that he would not be led a captive to Vienna. He was saved by one of those unforeseen events, by which Providence so often confounds and defeats all the calculations of men. The Empress Elizabeth died, and was succeeded by Peter the Third, who entertained the most extravagant admiration for Frederick. Russia, from being a formidable enemy, became suddenly an ally. The face of things changed at once. The rival powers were again balanced, and the decision of this terrible game of ambition appeared as far off as ever.

But all parties were by this time wearied and exhausted; all wished for peace, and none would stoop to ask it. At length, one of Maria Theresa's officers, who had been wounded and taken prisoner,* ventured to hint to Frederick that his imperial mistress was not unwilling to come to terms. This conversation took place at the castle of Hubertsberg. The king, snatching up half a sheet of paper, wrote down in few words the conditions on which he was willing to make peace. The whole was contained in about ten lines. He sent this off to Vienna by a courier, demanding a definitive answer *within twelve days.* The Austrian ministers were absolutely out of breath at the idea; they wished to temporize—to delay. But Maria Theresa,

* Thiebault, Vingt Ans de Séjour à Berlin

with the promptitude of her character, decided at once; she accepted the terms, and the peace of Hubertsberg was concluded in 1763. By this treaty, all places and prisoners were given up. Not a foot of territory was gained or lost by either party. Silesia continued in possession of Prussia; the political affairs of Germany remained in precisely the same state a. before the war; but Saxony and Bohemia had been desolated, Prussia almost depopulated, and more than 500,000 men had fallen in battle.

France, to whom the Austrian alliance seems destined to be ever fatal, lost in this war the flower of her armies, half the coined money of the kingdom, almost all her possessions in America and in the East and West Indies—her marine, her commerce, and her credit;* and those disorders were fomented, those disasters precipitated, which at length produced the revolution, and brought the daughter of Maria Theresa to the scaffold.

Immediately after the peace of Hubertsberg, the Archduke Joseph was elected King of the Romans, which insured him the imperial title after the death of his father.

At the conclusion of the seven years' war, Maria Theresa was in the forty-eighth year of her age. During the twenty-four years of her public life, the eyes of all Europe had been fixed upon her in hope, in fear, in admiration. She had contrived to avert from her own states the worst of those evils she had brought on others. Her subjects beheld her with a love and reverence little short of idolatry. In the midst of her weaknesses, she had displayed many virtues; and if she had committed great errors, she had also performed great and good actions But, besides being an empress and a queen. Maria

* Vide Siècle de Louis XV

Theresa was also a wife and a mother; and while she was guiding the reins of a mighty government, we are tempted to ask, where was her husband? and where her children?

Maria Theresa's attachment to her husband had been fond and passionate in her youth, and it was not only constant to death, but survived even in the grave. Francis was her inferior in abilities. His influence was not felt, like hers, to the extremity of the empire; but no man could be more generally beloved in his court and family. His children idolized him, and he was to them a fond and indulgent father. His temper was gay, volatile, and unambitious; his manners and person captivating. Although his education had been neglected, he had traveled much, had seen much, and, being naturally quick, social, and intelligent, he had gained some information on most subjects. In Italy he had imbibed a taste for the fine arts; he cultivated natural history, and particularly chemistry. While his wife was making peace and war, and ruling the destinies of nations, he amused himself among his retorts and crucibles, in buying pictures, or in superintending a ballet or an opera.

Francis expended immense sums in the study of alchymy;* he also believed that it was possible, by fusion, to convert several small diamonds into a large one, for it was not then

* We find that, during the reign of Maria Theresa, the pursuit of the philosopher's stone was not only the fashion at Vienna, but was encouraged by the government. A belief in the doctrines of magic and in familiar spirits was also general, even among persons of rank. Princes, ministers, and distinguished military commanders were not exempt from this puerile superstition.

"Professor Jaquin," says Wraxall, writing from Vienna, "is empowered by the empress to receive proposals from such as are inclined to enter on the attempt to make gold,—in other words, to find the philosopher's stone. They are immediately provided by him with a room, charcoal, utensils, crucibles, and every requisite, at her imperial majesty's expense."

known that the diamond was a combustible substance. His attempts in this way cost him large sums. He was fond of amassing money, apparently not so much from avarice as from an idea that wealth would give him a kind of power independent of his consort. Many instances are related of his humanity and beneficence, and his private charities are said to have been immense.

During the life of Francis, Vienna was a gay and magnificent capital. There was a fine opera, for which Gluck and Hasse composed the music, and Noverre superintended the ballets. He was fond of masks, balls, and fêtes; and long after the empress had ceased to take a pleasure in these amusements, she entered into them for her husband's sake. All accounts agree that they lived together in the most cordial union; that Maria Theresa was an example of every wife-like virtue—except submission; and Francis a model of every conjugal virtue—except fidelity. Such exceptions might have been supposed fatal to all domestic peace, but this imperial couple seem to present a singular proof to the contrary.

Francis submitted without a struggle to the ascendency of his wife; he even affected to make a display of his own insignificance, as compared with her grandeur and power. Many instances are related of the extreme simplicity of his manners. Being once at the levée, when the empress-queen was giving audience to her subjects, he retired from the circle, and seated himself in a distant corner of the apartment, near two ladies of the court. On their attempting to rise, he said, "Do not mind me; I shall stay here till the court is gone, and then amuse myself with looking at the crowd." One of the ladies (the Countess Harrach) replied, "As long as your imperial majesty is present, the *court* will be here" "You mistake," replied Francis;

"the empress and my children are the court—I am here but as a simple individual."*

In the summer of 1765, the imperial court left Vienna for Inspruck, in order to be present at the marriage of the Archduke Leopold with the Infanta of Spain. The emperor had previously complained of indisposition, and seemed overcome by those melancholy presentiments which are often the result of a deranged system, and only remembered when they happen to be realized. He was particularly fond of his youngest daughter, Marie Antoinette, and, after taking leave of his children, he ordered her to be brought to him once more. He took her in his arms, kissed, and pressed her to his heart, saying, with emotion, " J'avais besoin d'embrasser encore cette enfant!" While at Inspruck he was much indisposed, and Maria Theresa, who watched him with solicitude, appeared miserable and anxious; she requested that he would be bled. He replied, with a petulance very unusual to him, " Madame, voulez vous que je meurs dans la saignée?" The heavy air of the valleys seemed to oppress him even to suffocation, and he was often heard to exclaim, " Ah! si je pouvais seulement sortir de ces montagnes du Tyrol!" On Sunday, August 18th, the empress and his sister again entreated him to be bled. He replied, " I must go to the opera, and I am engaged afterward to sup with Joseph, and cannot disappoint him; but I will be bled to-morrow." The same evening, on leaving the theatre, he fell down in an apoplectic fit, and expired in the arms of his son.

A scene of horror and confusion immediately ensued. While her family and attendants surrounded the empress, and the officers of the palace were running different ways in consterna-

* Coxe's Memoirs.

tion, the body of Francis lay abandoned on a little wretched pallet in one of the ante-rooms, the blood oozing from the orifices in his temples, and not even a valet near to watch over him !

The anguish of Maria Theresa was heightened by her religious feelings; and the idea that her husband had been taken away in the midst of his pleasures, and before he had time to make his peace with God, seemed to press fearfully upon her mind. It was found necessary to remove her instantly. She was placed in a barge, hastily fitted up, and, accompanied only by her son, her master of horse, and a single lady in waiting, she proceeded down the river to Vienna.

Previous to her departure, a courier was dispatched to the three archduchesses, who had been left behind in the capital, bearing a letter which the empress had dictated to her daughters on the day after her husband's death. It was in these words :—

" Alas! my dear daughters, I am unable to comfort you! Our calamity is at its height; you have lost a most incomparable father, and I a consort—a friend—my heart's joy, for forty-two years past! Having been brought up together, our hearts and our sentiments were united in the same views. All the misfortunes I have suffered during the last twenty-five years were softened by his support. I am suffering such deep affliction, that nothing but true piety and you, my dear children, can make me tolerate a life which, during its continuance, shall be spent in acts of devotion. Pray for our good and worthy master.* I give you my blessing, and will ever be your good mother,　　　　　　　　　　　　　MARIA THERESA."

The remains of Francis the First were carried to Vienna,

* The Emperor Joseph.

and, after lying in state, were deposited in the family-vault under the church of the Capuchins. When Maria Theresa was only six-and-twenty, and in the full bloom of youth and health, she had constructed in this vault a monument for herself and her husband. Hither, during the remainder of her life, she repaired on the 18th of every month, and poured forth her devotions at his tomb. Her grief had the same fixed character with all her other feelings. She wore mourning to the day of her death. She never afterward inhabited the state apartments in which she had formerly lived with her husband, but removed to a suite of rooms, plainly and even poorly furnished, and hung with black cloth. There was no affectation in this excess of sorrow. Her conduct was uniform during sixteen years. Though she held her court and attended to the affairs of the government as usual, she was never known to enter into amuse-ments, or to relax from the mournful austerity of her widowed state, except on public occasions, when her presence was absolutely necessary.

Maria Theresa was the mother of sixteen children. The un-happy Marie Antoinette, wife of the dauphin, afterward Louis XVI., was her youngest daughter. She was united to the dau-phin in 1770, and thus was sealed an alliance between Austria and France—the great object of her wishes, which Maria Theresa had been engaged for years in accomplishing—for, in placing a daughter upon the throne of France, she believed that she was securing a predominant influence in the French cabinet, and that she was rendering, by this grand scheme of policy, the ancient and hereditary rival of her empire, subservient to the future aggrandizement of her house.

Maria Theresa lived in the interior of her palace with great simplicity. In the morning an old man, who could hardly be entitled a chamberlain, but merely what is called on the continent a *frotteur*, entered her sleeping-room, about five or six o'clock in the morning, opened the shutters, lighted the stove, and arranged the apartment. She breakfasted on a cup of milk-coffee; then dressed and heard mass. She then proceeded to business. Every Tuesday she received the ministers of the different departments; other days were set apart for giving audience to foreigners and strangers, who, according to the etiquette of the imperial court, were always presented singly, and received in the private apartments. There were stated days on which the poorest and meanest of her subjects were admitted almost indiscriminately; and so entire was her confidence in their attachment and her own popularity, that they might whisper to her, or see her alone, if they required it. At other times she read memorials, or dictated letters and dispatches, signed papers, &c. At noon, her dinner was brought in, consisting of a few dishes, served with simplicity; she usually dined alone, like Napoleon, and for the same reason—to economize time. After dinner she was engaged in public business till six; after that hour her daughters were admitted to join in her evening prayer. If they absented themselves, she sent to know if they were indisposed; if not, they were certain of meeting with a maternal reprimand on the following day. At half past eight or nine, she retired to rest. When she held a drawing-room or an evening-circle, she remained till ten or eleven, and sometimes played at cards. Before the death of her husband, she was often present at the masked balls, or *ridottos*, which were given at court during the carnival; afterward, these entertainments and the number of fêtes, or *gala-days*, were gradually diminished in number. During the last years of her life, when she became very infirm, the nobility and foreign ministers generally assembled at the houses of Prince Kaunitz and Prince Collerado.

On the first day of the year, and on her birth-day, Maria Theresa held a public court, at which all the nobility, and civil and military officers who did not obtain access at other times, crowded to kiss her hand. She continued this custom as long as she could support herself in a chair.

Great part of the summer and autumn were spent at Schönbrunn, or at Lachsenburg. In the gardens of the former palace there was a little shaded alley, communicating with her apartments. Here, in the summer days, she was accustomed to walk up and down, or sit for hours together; a box was buckled round her waist, filled with papers and memorials, which she read carefully, noting with her pencil the necessary answers or observations to each.

It was the fault or rather the mistake of Maria Theresa to give up too much of her time to the petty details of business; in her government as in her religion she sometimes mistook the form for the spirit, and her personal superintendence became at length more like the vigilance of an inspector-general, than the enlightened jurisdiction of a sovereign. She could not, however, be accused of selfishness or vanity in this respect, for her indefatigable attention to business was without parade, and to these duties she sacrificed her pleasures, her repose, and often her health.

Much of her time was employed in devotion; the eighteenth day of every month was consecrated to the memory of her husband;* and the whole month of August was usually spent in retirement, in penance and in celebrating masses and requiems for the repose of his soul. Those who are " too proud to wor

* Francis died on the 18th of August.

ship, and too wise to feel," may smile at this—but others, even those who do not believe in the efficacy of requiems and masses, will respect the source from which her sorrow flowed, and the power whence it sought for comfort.

After the death of her husband she admitted her son, the emperor Joseph, to the co-regency or joint-government of all her hereditary dominions, without prejudice to her own supreme jurisdiction.   They had one court, and their names were united in all the edicts ; but what were the exact limits of their respective prerogatives none could tell.   The mother and son occasionally differed in opinion ; he sometimes influenced her against her better judgment and principles ; but during her life she held in some constraint the restless, ambitious, and despotic spirit of the young emperor.   The good terms on which they lived together, her tenderness for him, and his dutiful reverence toward her, place the maternal character of Maria Theresa in a very respectable point of view.   Prince Kaunitz had the chief direction of foreign affairs, and although the empress placed unbounded confidence in his integrity and abilities, and indulged him in all his peculiarities and absurdities, he was a minister, and not a favorite.

She founded or enlarged in different parts of her extensive dominions several academies for the improvement of the arts and sciences ; instituted numerous seminaries for the education of all ranks of people ; reformed the public schools, and ordered prizes to be distributed among the students who made the greatest progress in learning, or were distinguished for propriety of behavior or purity of morals.   She established prizes for those who excelled in different branches of manufacture, in geometry, mining, smelting metals, and even spinning.   She particularly turned her attention to the promotion of agriculture, which in a medal struck by her order, was entitled the " Art which nourishes all other arts," and founded a society of agriculture at Milan, with bounties to the peasants who obtained the best crops. She confined the rights of the chase, often so pernicious to the husbandman, within narrow limits, and issued a decree, enjoining all the nobles who kept wild game to maintain their fences in good repair, permitting the peasants to destroy the wild-boars which ravished the fields. She also abolished the scandalous power usurped by the landholders of limiting the season for mowing the grass within the forest, and their precincts, and mitigated the feudal servitude of the peasants in Bohemia.

Among her beneficial regulations must not be omitted the introduction of inoculation, and the establishment of a small-pox hospital. On the recovery of her children from a disorder so fatal to her own family, Maria Theresa gave an entertainment which displayed the benevolence of her character. Sixty-five children, who had been previously inoculated at the hospital, were regaled with a dinner in the gallery of the palace at Schönbrunn, in the midst of a numerous court; and Maria Theresa herself, assisted by her offspring, waited on this delightful group, and gave to each of them a piece of money. The parents of the children were treated in another apartment; the whole party was admitted to the performance of a German play, and this charming entertainment was concluded with a dance, which was protracted till midnight.

Perhaps the greatest effort made by the empress-queen, and which reflects the highest honor on her memory, was the reformation of various abuses in the church, and the regulations which she introduced into the monasteries.

She took away the pernicious right which the convents and

churches enjoyed of affording an asylum to all criminals without distinction ; she suppressed the Inquisition, which, though curbed by the civil power, still subsisted at Milan. She suppressed the society of Jesuits, although her own confessor was a member of that order, but did not imitate the unjust and cruel measures adopted in Spain and Portugal, and softened the rigor of their lot by every alleviation which circumstances would permit.

To these particulars may be added, that Maria Theresa was the first sovereign who threw open the royal domain of the Prater to the use of the public. This was one of the most popular acts of her reign. She prevailed on Pope Clement XIV., (Ganganelli), to erase from the calendar many of the saints' days and holydays, which had became so numerous as to affect materially the transactions of business and commerce, as well as the morals of the people. It is curious that this should have proved one of the most unpopular of all her edicts, and was enforced with the utmost difficulty. Great as was the bigotry of Maria Theresa, that of her loving subjects appears to have far exceeded hers. She also paid particular attention to the purity of her coinage, considering it as part of the good faith of a sovereign.

It must, however, be confessed that all her regulations were not equally praiseworthy and beneficial. For instance, the censorship of the press was rigorous and illiberal, and the prohibition of foreign works, particularly of French and English literature, amounted to a kind of proscription. We are assured that " the far greater number of those books which constitute the libraries of persons distinguished for taste and refinement, not merely in France or England, but even at Rome or Florence, were rigorously condemned, and their entry was attended with no less difficulty than danger." That not only works of an immoral and a rebellious tendency, but "a sentence reflecting on the Catholic religion; a doubt thrown upon the sanctity of some hermit or monk of the middle ages; any publication wherein superstition was attacked or censured, however slightly, was immediately noticed by the police, and prohibited under the severest penalties."

The impediments thus thrown in the way of knowledge and the diffusion of literature, in a great degree neutralized the effect of her munificence in other instances. It must be allowed that, though the rise of the modern German literature, which now holds so high a rank in Europe, dates from the reign of Maria Theresa, it owes nothing to her patronage. Not that, like Frederick II., she held it in open contempt, but that her mind was otherwise engaged. Lessing, Klopstock, Kant, and Winkelman, all lived in her time, but none of them were born her subjects, and they derived no encouragement from her notice and patronage.

But the great stain upon the character and reign of Maria Theresa—an event which we cannot approach without pain and reluctance—was the infamous dismemberment of Poland in 1772. The detailed history of this transaction occupies volumes; but the manner in which Maria Theresa became implicated, her personal share in the disgrace attached to it, and all that can be adduced in palliation of her conduct, may be related in very few words.

The empress-queen had once declared that, though she might make peace with Frederick, no consideration should ever induce her to enter into an alliance in which he was a party. To prevent the increase of his power, and to guard against his encroaching ambition, his open hostility, or his secret enmity, had

20

long been the ruling principle of the cabinet of Vienna. Under
the influence of her son, and of the Russian government, and
actuated by motives of interest and expediency, Maria Theresa
departed from this line of policy, to which she had adhered for
thirty years.

The first idea of dismembering and partitioning Poland un-
doubtedly originated with the court of Prussia.

The negotiations and arrangements for this purpose were carried on with the profoundest secrecy, and each of the powers
concerned was so conscious of the infamy attached to it, and so
anxious to cast the largest share of blame upon another, that no
event of modern history is involved in more obscurity or more
perplexed by contradictory statements and relations. It is really
past the power of a plain understanding to attempt to disentangle
this dark web of atrocious policy. From the discovery of some
of the original documents within the last few years, a shade of
guilt nas been removed from the memory of Maria Theresa;
for it appears that the treaty which originated with Frederick
was settled between Prince Henry of Prussia and Catherine the
Second, in 1769 ; and that it was then agreed that, if Austria
refused to accede to the measure, Russia and Prussia should
sign a separate treaty—league against her, seize upon Poland,
and carry the war to her frontiers. Maria Theresa professed
to feel great scruples, both religious and political, in participating
either in the disgrace or advantages of this transaction, but she
was overruled by her son and Kaunitz, and she preferred a share
of the booty to a terrible and precarious war. That armies
should take the field on a mere point of honor, and potentates
" greatly find quarrel in a straw," is nothing new ; but a war
undertaken upon a point of honesty, a scruple of conscience—
or from a generous sense of the right opposed to the wrong—

this, certainly, would have been unprecedented in history; and Maria Theresa did not set the example. When once she had acceded to this scandalous treaty, she was determined, with her characteristic prudence, to derive as much advantage from it as possible, and her demands were so unconscionable, and the share she claimed was so exorbitant, that the negotiation had nearly been broken off by her confederates. At length, a dread of premature exposure, and a fear of the consequent failure, induced her to lower her pretensions, and the treaty for the first partition of Poland was signed at Petersburg on the 3d of August, 1772.

The situation of Poland at this time, divided between a licentious nobility and an enslaved peasantry, torn by faction, desolated by plague and famine, abandoned to every excess of violence, anarchy, and profligacy; the cool audacity of the imperial swindlers, who first deceived and degraded, then robbed and trampled upon that unhappy country; the atrocious means by which an atrocious purpose was long prepared, and at length accomplished; the mixture of duplicity, and cruelty, and bribery; the utter demoralization of the agents and their victims, of the corrupters and the corrupted—altogether presents a picture which, when contemplated in all its details, fills the mind with loathing and horror. By the treaty of partition, to which a committee of Polish delegates, and the king at their head, were obliged to set their seal, Russia appropriated all the north-eastern part of Poland—Frederick obtained all the district which stretches along the Baltic, called Western Prussia—Maria Theresa seized on a large territory to the south of Poland, including Red Russia, Gallicia, and Lodomeria. The city and palatinate of Cracow and the celebrated salt-mines of Vilitzka were included in her division.

In reference to Maria Theresa's share in the spoliation of Poland, I cannot forbear to mention one circumstance, and will leave it without a comment. She was particularly indignant against the early aggression of Frederick, as not only unjust and treacherous, but *ungrateful*, since it was owing to the interference of her father, Charles the Sixth, that Frederick had not lost his life either in a dungeon or on a scaffold at the time that he was arrested with his friend Katt.* In the room which Maria Theresa habitually occupied, and in which she transacted business, hung two pictures, and only two ; one was the portrait of John Sobieski, King of Poland, whose heroism had saved Vienna when besieged by the Turks in 1683—the other represented her grandfather, Leopold, who owed the preservation of his country, his capital, his crown, his very existence, to the intervention of the Poles on that memorable occasion.

After the partition of Poland, Maria Theresa appeared at the height of her grandeur, power, and influence, as a sovereign. She had greatly extended her territories ; she had an army on foot of two hundred thousand men ; her finances were brought into such excellent order that, notwithstanding her immense expenses, she was able to lay by in her treasury not less than two hundred thousand crowns a year. She lived on terms of harmony with her ambitious, enterprising, and accomplished son and successor, which secured her domestic peace and her political strength ; while her subjects blessed her mild sway, and bestowed on her the title of " mother of her people."

The rest of the reign of Maria Theresa is not distinguished by any event of importance till the year 1778, when she was

---

* Vide Life of Frederick the Great. Katt, as it is well known, was beheaded in his sight ; and Frederick had very nearly suffered the fate of Don Carlos—that of being assassinated by his crack-trained father.

again nearly plunged into a war with her old adversary, Frederick of Prussia.

The occasion was this,—the Elector of Bavaria died without leaving any son to succeed to his dominions, and his death was regarded by the court of Vienna as a favorable opportunity to revive certain equivocal claims on the part of the Bavarian territories. No sooner did the intelligence of the elector's indisposition arrive at Vienna than the armies were held in readiness to march. Kaunitz, spreading a map before the empress and her son, pointed out those portions to which he conceived that the claims of Austria might extend; and Joseph, with all the impetuosity of his character, enforced the views and arguments of the minister. Maria Theresa hesitated—she was now old and infirm, and averse to all idea of tumult and war. She recoiled from a design of which she perceived at once the injustice as well as the imprudence; and when at last she yielded to the persuasions of her son, she exclaimed, with much emotion, "In God's name, only take what we have a right to demand! I foresee that it will end in war. My wish is to end my days in peace."

No sooner was a reluctant consent wrung from her than the Austrians entered Bavaria, and took forcible possession of the greatest part of the electorate.

The King of Prussia was not inclined to be a quiet spectator of this scheme of aggrandizement on the part of Austria, and immediately prepared to interfere and dispute her claims to the Bavarian succession. Though now seventy years of age, time had but little impaired either the vigor of his mind or the activity of his frame; still, with him "the deed o'ertook the purpose," and his armies were assembled and had entered Bohemia before the court of Vienna was apprised of his movements.

To Frederick was opposed the young Emperor Joseph, at tue head of a more numerous force than had ever before taken the field under the banners of Austria, supported by the veteran generals, Loudon and Lacy, and burning for the opportunity, which his mother's prudence had hitherto denied him, to distinguish himself by some military exploit, and encounter the enemy of his family on the field of battle.

But how different were all the views and feelings of the aged empress! how changed from what they had been twenty years before! She regarded the approaching war with a species of horror; her heart still beat warm to all her natural affections; but hatred, revenge, ambition—sentiments which had rather been awakened there by circumstances than native to her disposition—were dead within her. When the troops from different parts of her vast empire assembled at Vienna, and marched with all their military ensigns past the windows of her palace, she ordered her shutters to be closed. Her eyes were constantly suffused with tears, her knees continually bent in prayer. Half-conscious of the injustice of her cause, she scarcely dared to ask a blessing on her armies; she only hoped by supplication to avert the immediate wrath of Heaven.

All the preparations for the campaign being completed, the emperor and his brother Maximilian set off for the camp at Olmutz in April, 1778. When they waited on the empress to take their leave and receive her parting benediction, she held them long in her arms, weeping bitterly; and when the emperor at length tore himself from her embraces, she nearly fainted away.

During the next few months she remained in the interior of her palace, melancholy and anxious, but not passive and inactive. She was revolving the means of terminating a war which she detested   Her evident reluctance seems to have paralyzed her generals: for the whole of this campaign, which had opened with such tremendous preparations, passed without any great battle or any striking incident except the capture of Habelschwert, which as it opened a passage into Silesia, was likely to be followed by important consequences. When Colonel Palavicini arrived at Vienna with the tidings of this event, and laid the standards taken from the enemy at the feet of the empress, she received him with complacency; but when he informed her that the town and inhabitants of Habelschwert had suffered much from the fury of the troops, she opened her bureau, and taking out a bag containing five hundred ducats, "I desire," said she, "that this sum may be distributed in my name among the unfortunate sufferers whose houses or effects have been plundered by my soldiery; it will be of some little use and consolation to them under their misfortunes."

She still retained something of the firmness and decision of her former years; age, which had subdued her haughty spirit, had not enfeebled her powers; and in this emergency she took the only measures left to avert the miseries of a terrible and unjust war. Unknown to her son, and even without the knowledge of Kaunitz, she acted for herself and for her people, with a degree of independence, resolution, and good feeling, which awakens our best sympathies, and fills us with admiration both for the sovereign and the woman. She dispatched a confidential officer with a letter addressed to the King of Prussia, in which she avowed her regret that in their old age Frederick and herself "should be about to tear the gray hairs from each other's head."* "I perceive," said she, " with extreme sensibility, the breaking out of a new war. My age and my earnest desire for maintaining peace are well

* Her own words.

known and I cannot give a more convincing proof than by the present proposal. My maternal heart is justly alarmed for the safety of my two sons and my son-in-law, who are in the army. I have taken this step without the knowledge of my son the emperor, and I entreat, whatever may be the event, that you will not divulge it. I am anxious to re-commence and terminate the negotiation hitherto conducted by the emperor, and broken off to my extreme regret. This letter will be delivered to you by Baron Thugut, who is intrusted with full powers. Ardently hoping that it may fulfill my wishes conformably to my dignity, I entreat you to join your efforts with mine to re-establish between us harmony and good intelligence, for the benefit of mankind and the interest of our respective families."*

This letter enclosed proposals of peace on moderate terms. The king's answer is really honorable to himself as well as to the empress-queen :—

" Baron Thugut has delivered to me your imperial majesty's letter, and no one is or shall be acquainted with his arrival. It was worthy of your majesty's character to give these proofs of magnanimity and moderation in a litigious cause, after having so heroically maintained the inheritance of your ancestors. The tender attachment which you display for your son the emperor and the princess of your blood, deserves the applause of every feeling mind, and augments, if possible, the high consideration which I entertain for your sacred person. I have added some articles to the propositions of Baron Thugut, most of which have been allowed, and others will, I hope, meet with little difficulty. He will immediately depart for Vienna, and will be able to return in five or six days, during which time I will act with such

* Coxe's Memoirs of the House of Austria, vol. ii. p. 531.

caution that your imperial majesty 'may have no cause of apprehension for the safety of any part of your family, and particularly of the emperor, whom I love and esteem, although our opinions differ in regard to the affairs of Germany."

It is pleasing to see these two sovereigns, after thirty-eight years of systematic hostility, mutual wrongs, and personal aversion, addressing each other in terms so conciliatory, and which, as the event showed, were at this time sincere.

The accommodation was not immediately arranged. Frederick demurred on some points, and the Emperor Joseph, when made acquainted with the negotiation, was indignant at the concessions which his mother had made, and which he deemed humiliating—as if it *could* be humiliating to undo wrong, to revoke injustice, to avert crime, and heal animosities. But Maria Theresa was not discouraged, nor turned from her generous purpose. She was determined that the last hours of her reign should not, if possible, be stained by bloodshed or disturbed by tumult. She implored the mediation of the Empress of Russia. She knew that the reigning foible of the imperial Catherine, like that of the plebeian Pompadour, was vanity—intense, all-absorbing vanity—and might be soothed and flattered by the same means. She addressed to her, therefore, an eloquent letter, in which praise, and deference, and argument were so well mingled, and so artfully calculated to win that vain-glorious but accomplished woman, that she receded from her first design of supporting the King of Prussia, and consented to interfere as mediatrix. After a long negotiation and many difficulties, which Maria Theresa met and overcame with firmness and talent worthy of her brightest days, the peace was signed at Teschen, in Saxony, on the 13th of May, the birth-day of the empress-queen.

The treaty of Teschen was the last political event of Maria Theresa's reign in which she was actively and personally concerned Her health had been for some time declining, and for several months previous to her death she was unable to move from her chair without assistance ; yet, notwithstanding her many infirmities, her deportment was still dignified, her manner graceful as well as gracious, and her countenance benign.

She had long accustomed herself to look death steadily in the face, and when the hour of trial came, her resignation, her fortitude, and her humble trust in Heaven never failed her She preserved to the last her self-possession and her strength of mind, and betrayed none of those superstitious terrors which might have been expected and pardoned in Maria Theresa.

Until the evening preceding her death, she was engaged in signing papers, and in giving her last advice and directions to her successor ; and when, perceiving her exhausted state, her son entreated her to take some repose, she replied steadily,— "In a few hours I shall appear before the judgment-seat of God, and would you have me sleep ?"

Maria Theresa expired on the 29th of November, 1780, in her sixty-fourth year ; and it is, in truth, most worthy of remark, that the regrets of her family and her people did not end with the pageant of her funeral, nor were obliterated by the new interests, new hopes, new splendors of a new reign. Years after her death she was still remembered with tenderness and respect, and her subjects dated events from the time of their "mother," the empress. The Hungarians, who regarded themselves as her own especial people, still distinguish their country from Austria and Bohemia, by calling it the "territory of the queen."

Charlotte Corday.

CHARLOTTE CORDAY.

HAD Charlotte Corday lived in the days of the Greek or Roman republics, the action which has given celebrity to her name would have elevated her memory to the highest rank of civic virtue. The Christian moralist judges of such deeds by a different standard. The meek spirit of the Saviour's religion raises its voice against murder of every denomination, leaving to Divine Providence the infliction of its will upon men like Marat, whom, for wise and inscrutable purposes, it sends, from time to time, as scourges upon earth. In the present instance, Charlotte Corday anticipated the course of nature but a few weeks, perhaps only a few days; for Marat, when she killed him, was already stricken with mortal disease. Fully admitting, as I sincerely do, the Christian precept in its most comprehensive sense, I am bound to say, nevertheless, that Charlotte Corday's error arose from the noblest and most exalted feelings of the human heart; that she deliberately sacrificed her life to the purest love of her country, unsullied by private feelings of any kind; and that, having expiated her error by a public execution, the motive by which she was actuated, and the lofty heroism she displayed, entitle her to the admiration of posterity.

Marie Adelaide Charlotte, daughter of Jean François Corday d'Armans, and Charlotte Godier, his wife, was born in 1768, at St. Saturnin, near Seez, in Normandy. Her family belonged to the Norman nobility, of which it was not one of the least ancient, and she was descended, on the female side, from the great Corneille. She was educated at the Abbey of the Holy Trinity, at Caen, and from her earliest youth evinced superior intellectual endowments.

From a peculiar bent of mind very uncommon in females, especially at that period, Charlotte Corday devoted herself to the study of politics and the theory of government. Strongly tinctured with the philosophy of the last century, and deeply read in ancient history, she had formed notions of pure republicanism which she hoped to see realized in her own country. A friend at first to the revolution, she exulted in the opening dawn of freedom ; but when she saw this dawn overcast by the want of energy of the Girondins, the mean and unprincipled conduct of the Feuillans, and the sanguinary ferocity of the Mountain party, she thought only of the means of averting the calamities which threatened again to enslave the French people.

On the overthrow of the Girondins, and their expulsion from the Convention, Charlotte Corday was residing at Caen, with her relation, Madame de Broteville. She had always been an enthusiastic admirer of the federal principles of this party, so eloquently developed in their writings, and had looked up to them as the saviors of France. She was, therefore, not prepared for the weakness, and even pusillanimity, which they afterwards displayed.

The Girondist representatives sought refuge in the department of Calvados, where they called upon every patriot to take up arms in defence of freedom. On their approach to Caen, Charlotte Corday, at the head of the young girls of that city, bearing crowns and flowers, went out to meet them. The civic crown was presented to Lanjuinais, and Charlotte herself placed it upon his head—a circumstance which must constitute not the least interesting recollection of Lanjuinais' life.

Marat was, at this period, the ostensible chief of the Mountain party, and the most sanguinary of its members. He was a monster of hideous deformity, both in mind and person ; his lank and distorted features, covered with leprosy, and his vulgar and ferocious leer, were a true index of the passions which worked in his odious mind. A series of unparalleled atrocities had raised him to the highest power with his party ; and though he professed to be merely passive in the revolutionary government, his word was law with the Convention, and his fiat irrevocable. In everything relating to the acquisition of wealth, he was incorruptible, and even gloried in his poverty. But the immense influence he had acquired, turned his brain, and he gave full range to the evil propensities of his nature, now unchecked by any authority. He had formed principles of political faith in which, perhaps, he sincerely believed, but which were founded upon his inherent love of blood, and his hatred of every human being who evinced talents or virtue above his fellow-men. The guillotine was not only the altar of the distorted thing he worshiped under the name of Liberty, but it was also the instrument of his pleasures—for his highest gratification was the writhings of the victim who fell under its axe. Even Robespierre attempted to check this unquenchable thirst for human blood, but in vain—opposition only excited Marat to greater atrocities. With rage depicted in his livid features, and with the howl of

demoniac, he would loudly declare that rivers of blood could alone purify the land, and must therefore flow. In his paper entitled, " L'Ami du Peuple," he denounced all those whom he had doomed to death, and the guillotine spared none whom he designated.

Charlotte Corday, having read his assertion in this journal, (that three hundred thousand heads were requisite to consolidate the liberties of the French people,) could not contain her feelings. Her cheeks flushed with indignation,—

" What !" she exclaimed, " is there not in the whole country a man bold enough to kill this monster ?"

Meanwhile, an insurrection against the ruling faction was in progress, and the exiled deputies had established a central assembly at Caen, to direct its operations. Charlotte Corday, accompanied by her father, regularly attended the sittings of this assembly, where her striking beauty rendered her the more remarkable, because from the retired life she led, she was previously unknown to any of the members.

Though the eloquence of the Girondins was here powerfully displayed, their actions but little corresponded with it. A liberating army had been formed in the department, and placed under the command of General Felix Wimpfen. But neither this general nor the deputies took any measures worthy of the cause ; their proceedings were spiritless and emasculate, and excited, without checking, the faction in power. Marat denounced the Girondins in his paper, and demanded their death as necessary for the safety of the republic.

Charlotte Corday was deeply afflicted at the nerveless measures of the expelled deputies, and imagining that, if she could succeed in destroying Marat, the fall of his party must necessarily ensue, she determined to offer up her own life for the good of her country. She accordingly called on Barbaroux, one of the Girondist leaders, with whom she was not personally acquainted, and requested a letter of introduction to M. Duperret, a deputy, favorable to the Girondins, and then at Paris Having also requested Barbaroux to keep her secret, she wrote to her father, stating, that she had resolved to emigrate to England, and had set out privately for that country, where alone she could live in safety.

She arrived at Paris at the beginning of July, 1793, and immediately called upon M. Duperret. But she found this deputy as devoid of energy as of talent, and therefore only made use of him to assist her in transacting some private business.

A day or two after her arrival, an incident occurred, which is worthy of a place here.

Being at the Tuileries, she seated herself upon a bench in the garden. A little boy, attracted no doubt by the smile with which she greeted him, enlisted her as a companion of his gambols. Encouraged by her caresses, he thrust his hand into her half-open pocket and drew forth a small pistol.

" What toy is this ?" said he.

" It is a toy," Charlotte replied, " which may prove very useful in these times."

So saying, she quickly concealed the weapon, and looking round to see whether she was observed, immediately left the garden.

On the 11th of July, Charlotte Corday attended the sitting of the Convention, with a determination to shoot Marat in the midst of the assembly. But he was too ill to leave his house ; and she had to listen to a long tirade against the Girondins, made by Cambon, in a report on the state of the country.

On the 12th, at nine o'clock in the evening, she called on M. Prud'homme, a historian of considerable talent and strict veracity, with whose writings on the revolution she had been much struck.

" No one properly understands the state of France," said she, with the accent of true patriotism ; " your writings alone

21

have made an impression upon me, and that is the reason why I have called upon you. Freedom, as you understand it, is for all conditions and opinions. You feel, in a word, that you have a country. All the other writers on the events of the day are partial, and full of empty declamation—they are wholly guided by factions, or, what is worse, by coteries."

M. Prud'homme says, that, in this interview, Charlotte Corday appeared to him a woman of most elevated mind and striking talent.

The day after this visit, she went to the Palais Royal and bought a sharp-pointed carving-knife, with a black sheath. On her return to the hotel in which she lodged—Hotel de la Providence, Rue des Augustins—she made her preparations for the deed she intended to commit next day. Having put up her papers in order, she placed a certificate of her baptism in a red pocket-book, in order to take it with her, and thus establish her identity. This she did because she had resolved to make no attempt to escape, and was therefore certain she should leave Marat's house for the conciergerie, preparatory to her appearing before the revolutionary tribunal.

Next morning, the 14th, taking with her the knife she had purchased, and her red pocket-book, she proceeded to Marat's residence, at No. 18, Rue de l'Ecole de Médicine. The representative was ill, and could not be seen, and Charlotte's entreaties for admittance on the most urgent business were unavailing. She therefore withdrew, and wrote the following note, which she herself delivered to Marat's servant :—

" CITIZEN REPRESENTATIVE,

" I am just arrived from Caen. Your well-known patriotism leads me to presume that you will be glad to be made acquainted with what is passing in that part of the republic. I will call on you again in the course of the day; have the goodness to give orders that I may be admitted, and grant me a few minutes' conversation I have important secrets to reveal to you.

"CHARLOTTE CORDAY."

At seven o'clock in the evening she returned, and reached Marat's ante-chamber; but the woman who waited upon him refused to admit her to the monster's presence. Marat, however, who was in a bath in the next room, hearing the voice of a young girl, and little thinking she had come to deprive him of life, ordered that she should be shown in. Charlotte seated herself by the side of the bath. The conversation ran upon the disturbances in the department of Calvados, and Charlotte, fixing her eyes upon Marat's countenance as if to scrutinize his most secret thoughts, pronounced the names of several of the Girondist deputies.

"They shall soon be arrested," he cried with a howl of rage, "and executed the same day."

He had scarcely uttered these words, when Charlotte's knife was buried in his bosom.

"Help!" he cried, "help! I am murdered." He died immediately.

Charlotte might have escaped, but she had no such intention. She had undertaken, what she conceived, a meritorious action, and was resolved to stay and ascertain whether her aim had been sure. In a short time, the screams of Marat's servant brought a crowd of people into the room. Some of them beat and ill-used her, but, the Members of the Section having arrived, she placed herself under their protection. They were all struck with her extraordinary beauty, as well as with the calm and lofty heroism that beamed from her countenance. Accustomed as they were to the shedding of human blood, they could not behold unmoved this beautiful girl, who had not yet reached her twenty-fifth year, standing before them with unblenching eye, but with modest dignity, awaiting their fiat of death, for a deed which she imagined would save her country from destruction. At length Danton arrived, and treated her with the most debasing indignity, to which she only opposed silent contempt. She was then dragged into the street, placed in a coach, and Drouet was directed to conduct her to the conciergeric. On her way thither, she was attacked by the infuriated multitude. Here, for the first time, she evinced symptoms of alarm. The possibility of being torn to pieces in the streets, and her mutilated limbs dragged through the kennel and made sport of by the ferocious rabble, had never before occurred to her imagination. The thought now struck her with dismay, and roused all her feelings of female delicacy. The firmness of Drouet, however, saved her, and she thanked him warmly.

"Not that I feared to die," she said ; "but it was repugnant to my woman's nature to be torn to pieces before everybody."

Whilst she was at the conciergerie, a great many persons obtained leave to see her ; and all felt the most enthusiastic admiration on beholding a young creature of surpassing loveliness, with endowments that did honor to her sex, and a loftiness of heroism to which few of the stronger sex have attained, who had deliberately executed that which no man in the country had resolution to attempt, though the whole nation wished it, and calmly given up her life for the public weal.

Charlotte's examination before the revolutionary tribunal is remarkable for the dignified simplicity of her answers. I shall only mention one which deserves to be handed down to posterity :

"Accused," said the president, "how happened it that thou couldst reach the heart at the very first blow? Hadst thou been practicing beforehand?"

Charlotte cast an indescribable look at the questioner.

"Indignation had roused my heart," she replied, "and it showed me the way to his."

When the sentence of death was passed on her, and all her property declared forfeited to the state, she turned to her counsel, M. Chauveau Lagarde,—

"I cannot, sir, sufficiently thank you," she said, "for the noble and delicate manner in which you have defended me; and I will at once give you a proof of my gratitude. I have now nothing in the world, and I bequeath to you the few debts I have contracted in my prison. Pray, discharge them for me."

When the executioner came to make preparations for her execution, she entreated him not to cut off her hair.

"It shall not be in your way," she said; and taking her stay lace she tied her thick and beautiful hair on the top of her head, so as not to impede the stroke of the axe.

In her last moments, she refused the assistance of a priest; and upon this is founded a charge of her being an infidel. But there is nothing to justify so foul a blot upon her memory. Charlotte Corday had opened her mind, erroneously perhaps, to freedom of thought in religion as well as in politics. Deeply read in the philosophic writings of the day, she had formed her own notions of faith. She certainly rejected the communion of the Roman Church; and it may be asked, whether the conduct of the hierarchy of France before the revolution was calculated to convince her that she was in error? But, because she refused the aid of man as a mediator between her and God, is it just to infer that she rejected her Creator? Certainly not. A mind like hers was incapable of existiug without religion; and the very action she committed may justify the inference that she anticipated the contemplation, from other than earthly realms, of the happiness of her rescued country.

As the cart in which she was seated proceeded towards the place of execution, a crowd of wretches in the street, ever ready to insult the unfortunate, and glut their eyes with the sight of blood, called out,—

" To the guillotine with her !"

" I am on my way thither," she mildly replied, turning towards them.

She was a striking figure as she sat in the cart. The extraordinary beauty of her features, and the mildness of her look, strangely contrasted with the murderer's red garment which she wore. She smiled at the spectators whenever she perceived marks of sympathy rather than of curiosity, and this smile gave a truly Raphaelic expression to her countenance. Adam Lux, a deputy of Mayence, having met the cart, shortly after it left the conciergerie, gazed with wonder at this beautiful apparition —for he had never before seen Charlotte—and a passion, as singular as it was deep, immediately took possession of his mind.

" Oh !" cried he, " this woman is surely greater than Brutus !"

Anxious once more to behold her, he ran at full speed towards the Palais Royal, which he reached before the cart arrived in front of it. Another look which he cast upon Charlotte Corday, completely unsettled his reason. The world to him had suddenly become a void, and he resolved to quit it. Rushing like a mad-man to his own house, he wrote a letter to the revolutionary tribunal, in which he repeated the words he bad already uttered at the sight of Charlotte Corday, and concluded by asking to be condemned to death, in order that he might join her in a better world. His request was granted, and he was executed soon after. Before he died, he begged the executioner to bind him with the very cords that had before encircled the delicate limbs of Charlotte upon the same scaffold, and his head fell as he was pronouncing her name.

Charlotte Corday, wholly absorbed by the solemnity of her last moments, had not perceived the effect she had produced upon Adam Lux, and died in ignorance of it. Having reached the foot of the guillotine, she ascended the platform with a firm step, but with the greatest modesty of demeanor. "Her countenance," says an eye-witness, "evinced only the calmness of a soul at peace with itself."

The executioner having removed the handkerchief which covered her shoulders and bosom, her face and neck became suffused with a deep blush. Death had no terrors for her, but her innate feelings of modesty were deeply wounded at being thus exposed to public gaze. Her being fastened to the fatal plank seemed a relief to her, and she eagerly rushed to death as a refuge against this violation of female delicacy.

When her head fell, the executioner took it up and bestowed a buffet upon one of the cheeks. The eyes, which were already closed, again opened, and cast a look of indignation upon the brute, as if consciousness had survived the separation of the head from the body. This fact, extraordinary as it may seem, has been averred by thousands of eye-witnesses; it has been accounted for in various ways, and no one has ever questioned its truth.

Before Charlotte Corday was taken to execution, she wrote a letter to her father entreating his pardon for having, without his permission, disposed of the life she owed him. Here the lofty-minded heroine again became the meek and submissive daughter—as, upon the scaffold, the energetic and daring woman was nothing but a modest and gentle girl.

The Mountain party, furious at the loss of their leader, attempted to vituperate the memory of Charlotte Corday, by attributing to her motives much less pure and praiseworthy than those which really led to the commission of the deed for which she suffered They asserted that she was actuated by revenge for the death of a man named Belzunce, who was her lover, and had been executed at Caen upon the denunciation of Marat. But Charlotte Corday was totally unacquainted with Belzunce —she had never even seen him. More than that, she was never known to have an attachment of the heart Her thoughts and feelings were wholly engrossed by the state of her country, and her mind had no leisure for the contemplation of connubial happiness. Her life was, therefore, offered up in the purest spirit of patriotism, unmixed with any worldly passion.

M. Prud'homme relates, that, on the very day of Marat's death, M. Piot, a teacher of the Italian language, called upon him. This gentleman had just left Marat, with whom he had been conversing on the state of the country. The representative, in reply to some observation made by M. Piot, had uttered these remarkable words :—

" They who govern are a pack of fools. France must have a chief; but to reach this point, blood must be shed, not *drop by drop*, but *in torrents*."

" Marat," added M. Piot to M. Prud'homme, " was in his bath, and very ill. This man cannot live a month longer."

When M. Piot was informed that Marat had been murdered, an hour after he had made this communication to M. Prud'—

homme, he was stricken with a sort of palsy, and would probably have died of fright, had not M .Prud'homme promised not to divulge this singular coincidence.

To the eternal disgrace of the French nation, no monument has been raised to the memory of Charlotte Corday, nor is it even known where her remains were deposited ; and yet, in the noble motive of her conduct, and the immense and generous sacrifice she made of herself, when in the enjoyment of everything that could make life valuable, she has an eternal claim upon the gratitude of her country.

Josephine

JOSEPHINE,

Josephine Rose Tascher de la Pagerie was born at Martinique on the 24th of June, 1763. At a very early age she came to Paris, where she married the Viscount Beauharnais, a man of talent and superior personal endowments, but not a courtier, as some writers have asserted, for he was never even presented at court. Beauharnais was a man of limited fortune, and his wife's dower more than doubled his income. In 1787, Madame Beauharnais returned to Martinique to nurse her aged mother, whose health was in a declining state; but the disturbances which soon after took place in that colony, drove her back to France. During her absence, the revolution had broken out, and on her return she found her husband entirely devoted to those principles upon which the regeneration of the French people was to be founded. The well-known opinions of the Viscount Beauharnais gave his wife considerable influence with the rulers of blood, who stretched their reeking sceptre over the whole nation; and she had frequent opportunities, which she never lost, of saving persons doomed by their sanguinary decrees. Among others, Mademoiselle de Bethisy was condemned, by the revolutionary tribunal, to be beheaded; but Madame Beauharnais, by her irresistible intercession, succeeded in obtaining the life and freedom of this interesting lady. The revolution, however, devouring, like Saturn, its own children, spared none of even its warmest supporters, the moment they came in collision with the governing party, then composed of ignorant and blood-thirsty enthusiasts. The slightest hesita tion in executing any of their decrees, however absurd or impracticable, was considered a crime deserving of death. Beauharnais had been appointed general-in-chief of the army of the North. Having failed to attend to some foolish order of the Convention, he was cited to appear at its bar and give an account of his conduct. No one appeared before this formidable assemby, but to take, immediately after, the road to the guillotine; and such was the case with the republican general Beauharnais. He was tried, and condemned; and, on the 23d of July, 1794, he was publicly beheaded at the Place de la Révolution. Meantime, his wife had been thrown into prison, where she remained until Robespierre's death, expecting each day to be led out to execution. Having at length recovered her freedom, she joined her children, Eugene and Hortense, who had been taken care of during their mother's captivity by some true and devoted, though humble friends. After the establishment of the Directory, Madame Tallian became all-powerful with the Director, Barras, to whom she introduced Madame Beauharnais.

Bonaparte at length became passionately attached to Madame Beauharnais, and married her on the 17th of February, 1796. She accompanied him to Italy, where by her powers of pleasing she charmed his toils, and by her affectionate attentions soothed his disappointments when rendered too bitter by the impediments which the jealousy of the Directory threw in the way of his victories.

Bonaparte loved Josephine with great tenderness; and this attachment can be expressed in no words but his own. In his letters, published by Queen Hortense, it may be seen how ardently his soul of fire had fixed itself to hers, and mixed up her life with his own. These letters form a striking record. A woman so beloved, and by such a man, could have been no ordinary person.

When Napoleon became sovereign of France, after having proved its hero, he resolved that his crown should also grace the brows of Josephine.

With his own hand he placed the small crown upon her head, just above the diamond band which encircled her forehead. It was evident that he felt intense happiness in thus honoring the woman he loved, and making her share his greatness.

It was truly marvelous to see Josephine at the Tuilleries, on grand reception days, as she walked through the Gallerie de Diane and the Salle des Maréchaux. Where did this surprising woman acquire her royal bearing? She never appeared at one of these splendid galas of the empire without exciting a sentiment of admiration, and of affection too—for her smile was sweet and benevolent, and her words mild and captivating, at the same time that her appearance was majestic and imposing.

She had some very gratifying moments during her greatness, if she afterwards encountered sorrow. The marriage of her son Eugene to the Princess of Bavaria, and that of her niece to the Prince of Baden, were events of which she might well be proud. Napoleon seemed to study how he could please her— he seemed happy but in her happiness.

He generally yielded to her entreaties—for the manner in which she made a request was irresistible. Her voice was naturally harmonious like that of most creoles, and there was a peculiar charm in every word she uttered. I once witnessed, at Malmaison, an instance of her power over the emperor   A soldier of the guard, guilty of some breach of discipline, had been condemned to a very severe punishment. Marshal Bessières was anxious to obtain the man's pardon; but as Napoleon had already given his decision, there was no hope unless the empress undertook the affair. She calmly listened to the Marshal, and, having received all the information necessary, said, with her musical voice and bewitching smile,—

"I will try if I can obtain the poor man's pardon."

When the emperor returned to the drawing-room, we all looked to see the expression his countenance would assume when she mentioned the matter to him. At first he frowned, but, as the empress went on, his brow relaxed; he then smiled, looked at her with his sparkling eyes, and said, kissing her forehead,—

"Well, let it be so for this once; but, Josephine, mind you do not acquire a habit of making such applications."

He then put his arm round her waist, and again tenderly kissed her. Now, what spell had she employed to produce such an effect? Merely a few words, and a look, and a smile; but each was irresistible.

Then came days of anguish and regret. She had given no heir to Napoleon's throne, and all hope of such an event was now past. This wrung her heart; for it was a check to Napoleon's ambition of family greatness, and a disappointment to the French nation. The female members of Napoleon's family disliked the empress—they were perhaps jealous of her influence—and the present opportunity was not lost to impress upon the emperor the necessity of a divorce. At length he said to Josephine,—

"We must separate; I must have an heir to my empire."

With a bleeding heart, she meekly consented to the sacrifice

The particulars of the divorce are too well known to be repeated here.

After this act of self-immolation, Josephine withdrew to
Malmaison, where she lived in elegant retirement—unwilling to
afflict the emperor with the news of her grief, and wearing a
smile of seeming content which but ill veiled the sorrows of her
heart. Yet she was far from being calm ; and in the privacy
of friendship, the workings of her affectionate nature would
sometimes burst forth. But she was resigned ; and what more
could be required from a broken heart ?

On the birth of the King of Rome, when Providence at
length granted the emperor an heir to his thrones, Josephine
experienced a moment of satisfaction which made her amends
for many days of bitterness. All her thoughts and hopes were
centered in Napoleon and his glory, and the consummation of
his wishes was to her a source of pure and unutterable satisfaction.

" My sacrifice will at least have been useful to him and
to France," she said with tearful eyes. But they were
tears of joy. Yet this joy was not unalloyed ; and the
feeling which accompanied it, was the more bitter because it
could not be shown. It was however, betrayed by these simple
and affecting words uttered in the most thrilling tone :—

" Alas ! why am I not his mother ?"

When the disasters of the Russian campaign took place, she
was certainly much more afflicted than the woman who filled
her place at the Tuilleries. When in private with any who
were intimate with her, she wept bitterly.

The emperor's abdication, and exile to Elba, cut her to the
soul.

" Why did I leave him ?" she said, on hearing that he had

set out alone for Elba ; " why did I consent to this separation ? Had I not done so, I should now be by his side, to console him in his misfortunes."

Josephine died at Malmaison, on the 29th of May, 1814, after a few days illness.   Her two children were with her during her last moments.

Her body was buried in the church of Ruel.   Every person of any note, then at Paris attended her funeral.   She was universally regretted by foreigners as well as by Frenchmen; and she obtained, as she deserved, a tribute to her memory, not only from the nation, whose empress she had once been, but from the whole of Europe, whose proudest sovereigns had once been at her feet.

THE END.